Also by Paige Tyler

SWAT: Special Wolf Alpha Team

Hungry Like the Wolf
Wolf Trouble
In the Company of Wolves
To Love a Wolf
Wolf Unleashed
Wolf Hunt
Wolf Hunger
Wolf Rising
Wolf Instinct
Wolf Rebel

X-Ops

Her Perfect Mate
Her Lone Wolf
Her Secret Agent (novella)
Her Wild Hero
Her Fierce Warrior
Her Rogue Alpha
Her True Match
Her Dark Half
X-Ops Exposed

WOLF REBEL

PAIGE
TYLER

Published by Sourcebooks Casablanca, an imprint of Sourcebooks
P.O. Box 4410, Naperville, Illinois 60567-4410
(630) 961-3900
sourcebooks.com

Printed and bound in Canada.
MBP 10 9 8 7 6 5 4 3 2 1

With special thanks to my extremely patient and understanding husband. Without your help and support, I couldn't have pursued my dream job of becoming a writer. You're my sounding board, my idea man, my critique partner, and the absolute best research assistant a girl could ask for. Love you!

PROLOGUE

Chattanooga, Tennessee, October 2017

"SUSPICIOUS ACTIVITY REPORTED NEAR THE SOUTH END of Forest Lake Memorial."

Officer Rachel Bennett knew the police dispatcher was going to ask her to check it out before the guy called out the number of her patrol car. Why? Because she was just lucky that way. Cursing under her breath, she flipped on her lights, spun her vehicle around, crossed over the median, and headed north on Highway 27.

Rachel forced herself to ignore the chatter on the radio, gritting her teeth as the shift sergeant instructed her fellow Chattanooga PD officers to set up a perimeter north of Lookout Mountain, miles away from where she was. There'd been a high-speed chase, a crash into a ditch, and lots of gunfire. It was literally the triple crown of fun for a cop on a slow Tuesday night in Tennessee. The chase had drawn half the law enforcement officers in the area, both city and county. And when the vehicle's two armed occupants had escaped into the woods near the highway, that had drawn every other cop in this corner of the state. Hell, there were probably off-duty officers already rolling out of bed right that minute and yanking on their uniforms on the off chance they could get involved in the excitement.

And where was she heading while the rest of the police force ran through the woods looking for two armed felons? To a damn cemetery, most likely to chase off a prostitute and his or her trick looking to get freaky in a graveyard. Rachel had caught the suspicious activity call because it was her beat, but being forced to deal with sex-crazed perverts the night before Halloween while the other members of her department went after real criminals was frustrating as hell.

As Rachel crossed over the Tennessee River, the more built-up parts of Chattanooga quickly got left behind, replaced with stretches of dense woods, interspersed with quiet residential areas. A mile later, the woods disappeared almost entirely.

There was a thriving red-light district just before the bridge, but while that area had plenty of sidewalks for the guys and girls to display their wares, there weren't many good locations to conduct their business. The nearby parking lots were generally well lit, which scared the johns to death. And the dark alleys behind the buildings were a refuge for the homeless and druggies, neither of which was good for a prostitute's business. Nervous customers took longer to finish in that environment—if they could finish at all.

So, the working men and women of Chattanooga now had their clients drive them over the bridge to the suburbs, and for reasons that made sense to no one but them, the Forest Lake Cemetery had become their preferred location to get busy. Apparently, the privacy and soft grass made the time it took to get out there worthwhile. Rachel had no idea how the graveyard ambiance affected their bottom line though. She'd definitely never want to do it in a place like that.

Rachel turned into the cemetery, wishing for the hundredth time the place would install a gate that locked. The city had talked to the facility's management about it, but they were resistant to the idea. They claimed it was because they didn't want to keep people from being able to come in and out to visit their loved ones whenever they wanted. More likely it was because they didn't want to spend money protecting a place when there wasn't anything to steal.

She stopped the car a few yards inside the entrance, the beams of her headlights reflecting off the fog drifting silently across the graveyard. She flipped on her search light and swiveled it this way and that, but beyond confirming there was no one parked anywhere near the main building to her left, she didn't see much of anything. Thanks to the fog, she couldn't see more than twenty feet in any direction. Just the silhouettes of headstones, large and small, along with a few family-sized crypts.

Nope, not creepy at all. Especially this close to Halloween.

She'd been in this damn graveyard a dozen times in the past month, so she was familiar with the mazelike network of narrow, curvy footpaths that weaved through the different parts of the tree-shrouded cemetery. The place had been fashioned that way on purpose, to give mourners a sense of privacy while they were there, but it also meant, if there was someone in the cemetery looking for action, it could take a while to find them.

She grabbed her car's radio and thumbed the button. "This is unit 220. Any additional information from the reporting party about Forest Lake?"

"Negative, 220," the dispatcher replied. "The reporting party said they heard a female screaming when they drove past the cemetery. No further contact since, though there was an earlier report of someone seeing a man in a clown costume walking near that same area."

Rachel groaned. She frigging hated clowns with a gut-twisting passion. Then again, was there anyone on the planet who actually liked them?

"10-4," she said into the radio.

She considered asking for backup but decided against it. Since the call had come into dispatch ten minutes ago, there was little chance whoever had screamed was still there.

Rachel drove around the cemetery, but with the ever-present fog and random patches of trees, she couldn't see a damn thing. Worse, between the hum of the vehicle's heater and the noise from the radio, it was impossible to hear anything either, even with the window down. Knowing she'd never find anything if she kept trying to do this search from her car, she turned around and headed back to the main building, figuring that would be the best place to park while she continued the search on foot.

Letting the dispatcher know she was getting out of the vehicle to look around, she shoved open the door. She shivered, trying to keep her teeth from chattering the moment the freezing fall wind hit her. Crap. It shouldn't be this cold in Chattanooga already. The weather forecast had mentioned a possibility of snow tonight, and from the way her breath frosted in the air, she could believe it.

She turned down the volume on the mobile radio attached to her equipment belt, putting some distance between herself and the distracting sound of the patrol car's hot engine ticking, straining her ears to pick up anything suspicious. She kept one hand on the weapon holstered on her hip as she moved away from the car and farther into the graveyard, letting her eyes and ears slowly adjust to the darkness and the night sounds around her as she swung her flashlight back and forth.

The moon was out tonight, but with the fog, it was like she was walking around in a bubble, cut off from everything around her. She couldn't see or hear anything. There could be someone standing only a few yards away and she'd never know it. Crap, there could be a psycho in a clown costume behind the next tombstone for all she knew.

Rachel shivered as tingles ran up her back. She cursed silently. She refused to let her unreasonable fear of clowns freak her out.

She walked slowly along the paths that separated the various sections of the graveyard from each other, stopping occasionally to shine her flashlight into the woods that lined the east side of the cemetery. After ten minutes, she gave up any hope of finding a vehicle. After twenty, she was convinced the entire call had been a hoax. There was nobody out here.

She hadn't gone more than a half dozen steps back toward her patrol car when a cracking sound from off to the right made her turn.

Any country girl who'd spent time in the woods knew that sound. Someone had stepped on a big stick, breaking it.

She immediately headed that way, aiming her flashlight in the direction of the noise, her other hand still resting on her weapon. She couldn't see anyone, but her instincts were telling her someone was out there beyond the edge of the glowing beam, in the brambles near the base of one of the trees.

"Whoever is out there, this is Officer Bennett from the

Chattanooga Police Department!" she shouted. "Stand up and move toward the sound of my voice or I'll release my K9 and you will get bit."

She didn't expect whoever it was to do as she asked. That line about having a dog with her almost never worked, so she was shocked when she heard a desperate scream in the darkness and then a series of crashing sounds as a girl ran toward her, slamming through tree branches and undergrowth like her life depended on it.

Rachel immediately had her Sig Sauer out of its holster, ready to take down whoever was chasing the girl. The teen collapsed to her knees the moment she cleared the wood line, crying, shaking, and gasping for breath in the circle of Rachel's flashlight.

Slipping the flashlight in her belt, Rachel hurried over and dropped to a knee beside the terrified girl, wrapping one arm around her shoulders and pulling her close while keeping her .45 caliber pointed at the dark woods.

The girl wore nothing but a thin T-shirt, pink leggings, and ragged socks. No wonder she was shaking. She didn't even have any shoes on. The socks and leggings were shredded from running through the woods, and she was bleeding from myriad cuts and scrapes. But it was the deep, bloody lacerations crisscrossing the kid's back and one arm Rachel was more concerned about. The girl had a hand clasped over the wound on her arm, but blood was still leaking out from between her fingers.

Rachel let the girl go long enough to reach up and thumb the button on the mic attached to the webbing on her vest. "Dispatch, this is 220. I need immediate backup and EMS at my location. One female victim with severe lacerations across her back and arm as well as possible hypothermia. Unknown assailant."

The dispatcher asked a few questions about Rachel's exact location in the graveyard and how far she was from her patrol car, but the best she could do at the moment was provide a general direction and distance from the entrance. She also couldn't answer the most pressing question—whether the scene was secure.

"Who did this to you?" Rachel whispered to the girl, glancing quickly at the wounds along the girl's back before looking off into the trees again. "Do you know where he is?"

The girl only cried harder, latching her arms around Rachel's waist and holding on for dear life. The poor thing might have been too traumatized to even speak.

"It was a clown," she whispered brokenly, her face buried in Rachel's shoulder.

Rachel thought for a minute she'd heard wrong. Then she started praying she'd heard wrong. But when the girl lifted her head and looked up at her with terror on her face, she knew she hadn't heard wrong at all.

Crap.

"A clown?"

The girl nodded, seeming to draw strength from Rachel's presence. "He wasn't wearing a mask though. He had on face paint. Like you see in a circus. I was in the backyard near the fire pit, talking to my friend on the phone, when he grabbed me and dragged me into the woods. I tried to fight him, but he had a knife. I thought he was going to kill me." She swallowed hard. "I still can't believe I got away."

"Where is he now?"

The teen shook her head. "I don't know. I hit him in the

head with a rock, but I didn't knock him out. I heard him come after me."

Cursing silently, Rachel called the dispatcher again with an update on the attacker, saying there was a man somewhere in the cemetery wearing clown makeup and carrying a knife. The dispatcher immediately put the information out on the radio. A moment later, officers began calling in their location and ETA—estimated time of arrival—to Forest Lake Memorial. Unfortunately, they were all on the far side of the city, which meant Rachel was on her own for at least ten minutes.

That might not seem like much, but those ten minutes were a lifetime when there was some weirdo out there with a knife.

She didn't hear anything right then that made her think the clown was nearby, but that didn't provide much comfort. The truth was that she hadn't heard a peep out of the girl either, and she'd been hiding in the woods twenty feet away. Rachel sure as hell didn't like the idea of the clown being that close to her and the kid.

Rachel couldn't stay out there in the middle of the graveyard waiting for help to arrive, letting the girl bleed to death. She needed to get the girl back to the car and put some bandages over those wounds.

"What's your name?" she asked gently, sliding her free arm around the girl again while still keeping one eye on the fog-shrouded night.

The girl stared at Rachel for all of a second before a slight smile graced her face. After everything that had happened, it was amazing she could still smile. "Hannah," she said even as her teeth chattered from the cold. "Hannah Freeman."

"Nice to meet you, Hannah. My name is Rachel. What do you think about getting out of this place? I have a nice warm car waiting back at the entrance. How does that sound?"

Hannah's smile widened for a moment but then disappeared. "That sounds good, but I'm not sure if I can walk that far."

It was Rachel's turn to smile. "No problem. I can help you."

Hannah's legs were complete rubber. There was no way she'd be able to walk back to the cruiser, even with help. Rachel had no idea how the girl had made it this far.

Hating to do it but having no choice, Rachel holstered her weapon then scooped Hannah up in her arms. The girl cried out softly in pain as the sleeve of Rachel's uniform jacket scraped against the open wounds on her back.

"I'm sorry," Rachel whispered as she turned and headed back toward her patrol car. "I know this hurts, but there's no other way to do this."

"I don't care." Hannah's hand came up to clutch Rachel's jacket in a death grip. "Just don't let him hurt me again. Please."

"Shh." Rachel's heart seized in her chest at the pain in the girl's words. Damn that effing clown, whoever he was. "I won't let anyone hurt you. I promise."

Hannah buried her face in Rachel's tactical vest, somehow making herself even smaller than she already was. A few more sobs that sounded almost like relief slipped out and all Rachel wanted to do right then was squeeze her tight and make her feel safe again. But giving her a hug wouldn't do that. Getting her back to the car and some medical help wouldn't, either. Finding that damn clown and getting him off the streets was the only thing that would do that.

Rachel moved quickly, glad Hannah was so petite. Rachel was strong—you had to be with this job—but if the girl had been any heavier, there was no way she could have carried her. She considered retracing her steps back to the car but then realized it would be a long trip with Hannah in her arms. Plus, keeping to the roads and gravel pathways would force her to go past several areas heavily shrouded in trees. With that damn clown still out there somewhere, it was a risk she wasn't willing to take, especially since her hands weren't free.

Hoping she was making the right decision, she turned off the path she was on, heading straight across the fog-shrouded cemetery in the direction of the main building and the front entrance. It was risky, going cross-country like this, but if her sense of direction was right, they'd be back at her patrol car in half the time it would take if they went the long way around.

Within seconds, the blurry outline of various shaped headstones and grave markers began to appear out of the darkness ahead of them. Rachel strained to hear the sounds of approaching sirens, but so far the only noise was her footsteps in the cold, crunchy grass, Hannah's occasional moans of pain, and the chatter of the radio as her fellow officers called in their updated ETAs.

Hannah was nearly unconscious in her arms by the time Rachel saw the hazy outline of the main cemetery building. She picked up her pace, almost running across the parking lot. Off in the distance, sirens echoed faintly in the night and she prayed the paramedics would be part of the first group to arrive.

Rachel was so eager to get Hannah into the warmth and safety of the car she didn't hear the crunch of gravel behind them until it was almost too late. She snapped her head around in time to see a huge man in clown makeup sprinting out of the fog, a big knife in his hand.

For the first time since becoming a cop, Rachel froze. Between the white greasepaint covering his face, the bloodred markings around his eyes, and the menacing red grin permanently etched around his mouth, he was like a nightmare come to life. Even his teeth, which he'd somehow tricked out to make it look as if they'd been filed down to sharp points like some kind of monster, screamed evil. A bright-orange fright wig completed the look, turning the big man into the most disturbing thing she'd ever seen, despite the big, bright-red nose he sported.

The clown was less than a foot away when Rachel finally snapped out of her daze. She instinctively curled around Hannah in an effort to protect her, praying the Kevlar fibers in her tactical vest would protect her own body.

Rachel flew forward like she'd been hit by a Mack truck. Her knees slammed into the gravel and Hannah sailed out of her arms with a high-pitched scream. A lightning bolt of fiery agony in her right shoulder blade let her know the demented clown's knife had punched right through the vest. Shock kept her from feeling the full extent of the damage, she was sure, but she had a feeling the blade had gone deep enough to puncture a lung. The pain from the wound made her whole body go rigid, and for one terrified moment, she thought she might not make it home that night.

She screamed as the clown ripped the knife out. Crap, it hurt even more coming out than it had going in. Fighting off dizziness, she rolled to the side to avoid the next attack she was sure was coming her way. Another piercing scream echoed in the cemetery, and she worried the man was going after Hannah, but when she looked over her shoulder, it was to find the psycho coming at her again.

She managed to get her Sig out, but the stabbing pain in her back kept her from moving as fast as she usually did, and the damn weapon slipped out of her hand when the clown landed on top of her, crushing what seemed like every trace of air out of her already-damaged lungs.

Rachel punched, scratched, kicked, and shoved, but the man on top of her easily weighed over 250 pounds, and most of it seemed to be muscle. He was insanely strong—or maybe just insane. Eyes practically glowing red, he went for her throat, and those teeth she'd thought only looked sharp were actually as pointy and dangerous as they looked. The pain as they tore through the coarse fabric of her clothing and vest straight into her shoulder was nearly as bad as when he'd plunged the knife into her back.

She tried to reach her Taser, but the a-hole had her left arm pinned. There was no way she could get at her telescoping baton with him on top of her, either. So, she did the only thing she could. She reached down to the other side of her belt and grabbed her radio. She brought it up and smashed it against the side of her attacker's head, hard. The plastic shattered into pieces, but it got the madman's attention—and his teeth out of her shoulder.

She dropped the remnants of the radio and punched out blindly, feeling her fist connect with a jaw that felt like steel. Something popped in her clenched hand with a spasm of pain, but she ignored it, punching him over and over. One of the blows caught him in the eye and he reared back with a shout of anger.

Rachel was sure she had him on the ropes then. Until the knife slashed down again with a thud so solid she thought, at first, he'd missed her completely and struck the gravel-covered ground. But then searing pain exploded in the left side of her chest and she knew he hadn't missed. Her scream of agony must have shocked the hell out of the clown because he jerked back, tilting his head sideways like a confused animal.

She grit her teeth against the pain and threw another punch at him. Her aim was crap and she completely missed his face, but she hit him in the throat, which was actually much better. The clown clutched at his neck with both hands, coughing and gagging like he was dying. She followed that up with a kick to the face, knocking off his stupid, red clown nose and breaking his real one with the heel of her heavy patrol shoe. Blood running down his face, he collapsed to the ground, coughing harder. Hopefully, she'd crushed his larynx and he'd choke to death.

Just in case he didn't, she rolled over, trying to figure out where her Sig had gone. She couldn't find it in the dark, but the move sent a spike of pain lancing through her chest. *Crap.* The knife was still in her. How the hell hadn't she noticed it?

Rachel glanced down and almost passed out when she saw how deeply the knife was buried in her chest, and she momentarily wondered how it was possible for her to still be alive. Taking a breath, she wrapped her hand around the handle. She remembered a first-aid class saying something about leaving the knife where it was, that it could cause more damage on the way out. They were probably right, but there was no way in hell she was leaving it where it was. Not with that idiot clown already dragging himself to his feet. And definitely not when he could take it out and stab her again.

Tightening her grip, she clenched her jaw and tugged on the knife. It took more force than she would have thought necessary, but the first stomach-twisting sensation of the blade sliding out distracted her from that fact. Then the soul-searing pain arrived, threatening to overwhelm her. For a moment, she was tempted to give in to the blackness threatening to consume her, but then Hannah screamed.

Rachel lifted her head to see the clown turning his attention to the girl. If Rachel lost consciousness, Hannah was dead. And Rachel had promised not to let the bastard hurt her again.

The sirens in the distance were gradually coming closer, but they were still too far away to matter.

Tossing the knife away, Rachel scrambled to her feet to go after the insane man in the clown makeup. It might have been smarter to keep the weapon, but in truth, she feared that, in her condition, he'd take the blade away from her and use it on Hannah.

For a big man, he was ridiculously fast. He lunged for Hannah, wrapping his huge hand around her ankle and dragging her toward him with a grunt. Hannah kicked at him with her free foot, trying to get away by pulling herself across the gravel as she screamed at the top of her lungs.

The clown continued to crawl forward, moving like some deranged monster, so focused on Hannah all of a sudden it was like Rachel didn't even exist. Maybe he assumed she was too weak to come after him—or already dead. Either way, he didn't notice her behind him pointing her Taser at his back.

Rachel waited until she was two feet away to squeeze the trigger—so close she couldn't possibly miss. The barbed probes deployed with a pop, stabbing him through the shirt he wore. The Taser clicked like crazy in her grip as it dumped thousands of volts into the man. He groaned but didn't seem nearly as fazed by it as she'd expected.

Not wanting to lose even that small advantage, Rachel reached behind her back and pulled out her cuffs, then jumped on his back. If she could get his arms restrained, she and Hannah might just make it until backup—and EMS—arrived.

The clown immediately lost interest in Hannah, releasing his hold on the girl and turning on Rachel with a vicious roar. She still had the trigger on the Taser depressed and it was still clicking like it should. By now, he should have been screaming in pain and writhing around on the ground, but it wasn't having any real effect on him. Wrapping one hand around her throat, he grabbed her left shoulder with the other, nearly crushing her bones as he shoved his thumb into the stab wound in her chest.

Rachel tried to scream as the pain hit her, but the hand around her neck made that impossible, and all that came out was a strangled sound. She swung a punch at him, hoping to get him to release her. She didn't realize until her fist connected with the side of his face that she was still holding her cuffs in her hand.

His head rocked back hard, but it seemed like he'd barely noticed the blow from the heavy steel cuffs, despite the blood that ran down his paint-smeared cheek. If anything, it seemed to piss him off even more and he tightened his grip around her throat.

Rachel's vision started to dim and she knew she was going to die. This freak was going to kill her, then he was going to kill Hannah.

Like hell.

She punched him again and again and again. She didn't aim, didn't even think, but simply fought for her life…and for Hannah's.

Rachel wasn't sure how many times she hit him, but at some point, she realized he wasn't moving and that his hand was no longer wrapped around her neck. Her arms were so weak she could barely lift them any longer. She had no idea where the Taser was. And those damn sirens still seemed so far away.

She used what little strength she had left to roll the clown over onto his front, then yanked an arm behind his back and got one of the cuffs around his wrist. Even semiconscious, he was strong enough to resist her efforts and she couldn't get his arm around to cuff that wrist. It didn't help that it was coated in so much of his blood she couldn't get a grip on it.

That was when she realized it wasn't his blood but hers.

She was bleeding to death.

Refusing to think about what that meant, Rachel tried to pull the man's left arm around, but the stab wounds in her chest and back were making it difficult to get a breath. Her vision was getting fuzzy, too. Suddenly, it was like she was viewing everything through a curtain. One that was getting thicker by the second.

She was close to giving up when a slender pair of hands reached out and covered her own. Rachel lifted her head to see Hannah kneeling beside her. Even in the darkness, the young girl's face looked pale. She'd lost almost as much blood as Rachel.

Hannah didn't say anything as she helped get the clown's left arm back behind his back, then worked with Rachel to get the cuff on his wrist. Once that was done, it was like every ounce of energy left in Rachel's body evaporated and she slumped down to the ground on one hip.

Suddenly, she was surrounded by warmth as Hannah moved close and settled down at her side. The girl wrapped an arm around her, resting her cheek on Rachel's shoulder. "Thank you for saving me. And for not leaving me. Or letting him hurt me."

"I made a promise," Rachel said softly. "I never go back on a promise."

Hannah didn't say anything for a moment. "He's not really a clown, is he?"

Rachel shook her head, alarmed at how dizzy even that simple movement made her. "I'm pretty sure he's not. But if he is, then he's the worst clown in the world."

Hannah lifted her head from Rachel's shoulder to gaze into the fog at the blue and red flashing lights of the police cars that were coming closer. After a moment, she put her head on Rachel's shoulder again.

"I don't like clowns," Hannah said.

"No one likes clowns," Rachel replied.

Her vision was getting dimmer by the second and breathing was almost too painful to bother with. She wasn't going to make it until help arrived.

"Rachel!"

She jumped at the panic in Hannah's voice. That's when Rachel realized she'd fallen over and was lying on the ground near the clown, staring straight into his open eyes. She freaked, horrified he'd fully regained consciousness at the same time she was losing hers. The thought of what he could do to Hannah even though he was in cuffs terrified her.

"Rachel, you have to stay awake!" Hannah shook Rachel's shoulder. "They're almost here. I can see the red and blue lights."

Rachel tried to do as Hannah asked, but her eyelids were suddenly so heavy. Nothing hurt anymore, so that was good. On the downside, it was getting harder and harder to breathe. It struck her that she was dying. The fact that backup had arrived and that Hannah would be okay made her feel better about that.

But as she lay there on the cold ground, staring into the clown's glowing red eyes, Rachel realized she was still scared—of leaving Hannah behind after making her a promise and of being so close to this creepy-ass clown. More than anything, though, she was scared of dying. There was still so much she'd never had a chance to do with her life. Like learn to play a musical instrument like she wanted to, travel to exotic places she'd dreamed about, or even fall in love. Panic began to overwhelm her as she realized she was never going to get a chance to do any of it.

As that fear threatened to choke out what little breath she had left in her lungs, the clown grinned at her, his bloodied lips pulled wide as if he could sense her terror and it was the most amusing thing he'd ever seen.

That nightmarish smile of his—and the all-consuming fear she felt—was the last thing she remembered before everything went black.

CHAPTER 1

Dallas, Texas, Present Day

"Don't take this the wrong way, but you look like crap."

From where she sat on the bench lacing her boots in the SWAT team's locker room on the second floor of the admin building, Rachel glanced up to see fellow officer Khaki Blake regarding her with concern. Tall with long, dark hair and brown eyes, Khaki was the only other female werewolf on the Dallas PD SWAT Team. But more than that, she was Rachel's best friend. And when friends started a conversation with *don't take this the wrong way*, it was because they knew you would.

"We just ran ten miles cross-country for physical training this morning," Rachel pointed out, returning her attention to her boots. "How do you expect me to look?"

"I didn't say you looked tired. I said you look like crap."

"What's the difference?" Rachel asked, not sure she wanted to know.

"Tired means you stayed up late binging something on Netflix," her friend said. "You look like you haven't slept in a week."

Rachel finished lacing her boots, then sat up with a sigh. In addition to the showers and locker room, there were also a handful of cots as well as a kitchenette. If you had to work a double shift, it was nice to be able to come up here to catch some rest.

Beside Khaki on the opposite bench, a black cat named Kat that belonged to one of their teammates regarded Rachel thoughtfully. Unlike Tuffie, the playful pit-bull mix the SWAT pack had adopted the previous summer, Kat acted like she owned the place. When she wasn't up here watching the guys clean up after PT or hanging out with her rescuer, Connor, she wandered the compound looking bored. If the expression in her feline gaze now was any indication, she completely agreed with Khaki. It was times like these that made Rachel think the animal knew a whole hell of a lot more about the world than any cat should.

"I haven't been sleeping much lately," she said quietly.

Khaki frowned. "You're still having nightmares, aren't you?"

Rachel nodded. She hated admitting it, but it wasn't like Khaki didn't already know about the hellish dreams. Her friend had quickly picked up on the fact that something was bothering Rachel after she and some of their pack mates had come back fresh from a fight with a nest of vampires in Los Angeles a few weeks ago.

It might be stupid, especially since she and her pack mates were werewolves, but discovering vampires existed had shocked the hell out of all of them, including Rachel. So, when Khaki assumed she was a little off because of what happened in California, Rachel hadn't corrected her. It'd seemed easier to let her friend think she was suffering PTSD from the fight with the bloodsuckers than to admit she'd been dealing with nightmares—and other things—ever since werewolf hunters had attacked the SWAT compound two months ago. That night, she'd screwed up and let one of the hunters get away, even when she'd had the man right in her sights.

A little while after, she'd started picking up bizarre scents that none of the other werewolves in her pack seemed to notice. Scents that both attracted and scared the hell out of her. Even worse were the shadows she caught out of the corner of her eye—shadows that were frequently horrifying but, at other times, almost comforting.

As bad as her waking hours were, it was the nightmares that were causing her the most distress. She'd been having traumatic dreams ever since going through her change that night in the cemetery in Chattanooga, but they'd been nothing compared to the terrors she was experiencing lately. The endless horrors of being chased, hunted, and savagely attacked that she revisited on a nightly basis would jerk her out of sleep, heart pounding and sobbing in fear. They were the kind of things that made a person never want to go back to sleep for as long as they lived.

"You know," Khaki said as she stood up and strapped on the last of her gear, "there are people you can talk to about stuff like this. I know Cooper talked to a psychologist a few times and really thinks highly of her. I'm sure he could get you in to see her."

Rachel hadn't realized their pack mate had seen a psychologist. Before she could answer, footsteps at the base of the stairs interrupted her. She breathed a sigh of relief as she picked up Senior Corporal Xander Riggs's scent. It wasn't that she didn't appreciate Khaki's help, but she seriously didn't want a shrink poking around in her head. She already knew she had a few screws loose. If a therapist confirmed it, the department would put her on administrative leave. She couldn't let that happen.

Xander's voice floated up from below. "You two almost

done up there? The guys and I would like to clean up in this century. Unless you're cool with the idea of working alongside a bunch of sweaty male werewolves all day."

Rachel looked over at Khaki, who returned her smile.

"I could think of a lot worse ways to spend the day," her friend admitted. "Especially if we can convince them to take their shirts off."

Rachel laughed as Xander grumbled down below, making out like he was jealous. It was all an act, of course. No one could ever come between Khaki and Xander. He might be Khaki's squad leader on the SWAT team, but he was also *The One* for Khaki—her soul mate—just as she was for him. In any other SWAT team in the country, cops would never be allowed to have a relationship with a fellow officer. But in their world, it was something that was accepted. Finding a soul mate was extremely important to a werewolf. Not to mention rare.

Too bad there wasn't a chance of Rachel finding her soul mate among the Pack. While there wasn't a single guy on the team who wasn't sexy AF, unfortunately they were all like brothers to her. The idea of getting busy with any of them was enough to make her want to yak. Just her luck. Here she was, surrounded by the most amazing men she'd ever been around in her life, and none of them did a thing for her.

"Oh, and Rachel," Xander called from below. "Gage wants to see you in his office."

Rachel had to fight to keep her inner wolf from coming out in pure self-defense as an inexplicable terror overtook her.

Sergeant Gage Dixon was the commander of the Dallas SWAT team, as well as alpha of their pack of alphas. When

Rachel had shown up at the compound out of the blue, eager to join the Pack, he'd gone out of his way to welcome her and make her feel like this was the place she was supposed to be. But while he was a great guy and the best boss she'd ever worked for, there was a reason Gage was the head of the Pack. The man was completely in charge and nothing ever got past him.

What if he knew there was something wrong with her and was going to tell her he was putting her on leave—or worse?

The panic must have shown on her face because Khaki sat down beside her and gently touched her arm.

"Relax," Khaki said. "There's no way Gage could know about the nightmares. He probably just wants to talk about work stuff, maybe even something to do with that STAT unit you worked with out in LA."

Rachel's inner wolf retreated as she considered that. The Special Threat Assessment Team—aka STAT—was the joint CIA and FBI task force that had helped Rachel and the guys take down the vampires. Apparently, STAT had been aware of the existence of werewolves and other supernatural creatures for some time. While it was a little scary to have the Pack on the government's radar, at least the organization seemed to be interested in developing a working relationship with them. They'd even asked Gage if they could use members of the Pack to help them deal with some of their more dangerous cases. But the thing that had really convinced Rachel and the others to trust the STAT people was when they'd discovered that fellow werewolf and SWAT cop Zane Kendrick had found his soul mate in a member of the task force.

She gave Khaki a small smile. "You're probably right. I'm just tense from lack of sleep."

Standing up, she headed for the steps, stopping on the way to scratch Kat behind the ears.

"Don't think I didn't notice the slick way you avoided giving me an answer about getting some help with those nightmares," Khaki said, her voice making Rachel pause and look over her shoulder. "You have to stop going it alone, Rachel. If you're not going to see a psychologist, then at least find some good-looking guy and engage in a little pillow-talk therapy."

Rachel laughed and started down the stairs. "I'll keep that in mind."

Khaki's advice might be sound, but the truth of the matter was that Rachel hadn't slept with a guy since being attacked in Chattanooga and going through her change. At first, her life had been too insane, as she'd tried to learn how to control her inner wolf. Between moving to Dallas and spending time in LA, she hadn't had time to even think of dating. These days, she couldn't imagine simply picking up some random guy for a booty call. She wasn't sure she knew how to do that anymore. Even if the idea did sound inviting.

Rachel knocked once on Gage's open office door, then walked in, a donut wrapped in a napkin in hand. The offering was partly an attempt to put him in a good mood—in case he wasn't—and partly an apology for being late. It truly wasn't her fault that she'd been forced to take a detour over to the training building. There was no way he could expect her to ignore the delicious scent of donuts. She didn't know how it could be scientifically/biologically possible, but she was convinced she was addicted to the baked goodies.

"Someone brought donuts?" Gage asked, glancing up from his paperwork with an amused expression as she set the napkin with the Boston cream in the center of his desk calendar. She'd intended to bring him two but had gotten tempted by the sweet pastry on the way over from the other building and eaten one. The reminder of how delicious the yummy, chocolate-topped, cream-filled confection tasted made her want to reconsider offering one to Gage. "Is it a special occasion or just because it's Tuesday?"

Rachel sat down in one of the two chairs in front of his desk with a laugh. As far as she was concerned, a person didn't need a reason to eat donuts. "Cooper brought them in to celebrate. He and Everly found out last night that she's pregnant. He's pretty excited about becoming a dad, even if all the guys are ragging him about having a little Mini Cooper for the Pack to play with."

Gage chuckled, his dark eyes full of laughter. "It's nice to finally have some good news for a change. It's been a long time since we've had something as happy as a new baby to celebrate around here."

Rachel expected her boss to immediately get into why he'd wanted to see her, but instead, he turned his attention back to what he'd been doing before she walked in, scribbling something on one of the police department's official forms.

She sat patiently for a few minutes before nerves got the best of her. "Xander mentioned you wanted to talk to me about something?"

Gage nodded. "I do. But we're waiting for a few other people to join us."

His tone suggested this meeting had serious implications, almost certainly for her, and just like that, her mind immediately took off running in the worst possible direction. Gage had somehow found out about the nightmares and the rest of the problems she'd been having. As crushing as that was, it was even worse thinking about how he'd learned about them.

Only three people knew about her secret—Khaki, because she'd figured it out on her own; Diego Martinez, the teammate she'd shared a hotel room with in LA who'd witnessed her nightmares firsthand; and Zane, because Rachel had broken down out there and told him everything. And she did mean everything, right down to the haunting scents, bizarre images hovering on the edges of her peripheral vision, and the hunter she'd let escape.

She knew there was no way Khaki had told Gage, which meant it must have been one of the guys. If Diego had talked to Gage about the nightmares, it would be bad, but if Zane had told their boss everything she'd confided in him, she was beyond screwed.

Rachel clenched her teeth to keep from hyperventilating. Unfortunately, that did nothing to keep her fangs from extending and pulse from racing. The big problem with that? Gage was an experienced werewolf with exceptionally keen hearing. Easily good enough to hear her heart pounding like a drum.

He stopped scribbling to look at her. "Is something wrong? You seem tense all of a sudden."

Rachel considered shaking her head and waving off his concerns, but she knew that would never fly. Now that she had his attention, Gage wouldn't stop pushing until he had an answer. But she had to be careful with what she said because he was a walking lie detector. Distressed breathing patterns, spikes in her heart rate, even something as simple as wetting her lips would give her away.

"Are you going to eat that donut?" she asked, deciding to avoid the issue of answering his question entirely. "Because if you aren't, I'll take it." She hurried on before her boss could recognize the ploy for what it was—a blatant distraction. "Boston creams can get mushy if you let them sit around too long and I wouldn't want it to go to waste."

Gage laughed and nudged the napkin with the donut toward the edge of his desk. "We wouldn't want that. Go ahead and have it. I prefer plain glazed anyway. There are always lots of those left over."

Rachel reached out and snatched the baked goody, taking a big bite. There was the perfect ratio of cream to dough, meaning more of the former than the latter, and she closed her eyes as she chewed, indulging in all that sweetness. There was no way Gage could expect her to answer questions now, even if she wanted to. Her mouth was full. Besides, eating donuts always calmed her down.

Best. Comfort food. Ever.

Gage turned his attention to his form, leaving Rachel to finish her donut. Of course, the minute she was done, she went right back to worrying about who else was coming to the meeting and what they were going to talk about. She was still fretting over it when someone knocked on the door. She glanced over her shoulder to see Diego standing there all freshly showered and looking like he'd hardly taken time to brush his dark hair.

At six foot even, Diego was the shortest male alpha in the Pack, but what he lacked in height he more than made up for in width. Seriously, the guy's shoulders were as broad as a barn. But even though his size could be intimidating, he'd always been awesome with her. Those three weeks they'd spent sharing a hotel room in LA under the guise of being a couple, when nightmares had her waking up screaming every night, would have been a lot worse without Diego there to talk to. He'd never once asked what the dreams were about, as if knowing she didn't want to talk about them, but instead, sat up with her watching *Vikings* while they ate cheeseburgers from the fast-food place down the street.

Diego gave her a smile before turning to their boss. "The chief just got here and everyone else you asked to see is in the bull pen. You ready to meet with us?"

Gage clicked his pen closed with his thumb and straightened the papers he'd been working on, then got to his feet. "I'm ready."

Rachel stood and turned toward the door, wanting more than anything to bolt. But she forced herself to take a deep breath and stay where she was.

Diego entered Gage's office, followed by team medic, Trey Duncan, and Rachel's squad leader, Senior Corporal Mike Taylor. Tall and muscular, Trey had dark-blond hair while Mike's was close cropped and black. A moment later, a woman in DPD dress blues walked in carrying a thick file folder that looked similar to a personnel record.

Rachel's heart began thudding all over again. She suddenly had a sinking feeling this meeting had nothing to do with her nightmares but everything to do with the hunter she'd let get away.

Tall with medium brown skin and black hair swept back in a sleek bun, Shanette Leclair was the new chief of police, recently lured away from Detroit to take over for the current acting chief, Hal Mason. Everyone on the SWAT team had hoped Mason would be able to keep the job full-time, since he already knew they were werewolves, but the city council wanted someone from outside Dallas to come in and change the perception of the office, so Mason was back to being deputy chief. Rachel supposed she couldn't blame them, since the optics of the previous chief of police aligning himself with the people who'd attempted to kill off his own SWAT team was something of a public relations nightmare. Not as bad as her nightmares, but bad enough.

Leclair had a good reputation, both as a cop and a leader, but she was also known to be demanding as hell on the officers who worked for her. The fact that she'd chosen to meet with Rachel as well as some of her pack mates, instead of the entire SWAT team, for her first visit to the compound had to mean something significant. But if a reprimand was coming down, wouldn't Leclair want to meet with her alone?

Rachel relaxed as she realized that made sense. Maybe this meeting wasn't about her issues at all.

Then Zane walked in.

The sight of the tall, dark-haired Brit made her head start to spin. Like the others on the team, Zane was a friend as well as a pack mate, but right then, all she could think was that he'd told Gage about the hunter.

Crap.

She remembered that night clearly. Like mere minutes had passed instead of two months. Her pack mate Max and his bride Lana's wedding had been beautiful and the reception at the compound was the best party Rachel had ever been to. Then the hunters had attacked and everything went to hell.

Over the past year, hunters had become the boogeymen of the werewolf community, tracking down and executing their kind indiscriminately, as well as any humans who happened to be in their way—friends, loved ones, even kids. They were bloodthirsty and ruthless. It wasn't until Rachel and the guys had gone out to LA that they'd learned the hunters were hired by the vampires, employed to rid the world of werewolves.

Rachel had been outside the reception tent when a dozen hunters had stormed the SWAT compound and, in seconds, turned the place into a war zone, explosions and gunshots filling the night. She'd immediately pulled her gun to engage them, only to come up against a hunter pointing his weapon directly at her head. She'd barely started squeezing the trigger when the man collapsed face-first to the ground, shot by someone. To this day, she still didn't know who'd saved her life that night.

She'd ended up chasing a group of four hunters as they fled toward the perimeter fence and their getaway vehicle. One of the men had been limping painfully from a bullet wound in his upper thigh and there'd been a lot of blood running down the leg of his jeans. It was obvious the guy's femoral artery had been nicked and he had to be close to passing out from blood loss, but he'd moved quickly all the same.

Even so, no normal human was as fast as a werewolf, and Rachel had caught up with the group easily. Since the guy who was wounded had headed for the driver's door, that meant he had the key, so she aimed her weapon at him. She knew if she took him down first, the other three would be easy to neutralize.

But then the man turned and locked eyes with her, and in that split second, she froze. Her mind had screamed at her to pull the trigger, but her body wouldn't obey. All she could do was stand there and wait for him to put a bullet in her head. Instead, the hunter gazed at her for what seemed like an eternity, then joined his buddies already in the SUV and sped away.

Rachel was so focused on the memory she didn't even realize the meeting had started until someone nudged her knee with theirs. Giving herself a mental shake, she glanced over to find Diego staring at her like he thought she was on drugs. Then he motioned with his chin toward the far side of the small conference table in Gage's office. Crap, she didn't even remember sitting down.

She looked around the table, hoping no one else was aware she'd zoned out, but everyone was focused on Chief Leclair and the collection of documents and photos spread out on the table. Rachel was relieved to see that none of them had anything to do with Rachel or her run-in with that damn hunter.

"Jennifer Lloyd is the best assistant district attorney in Dallas County," Leclair said, spinning a photo around on the table so the rest of them could see it. "Which is why she was assigned as the prosecutor in the Alton Marshall trial."

The picture showed a pretty woman in her mid-to-late forties with shoulder-length, brunette hair and a serious expression on her face. Leclair picked up a photo of a man Rachel recognized as Alton Marshall and placed it beside Jennifer Lloyd's. He had calculating eyes and dark hair he wore slicked back from his face.

Rachel scanned the guy's rap sheet that Leclair handed out while Gage and Mike discussed the man with the new chief. Apparently, Marshall had been a low-level lieutenant for a local crime boss named Walter Hardy, whom the SWAT team had taken down a year and a half ago when the man had kidnapped Gage's wife.

"I read the reports on the hostage situation," Leclair said, studying Gage thoughtfully. "I'm impressed you were able to wipe out an entire organized crime syndicate without any injuries on our side."

"We were lucky," Gage told her. "Unfortunately, Marshall was out of the country that night, or we would have taken him down too."

Leclair nodded. "And with the connections he'd made there along with the muscle they were willing to loan him, Marshall was able to rebuild Hardy's crime syndicate in a shockingly short period of time. Since his return to the country in September, he's completely taken over the opiate drug trade in the southwestern part of the country and started making major inroads into human trafficking. As you can guess, Marshall has become a very rich man. But that money—and the speed at which he's acquired it—has made him sloppy. The DPD arrested him a month ago, and Jennifer has put together a solid case against him. Marshall has his lawyers doing everything they can to slow down his trial while his goons work behind the scenes to make all the witnesses and evidence disappear."

"And you want us to protect your witnesses," Mike said.

When Leclair didn't answer right away, Rachel looked up to see the chief regarding her tall, good-looking African American teammate with what could only be described as interest.

Crap. Was Leclair hot for Mike?

If the way the woman's heart suddenly beat faster was anything to go on, Rachel suspected the answer was definitely yes. Unfortunately, the chief got her act together too quickly for Rachel to be sure.

"Not the witnesses—Jennifer Lloyd," Leclair said. "Last night, someone put a bomb in her car while it was sitting at the courthouse. Jennifer was finishing up something and asked one of her investigators to bring her car around to the front of the building. The bomb got the investigator instead of her."

Gage frowned. "So, you want us to keep Jennifer Lloyd safe until the trial is over?"

Leclair nodded. "I know this isn't something your team normally gets involved in, and yes, I know the DA's office has a whole squad of people for this kind of thing, but I want her to have more protection than that." She sighed. "Jennifer and I went to college together. She'd hate the idea of me pulling strings on her behalf, and I know it's wrong to use my position to ask your people to do something like this, but I can't let her go this alone. I simply can't."

Gage shook his head. "You don't ever have to apologize for wanting to protect your friends and family. It's what any of us would do. If you need our help, you have it."

Leclair visibly relaxed at that. "Thank you."

"Corporal Kendrick will head up the security detail, working with Officers Bennett, Martinez, and Duncan. If you need additional personnel, don't hesitate to reach out to Senior Corporal Taylor. He'll get you anything you need."

Rachel heard Leclair's heart quicken at the mention of Mike's name, but nothing showed on her face. "Thanks for the offer, Commander, but I don't think it will be necessary to bring in more of your people. Jennifer's husband, Conrad, is as terrified as I am about this trial and has hired an entire private security firm to watch over her. The people he's employed are all prior military, and I have no doubt they'll do a good job. I simply want some of my own people sticking close to Jennifer, just in case."

Gage nodded, but Rachel could tell from the look on his face that he wasn't a fan of working with a private security firm. Not that he had anything against private security or prior military. It was the fact that having people like them around increased the likelihood someone would see something they weren't supposed to see—like glowing eyes, fangs, and claws.

The meeting wrapped up a little while later, after which Gage offered to take the chief over to the training building to meet the rest of the team.

"There might even be some donuts left," he said with a laugh.

Rachel wasn't too sure about that, though she hoped so. She was already craving another Boston cream.

"You okay?" Diego whispered as they followed everyone else out of the admin building and walked across the compound to the training one. "You seemed a million miles away for a while in there."

She nodded. "Just thinking about other stuff I guess."

Rachel could tell Diego wasn't buying that, but before he could call her on it, the pungent smell of leather and gun oil made her stop midstep and jerk her head around to scan the perimeter fence and the collection of parking lots and warehouses beyond.

"What is it?" Diego asked.

She didn't answer right away, too focused on the scents she'd smelled so many times over the past couple months wafting toward her on the morning breeze. But while they were familiar, there was something different, too. Something wild and dangerous.

As she sniffed the air, she studied the vehicles in the lots, then each warehouse, but didn't see anyone. Then again, she never did. The scents seemed to pop up, then disappear just as quickly, making her wonder if she truly was losing her sanity.

When she still didn't reply, Diego came around to stand in front of her. "Rachel, do you smell something?"

She shoved the scents of leather and gun oil away, immediately picking up on another one that was equally comforting but more real.

"Yeah—donuts." Giving him a smile, she stepped around him and continued toward the training building. "Let's go get some before they're all gone."

Diego caught up with her in time to grab the door and open it for her. Rachel murmured a quick thanks, refusing to look at him as she hurried inside so she wouldn't have to see the concern in his eyes.

Knox Lawson dropped to lay flat on the roof the moment Rachel snapped her head around and looked in his direction, terrified she'd seen him even though he was on the top of a two-story warehouse across the street from the DPD SWAT compound. He stayed there with his forehead planted on the gravel-and-tar roof for a slow count of thirty, the ground rough against his skin, before slowly lifting his head to look around. He breathed a sigh of relief when he saw the woman he'd been stalking for nearly two months had turned to make her way toward another building with her big coworker. Damn, that had been close. He was a good four hundred yards away from the SWAT compound and easily thirty feet above the ground, and yet Rachel had looked straight at him like she'd known exactly where he was.

He liked to think that wasn't possible, but the truth was, he didn't have a clue what a werewolf was capable of, especially a female werewolf. He'd recently come to the conclusion everything he'd learned from the other hunters on the subject had been complete and utter bullshit. For all he knew, werewolves could read minds and Rachel had known there was some guy nearby staring at her ass.

Knox realized with a start he was growling softly as he watched Rachel walk away. He bit his tongue until his suddenly too-sharp teeth pierced the flesh, making him growl again, this time for a completely different reason. But even as the metallic taste of blood filled his mouth, he still couldn't pull his gaze away from the woman's curvy figure. How could she look that good in a pair of uniform cargo pants? He'd seen hundreds of women—maybe thousands of them—in military uniforms and none of them had looked as alluring as Rachel.

His whole body suddenly tensed as the big guy with Rachel opened the door for her, stepping aside to let her enter the building first. Before Knox even realized what he was doing, he was halfway to his knees, ready to jump off the roof and leap the fence into the police compound to stop the other cop from putting a hand on her as he motioned her into the building.

Knox stopped himself just in time, fighting for control of the animal inside him that howled at even the possibility that another man might touch the woman he'd been obsessed with for weeks.

Inside the compound, Rachel disappeared through the door, her coworker never coming close to touching her. Knox dropped back down to the roof, breathing deeply and gasping through a sensation unlike anything he'd ever felt before. Well, unlike anything he'd ever felt before getting shot at this same compound back in December.

Knox swore he could feel muscles all over his body twisting and flexing like they were trying to assume a different shape, sweat breaking out along his spine, and those damn teeth making an even bigger mess out of his tongue. When he finally got himself back under control, he took another quick look to confirm Rachel truly was out of sight. Then he lay there, letting the sweat cool on his body as he berated himself for losing it again.

What the hell was wrong with him? Stalking this woman for months and swiping her junk mail to figure out her name was bad enough, but freaking out at the mere thought of someone touching her was completely insane. Then again, *insane* was a good way to describe his life lately.

Knox had bailed on the Navy a little less than a year ago. The SEALs had been something he'd poured his heart and soul into for eight years, and he thought he'd stay for at least twenty, maybe more. Then a man he'd barely even known had gotten killed on a mission, and his death had changed everything. Knox had tried to explain it to his teammates at

Coronado and to his family, but he'd never been able to put what he was feeling into words. Probably because he didn't want to. All anyone knew for sure was that one minute he'd loved being a SEAL more than anything, and the next, he couldn't do it anymore.

While neither his SEAL teammates nor his family had turned their backs on him, they hadn't tried to hide their disappointment, either. So he'd wandered around for a while—searching for what, he wasn't sure. He thought he'd found it when he fell in with the hunters. He thought he was saving the world from monsters, but the first time he'd seen what the hunters did to one of the werewolves they'd caught, he realized he'd made the biggest mistake of his life. The werewolves weren't the monsters; the hunters were. But by then, it was too late to back out.

The attack on the SWAT team at a frigging wedding reception of all places confirmed the hunters were psychotic. Yeah, they were werewolves, but still, they were frigging cops. Worse, there'd been women and kids at that party. He'd pointed that out, but the hunters didn't care.

When the shooting had started, Knox made the decision to bail, figuring he wouldn't be missed in the chaos. Afterward, they'd assume he was dead, right? It wasn't like they gave a damn about him.

Then he'd seen a gorgeous woman with long, blond hair running through the compound in a beautiful dress, a handgun held low and confident in her hand. That's when everything had really gone to hell. He hadn't wanted to believe she could be a werewolf, but from the way she moved, he knew she had to be.

His attention was so focused on the beautiful,

hypnotizing woman he almost missed the other hunter taking aim and planning to shoot her like the cowardly piece of crap he was. Knox didn't overthink the situation. He'd spent the past eight years of his life reacting when shit hit the fan, so he jumped in just in time to take the bullet intended for her.

The bullet had hit him in the thigh, pain ripping through him as it hit bone and kept going. His vision darkened as agony overwhelmed him, and he knew the impact of the round had probably cracked his femur. He'd shoved away the urge to pass out, spinning and firing his weapon for the first time since entering the compound, putting a round through the center of the hunter's chest.

Then he'd run, knowing he had to get out of there before he passed out. He had no desire to be involved with the hunters anymore, and if he stayed, he had no doubt he'd go to prison with them. He'd just reached the SUV they'd left near the perimeter when he felt a pricking sensation along his spine. He'd turned to find the blond woman staring at him with vivid green, glowing eyes, her weapon pointed straight at him. She was so damn perfect all he could do was stare back, even though he knew she was going to kill him.

But as the seconds dragged on, he realized she wasn't going to shoot him at all. For the life of him, he still couldn't understand why. The next thing he knew, the moment was over and he was jumping into the driver's seat of the getaway vehicle and speeding out of there. He'd been tempted to put a bullet in each of the hunters in the SUV with him, but in the end, he couldn't do that. He could deal with killing someone in the heat of combat, but murdering them in cold blood, not so much. Even if they were complete d-bags.

As a result, he'd been forced to babysit the three hunters, along with the dumbass Dallas chief of police, who was working with the a-holes, all the way back to LA, his leg bleeding and in pain the entire way. He'd tried to bail several times, but hadn't been able to, and before he knew what was happening, the vampires had elevated him from hunter to private security. He attempted to decline the promotion, but then one of the bloodsuckers had pointed out how easy it was to separate a man's head from his body, and he changed his mind.

Things got weird after that—if it was possible to get weirder than going from Navy SEAL to werewolf hunter to private security for a coven of vampires. But two days after the debacle in Dallas, the bullet wound in his leg had completely healed. That's when he'd realized something had changed. Knox hadn't known what was happening to him, and in the dark recesses of his mind, he'd been willing to admit—if only to himself—that he was scared as hell.

With everything happening in his screwed-up life right then, he'd never expected to see the beautiful werewolf from the wedding reception again—except maybe in his dreams. But Rachel had shown up in LA, and everything had spiraled completely out of control as he'd found himself inexplicably drawn to her. He'd barely understood what the hell he was doing as he followed her all over the city, then chased her back to Dallas after she and her friends wiped out the vampires.

It was scary, the hold a complete stranger had on him.

Knox was still on the roof, contemplating how much more bizarre the whole situation could get—beyond stalking a SWAT werewolf cop to her frigging place of employment—when his cell phone vibrated. Wondering who the hell could be calling him at this time of the morning, he pulled the phone out of his back pocket and rolled over, sitting up as he thumbed the green button and put the phone to his ear.

"Lawson. Who are you and what do you want?"

A deep, rumbling chuckle met his abrasive greeting and Knox knew who the caller was before the man said anything.

"Did I catch you in the middle of something with that lady friend of yours?" Theo Whittaker sneered. "You know, the one you never want to talk about."

Knox ground his jaw. Theo was his boss as well as the owner of Direct Action Private Security. The man was also a frigging d-bag. He was constantly talking about the women he banged and assumed every guy on the planet wanted to boast about it too.

Knox had never intended to work private security. In the world he came from, private security was something you ended up in, not something you aspired to do—kind of like porn or prostitution. But stalking a female werewolf back and forth across the country had gotten expensive. Ergo, he'd needed a job. DAPS paid good money and was easy to get into for someone with his résumé.

"I'm not with anyone," he said. "I told you before. There is no woman in my life. I was sleeping. You woke me up."

"Bullshit. I can practically hear the heavy breathing over the phone. What, did you just finish getting—ahem—intimate with her?"

Knox cursed silently. Stalking Rachel from the rooftop across the street from the SWAT compound was the most intimate he'd been with a woman since he'd gotten out of the Navy.

Damn, that was sad.

"Is there a reason you called?" he asked, refusing to engage his perverted boss on the subject.

"We got a new job," Theo said. "Some woman lawyer got herself on the bad side of a bunch of scary dudes, and her husband is paying us an ass-ton of money to keep her and their daughter safe. I need you to come with me to do a recon of their residence and start working up guard shifts. We'll need to work with the local cops, too, since they're going to be involved as well. I know this shit is your jam, so I want you with me from the jump."

Knox didn't bother to point out *this shit* was the jam of almost everyone in the company, since all of them were prior military. But if Theo wanted him to take point on this, whatever. It was a paycheck.

"So, this family we're protecting. It's just the three of them, right?" Knox asked, already working through the logistics of babysitting people he didn't know the first thing about. "The lawyer, her husband, and their daughter?"

"Yup. Mom's a looker, too," Theo said. "At least she is in the pictures I've seen of her. Wouldn't mind hitting that, I can tell you."

Knox shook his head. "Theo, you're a pig. You know that, right?"

The man laughed. "Hell yeah. And proud of it. Meet me at the office in thirty. Pick up breakfast on the way, would you?"

Knox hung up with a growl, his gums aching as his teeth threatened to rip their way right out again. He prayed he didn't have to work much with Theo on this job. The man had been with Army Special Forces for years before getting out to open DAPS, so he was capable, but it was damn hard being around the guy without ripping his throat out with your bare hands—or your teeth.

He groaned at the visual. He'd just imagined wanting to sink his teeth into another human being's throat. What the hell was wrong with him?

But the truth was, he knew what was wrong. And no matter how long he'd been putting it off, he was going to have to stop screwing around and finally talk to the only person who might be able to help him. And soon.

"But not today," he muttered.

Getting to his feet, he headed toward the back of the warehouse roof and the ladder attached to the side of the building.

CHAPTER 2

Rachel jerked upright in bed, screaming in terror loud enough to wake the dead until she realized it had all been another nightmare.

Crap, she was so over this.

She flopped back on the bed, groaning in disgust when she noticed her sheets were soaking wet with sweat. She covered her eyes with her forearm and licked her lips, making a face at the metallic tang of blood in her mouth courtesy of her fully extended fangs. She only hoped her screams hadn't woken her poor neighbors again.

Glancing over at the clock on her nightstand, she saw that it was only a few minutes past 2:00 a.m. Great. She'd gotten an entire three hours of sleep. Three more nights like this and it might add up to a full evening's rest.

With a sigh, she replayed the dream, trying to remember exactly what had scared her so much. But it was difficult recalling any details. Nothing more than images of something dark and vaguely shaped like a man chasing her, clawing, stabbing, and biting at her back and shoulders as she tried to get away. But no matter how fast she ran, she couldn't escape the thing in her dream. Even without being able to see it, she knew with every fiber of her soul that whatever it was hated her and wanted her dead. The worst part of the nightmare, beyond the pain and the fear, was hearing the thing laugh at her. Harsh, sick-sounding cackles that twisted her stomach into knots and made her want to curl up into a ball. The thing in her nightmare knew she was terrified and had reveled in that hopeless terror.

She reached up and fingered the necklace lying on her chest, toying with the Celtic shield knot charm hanging from the chain there. Hannah had given her the necklace right before Rachel had left Chattanooga for Dallas, and she never took it off. She and Hannah had become good friends during their recovery in the hospital and had spent a lot of time together afterward simply being there for each other after that traumatic night in the cemetery. Hannah had given her the Celtic knot for protection. Rachel had given her a wolf charm necklace for the same reason.

If it wasn't so late, Rachel would have jumped on the computer and checked in with Hannah that very second. The two of them texted and Skyped regularly since Rachel had moved, but giving her a call now was out of the question, so Rachel pushed back the paisley-print comforter and climbed out of bed, then stood there for a moment, waiting for the dizziness to pass. She always felt weak after a nightmare, but lately it seemed the episodes were getting worse. Or maybe the dreams were. Either way, it felt like someone had drained the energy completely from her body.

Since she wasn't getting any more sleep tonight no matter how exhausted she was, she decided to make some coffee. If she was going to be awake at this ungodly hour, she might as well be caffeinated, too. But first, she needed to rinse the taste of blood from her mouth.

Padding into the hallway, she wandered into the bathroom. The light in there was already on, as was every other light in her apartment, including the bedroom. Thanks to those damn nightmares, she couldn't stand to be in the dark anymore.

She studied her reflection in the big mirror above the vanity for a moment, groaning at the dark circles visible under her eyes. She shouldn't be surprised. She hadn't gotten a good night of sleep in forever. Holding her hair back from her face ponytail style, she turned on the faucet and cupped water in her hand.

While she rinsed her mouth, she thought about the meeting she and the guys had with Jennifer Lloyd at her office that morning. They'd gone there to discuss her schedule and daily routine, hoping to start working out the details of how they were going to keep her safe, but while the prosecutor had said all the right things about appreciating their help and doing anything to help make their jobs easier, she'd seemed kind of cavalier when it came to the threat she was facing, vetoing every suggestion Zane made regarding even simple changes to her itinerary. Maybe Jennifer was so focused on taking down Alton Marshall she couldn't think about anything else, even her own safety. It was hard to keep someone safe when they refused to believe they were in danger.

Rachel just finished rinsing her mouth when she felt something behind her. She couldn't say if it was a sound she'd heard, a flicker of movement out of the corner of her eye, or merely her inner wolf sensing a presence, but whatever it was, she quickly spun around ready to defend herself. She didn't see anything in the hallway just outside the door, so she tiptoed over to peek out. Her bedroom was empty, as was her living room—at least what she could see of them from where she stood. Holding on to the doorframe, she stepped into the hallway and sniffed the air, trusting her sense of smell to tell her if there was anyone in her apartment.

There wasn't.

There never was.

Even so, Rachel couldn't shake the feeling that someone was watching her. It was an unnerving sensation, and she swore the temperature in the apartment dropped ten degrees as goose bumps chased over her body.

Shivering, she turned to go back into the bathroom.

And froze.

Instead of her own reflection, a clown stared back at her from the mirror. Not just any clown, either, but the clown who'd tried to kill her in the graveyard that night.

Rachel screamed and stumbled back, fear gripping her even as she instinctively reached for a sidearm she wasn't wearing right then. She whirled around, sure she was about to be attacked from behind, but no one was there. She was just as alone in her apartment as she'd been five seconds ago.

That didn't stop her from thinking about running into the bedroom to grab her service-issued .45 caliber from her bedside table. But she quickly dismissed the idea. What the hell good would a gun do in a situation like this?

Telling herself she was seeing things, she slowly turned to face the mirror again, bracing herself for what she'd see there. The clown was gone and all she saw was her own reflection, fangs and claws extended, eyes bright green. She hadn't even realized she'd shifted.

Rachel took a step back, only a little relieved the clown was nowhere in sight because that confirmed she was insane. On top of the bizarre scents she kept picking up, the glimpses of shadows out the corner of her eye, and the terrifying nightmares, now she was having waking flashbacks. She was losing her already-tentative grip on reality. How much worse was this going to get?

She glanced at the mirror one more time before heading out of the bathroom and through the living room to the kitchen. She made coffee, impatiently waiting for it to brew and thinking about the monster that still haunted her dreams—and now apparently her bathroom.

Horace Watkins, the man who'd tried to kill her in the cemetery, really *had* been a clown. First on the rodeo circuit in the eighties, then in a traveling circus through the nineties and into the early two thousands, and finally, in an old folks home of all places. Horace had also been criminally insane, at least according to his court-appointed lawyer. Rachel figured he was, especially when the guy had actually demanded the judge allow him to stand trial in his clown makeup.

The judge had said no, and the people with doctorate degrees had decided Horace wasn't insane. Or if he was, at least he was still aware enough to face a jury. Thank God. Because that meant the man ended up with a thirty-year sentence in Riverbend Maximum Security Institute versus an undefined stay in a mental facility. Never mind that Horace claimed he didn't remember anything about that night or what he'd done.

Yeah right.

Rachel had a crazy urge to call the prison in Nashville right then to make sure the demented clown was still there but quickly pushed that ridiculous thought aside. The man who'd made a mess of her head was still locked up and would be until he was old and gray.

Pouring coffee into a mug, she added sweetener and cream, then headed across the living room toward the balcony, opened the door, and stepped outside, letting the chilly night air caress her exposed skin. Since she was only wearing shorts and a Captain America tank top, she probably should have grabbed the throw from the couch, but the cool air felt good. It was like a shock to the system she hoped would clear out the remnants of whatever the hell just happened in her bathroom.

She leaned against the balcony railing to do a little stargazing from the second-floor deck when two scents that were becoming overwhelmingly familiar hit her. It was the same combination of scents she'd picked up this morning at the compound.

But this time it wasn't some slight trace carried on the breeze. Instead, it was thick and heavy, like whoever the scents belonged to had been standing on the balcony mere seconds ago. It struck her then that this was the first time she'd attributed the smell to a person. Before now, she hadn't been quite sure.

Hand tightening on her mug, she swept the street below her apartment with her gaze, taking in every car parked on the curb and row of buildings on the other side of the street, following the smell with her nose. It was strongest in that direction and she inhaled deeply. The scents were richer and fuller than she'd sensed before. And they definitely belonged to a man. Of that she was sure. The scents possessed a subtle hint of something so tantalizing that Rachel found her eyes going slightly unfocused as she fixated on it. She'd never smelled anything so...perfect.

Suddenly, she caught sight of movement across the street, buried in the shadows of the alley that ran alongside the organic food store. She turned all her attention in that direction, her eyes shifting so she could see better. That's when she saw a man's silhouette in the darkness.

As if sensing her gaze on him, the man retreated farther

into the alley, and while she couldn't see him, she could tell he was still there somewhere.

Setting her cup on the small table in between the two chairs, Rachel gripped the balcony railing and vaulted over it to the ground below. Her bare feet hit the sidewalk hard, but she ignored the discomfort and took off running across the street, chasing after the shadow.

The rocks and stray pieces of glass in the alley dug into her feet, but she refused to let that slow her as she ran as hard as she could. For a werewolf like her, that was pretty damn fast. But the man ahead of her was fast, too—too fast to be a normal human.

Crap, she was chasing another werewolf. She almost stumbled to a halt at the realization, shocked she hadn't recognized the unique scent until now. How was it possible she hadn't known it for what it was? Maybe because it had changed since she'd first smelled it all those weeks ago. The werewolf part of the scent seemed new.

Growling, she picked up speed, her body partially shifting as she ran faster, refusing to let the man ahead of her get away. It took a while to corner him, but when her prey turned down a dead-end alley, she knew she had him.

He didn't stop running until he reached the brick wall at the end of the alley. Then he stood there and stared at it as if trying to figure out how to go through it. Dark-haired, he was tall with broad shoulders and sleek muscles filling out the T-shirt he wore. He looked left and right, breathing hard as he searched for an escape route.

"You're not getting out of this alley," Rachel told him, not even trying to disguise the anger in her voice. This guy had been stalking her for weeks. He was lucky she didn't rip him to shreds first and ask questions later. "Not until you tell me who the hell you are and what you want with me."

Squaring his shoulders as if resigned to his fate, he slowly turned to face her. His hair was short on the sides and longer on the top, and his face carried a few days' worth of scruff that emphasized his square jaw, making him look dangerous and even more attractive than he probably had a right to. His eyes were a deep, rich chocolate brown, piercing but somehow soft at the same time.

She was well on her way to getting lost in those eyes when she suddenly realized she recognized him. He was the hunter she'd let get away. A hunter who was a werewolf.

She would have made a crack about how insane this entire situation was, but the expression on his face stopped her. For a guy who had an obvious confidence about him, he looked completely and utterly lost.

He lifted his hands in a gesture of surrender. "I'm sorry I've been following you, but something's happening to me and I think you're the only one who can help." When she didn't say anything, he took a deep breath and continued. "This is going to sound crazy, but I think I'm turning into a werewolf."

Rachel couldn't help it. She laughed. It was either that or start crying at the poetic irony that would make poor William Shakespeare choke on his writing quill.

"You're a werewolf?" she said. "Well, all I can say to that is, no shit, Sherlock."

Knox had envisioned his first face-to-face meeting with Rachel hundreds of times. But in absolutely none of those visions had he imagined the woman laughing at him. Yet that was what she was doing, as if his confession that he thought he was turning into a werewolf was the funniest thing in the world.

He had to admit she was even more beautiful up close—in a wild, almost feral way—and he couldn't stop himself from staring. Her long, blond hair was in disarray from chasing him at light speed through the streets, and her fair skin was glistening with a light sheen of sweat. Which was crazy, considering she wasn't wearing much in the way of clothes, and the temperature had to be thirty degrees tonight.

He tried not to gawk at her long, toned legs, but he couldn't help it. They were as perfect as the rest of her, right down to her bare feet.

Knox didn't realize how hard he'd been staring at her body until he lifted his head to find her light-brown eyes locked on him, brow arched in an expression that might have been amusement. Or anger. He wasn't entirely sure which.

"What? You have a problem with being a werewolf?" she demanded, her southern drawl sexy as hell. "Oh, that's right. You're a hunter. You kill werewolves for fun and now you are one. Ain't that a bitch?"

Knox really wasn't sure what to say to that. This really wasn't the way he'd expected this conversation to go.

"So, are you going to help me, or what?" he asked.

For the first time, it occurred to him that he might have wasted his time chasing her all over the country. To her, he was one of the people who'd tried to kill werewolves like her—attacked her and her friends at a wedding reception no less. Why the hell would she ever want to do anything to help him? Damn, he'd been so stupid. But from the moment he'd seen her at that wedding reception at the SWAT compound, he'd felt like there was something there.

"What kind of help do you think I can give you?"

Her tone had softened, giving him hope. At least for a moment.

"I'm hoping you can tell me how this happened. Because I know I never got bitten by a werewolf. More importantly, how do I make it go away?"

Rachel regarded him thoughtfully, as if deciding whether she wanted to help him or not. Finally, she jerked her chin toward the mouth of the alley. "Come on. This conversation is going to take a while, and there's a pot of coffee in my apartment with my name on it."

Without waiting for an answer, she turned and headed toward the street. Knox stared after her for a moment, then hurried to catch up. She didn't say anything on the way to her place and he didn't want to press his luck by trying to engage her in conversation. When they got there, Rachel had to climb up to the balcony since she didn't have her key while she insisted he take the traditional way through the apartment building's front door then went up to the second floor and waited for her to let him in.

Rachel's place was small but appeared bigger thanks to the light-colored paint on the walls and open floor plan. The earthy tones she'd used to decorate gave the apartment a warm, homey feel, as did the landscape paintings and framed photos of what he assumed were family and friends on the built-in bookcase along one wall of the living room.

"Make yourself comfortable," she said, gesturing to the tan-colored couch and matching love seat.

Knox did as she suggested, opting for the love seat. He expected her to head into the kitchen for that coffee she mentioned, but instead, she walked down the hall and into what he presumed was the bathroom. A moment later, he heard the water running and what sounded like a soft grunt of pain.

"You okay in there?" he called.

"Just picking out pieces of glass I got stuck in my feet running after you. I'm fine."

That sounded painful. And made him feel guilty for making her chase him. He hadn't intended for that to happen. No, the original plan had been simple. Stop by Rachel's apartment and knock on her door. Instead, he'd hung around across the street from her building like the stalker he'd become until she went to bed. Or at least he thought she'd gone to bed. He wasn't quite sure because she hadn't shut off any of the lights.

He'd just been about to leave when he'd heard her scream. The terror in it had cut right through him and he'd lost it.

The next thing he knew, he was on her second-floor balcony. He'd been this close to busting through the sliding glass door when Rachel had wandered out of her bedroom, slick with sweat and looking like death warmed over. Despite how crappy she'd looked, Knox was relieved she was safe and unharmed. While he knew it wasn't possible, for a moment, it almost seemed like he could actually hear her heart pounding. The idea that something could scare a werewolf like her shocked him. He'd been so busy trying to wrap his mind around that he hadn't even realized she was walking toward the balcony.

He'd hurdled the railing, hitting the street below like a bag of bricks thrown from a moving car. The pain was intense but, oddly, not as bad as it probably should have been. Nothing broke, so it was definitely a small price to pay to avoid getting caught.

Not that his clumsy escape had done much good. Somehow, Rachel had seen him and leaped off the balcony like a graceful gazelle. She'd chased him down like a barefoot bloodhound on crack, catching him with ridiculous ease.

But on the bright side, it had broken the ice on the introductions.

Knox glanced up as Rachel walked into the living room still wearing the same tank top and shorts. While he didn't mind getting another look at those legs, he was more concerned about her injured feet.

"You sure you don't need to go to the hospital and get checked out?" he asked. "With the trash and crap in those alleys, you could get a serious infection."

"We don't get infections, as long as you get any foreign debris out of the wounds. Your body will take care of everything else. It's a werewolf thing."

She lifted one foot, showing him that the bloody lacerations were now replaced with scars that looked three or four days old, then continued into the kitchen. Taking two mugs out of the cabinet, she grabbed a package of popcorn from another, then stuck it in the microwave. She was making popcorn…at 0300 in the morning. Coffee and popcorn. Different but okay. Within moments, the smell of butter and the sounds of popping kernels filled the apartment, making his mouth water.

When the microwave beeped a minute later, Rachel dumped the popcorn in a bowl, then poured coffee into the mugs.

She glanced at him over the peninsula separating the kitchen from the living room. “Cream and sweetener?”

He nodded. “Please.”

Rachel added cream and two packs of sweetener to each mug, then set the bowl of popcorn on a wooden tray along with them and carried everything into the living room. Placing the tray on the table, she handed Knox a mug, taking the one with the Tennessee Volunteers logo for herself. Then she curled up on the other couch, gracefully tucking her long legs under her.

Knox tried to keep from staring at all that exposed skin, but it was damn tough. He hadn't seen skin that smooth and perfect in a long time. Well, ever, actually. He attempted to focus on the aroma of the hot, buttered popcorn instead, but then he picked up another scent even more mouthwatering—cinnamon with a hint of licorice jelly beans. He'd never smelled those two scents together before, but they completely worked. Probably because they were two of his favorite things. Maybe she had a candle or some of that potpourri stuff in her apartment.

Wonder why I didn't smell it before.

He swigged his coffee. “So, it's true then. I'm a werewolf?”

Rachel arched a brow as she leaned forward to grab a handful of popcorn. While Knox was focused on her face, he didn't miss the fact she wasn't wearing a bra under that Captain America tank top. He had superb vision and the low sides of the tank showed off a teasing amount of skin.

“Yeah, you're a werewolf,” she said. “But you knew that already or you wouldn't be here.”

Knox nodded. “I guess. I think I knew it when I survived that gunshot wound. I mean, I should have bled to death within a few hours. The fangs and claws were a dead giveaway, too. Not to mention the anger management issues I've been having lately."

She frowned. "How many times have you lost control?"

"Enough," he said noncommittally.

He supposed losing control was simply part of turning into a monster. He lost count of how many times he'd snarled at people for no reason in the past week. He'd even come close to putting a few guys at Theo's security firm through a wall when an episode of roughhousing had gotten out of hand. Fortunately, Theo hadn't gotten upset and fired his ass. In fact, he'd approved, saying he liked the way Knox had put them in their place. Apparently, the boss thought some of his employees had been getting soft lately.

As far as Knox was concerned, the random outbursts were one more in a long string of reasons he needed to get this problem fixed. But before he got into that, he needed to understand how the hell he'd ended up in this situation to begin with.

"How can I be a werewolf?" he asked. "I didn't get bitten."

He reached out with his free hand to snag some popcorn so she wouldn't see how tense he was now that they'd come down to the sixty-four-thousand-dollar question. It was buttery and perfectly salted.

"It doesn't work like that." She sipped her coffee. "Werewolves aren't created from a bite. That's myth and Hollywood make-believe. We're born this way."

He snorted. "Like hell. I wasn't like this before I got shot at that wedding reception."

She scooped up some more popcorn, then leveled her gaze at him. "Actually you were. Getting shot merely brought the werewolf out in you."

Okay, now he was really confused. "Maybe you better start from the beginning."

Rachel nibbled on a piece of popcorn, and he stared at her mouth, transfixed as she chewed. He was so distracted he almost missed what she was saying.

"The werewolf trait is in our DNA," she explained. "It remains dormant until something traumatic—usually painful and, a lot of the time, violent—happens and triggers it." She popped another piece of popcorn in her mouth with a shrug. "And poof, you're a werewolf."

And poof, you're a werewolf.

Well, damn. Could it be anymore underwhelming? At least if another werewolf had attacked and bitten him, he'd have a cool story to tell. The most he could admit to was getting shot in the leg due to an overdeveloped sense of morality.

"So, getting shot was all it took?" he said.

"Apparently," she replied. "If it was bad enough."

He grabbed another handful of popcorn. "The bullet went straight through my leg, but I'm pretty sure it cracked my femur on the way out. Which is something I wouldn't recommend, by the way, especially when you have to drive nonstop across the country."

Her mouth curved. "I'll keep that in mind."

"How about you?" he asked. "What happened to turn you into a werewolf?"

Rachel hesitated for a moment before answering. "I was a cop in Chattanooga, and I responded to a suspicious activity call in a graveyard. Long story short, I got attacked by a psychopathic clown with a big knife trying to kill a teenage girl. He stabbed me a couple times and I almost died."

Knox stared at her, wondering for half a second if she was joking. But from the haunted look in her eyes, it was obvious she wasn't. "Okay, you win."

"Were we competing for something?"

"No." He shrugged. "But if we were talking about most-badass origin story, you'd win, hands down."

She snorted and ate more popcorn.

"You know," he said. "When I thought about having this conversation with you, I had dozens of questions, but now, I find myself coming back to one question over and over."

She regarded him, her light-brown eyes thoughtful. "What's that?"

"Can you help me learn to control this thing inside me?"

Rachel paused, her mug of coffee halfway to her mouth, her expression hardening. "You and your hunter friends spent the past two years trying to eradicate my kind from existence. Why should I help you with anything?"

The disdain and hatred in the words stung way more than they should have. He was tempted to defend himself, but he wasn't sure she'd even believe him. "Because I'm a werewolf like you now. Doesn't that automatically get me into the club—or whatever you call it?"

"That would be the Pack, and no, it doesn't automatically get you in. Not by a long shot."

Knox cursed silently, resisting the urge to give in to his gut and say the hell with it and get up and walk out. He wasn't sure why he didn't. He'd spent his whole life depending on those instincts. They'd sure as hell kept him alive on more deployments than he could count. But lately, he hadn't made the best decisions, so instead of running, he stayed where he was.

"So being a werewolf doesn't get me anything. How about saving your life?" he countered. "What does that earn me?"

Rachel's eyes narrowed. "What are you talking about? I don't remember you saving my life."

"How do you think I got shot?" He reached for more popcorn, tossing some in his mouth. Now that he'd gotten used to the idea of eating popcorn at 0300 hours, he had to admit it was pretty good. "I was running across that damn compound, doing everything I could to get the hell out of there without spilling any blood when I saw you. Unfortunately, another hunter saw you at the same time and decided to pop a cap in you. I got shot because I stepped in front of a bullet with your name on it."

He waited for her to throw the bullshit flag, but instead, understanding dawned on her face, like she'd just remembered something.

"You shot the hunter who tried to kill me," she breathed. "Why would you do something like that when you were one of them?"

Knox opened his mouth and closed it again. Unfortunately, there wasn't a simple answer to the question. "It's a long and complicated story."

She shrugged. "So talk. It's not like I plan on getting any more sleep tonight."

"This might come as a shock, but while you can obviously go without your beauty rest and still look good, I can't. I need to go home and crash for a few hours before I drag my sweet southern ass into work. If you're willing to meet up again tomorrow night, I'll tell you why I took that bullet for you. In exchange, you can teach me how to control the werewolf I've turned into."

There was no sane reason for her to agree, which was why Knox was sure she was about to tell him to pound sand. He couldn't let that happen.

"You could have killed me that night. You had me in your sights with your finger on the trigger, but you didn't take me out," he reminded her. "Something tells me you had your reasons, and now, I'm hoping they're enough to make you agree to see me again."

Her eyes pierced him. "How many werewolves did you kill when you were a hunter?"

"None," he said without hesitation. "I won't try telling you I didn't see what those assholes did to your kind. To my kind, I guess. I never took part in any of it and I hate myself for standing by and letting it happen, but after I realized what I'd gotten myself into, I did everything I could to get out."

She seemed to consider that, then slowly nodded. "Okay. Come by tomorrow night at eight. I'll talk to you again and give you a chance to explain. But I'm not making any promises. If I don't like what you have to say, I'll tell the rest of my pack you're here and let them decide what to do with you."

He shuddered at that but refused to let his trepidation show. "Fair enough. Tomorrow night then."

Downing the rest of his coffee, Knox scooped up one more handful of popcorn, then stood and headed for the door. Once there, he paused with his hand on the knob to glance over his shoulder at Rachel. She looked exhausted, and he wanted to tell her to get some sleep, but he was pretty sure the concern would be wasted on her.

CHAPTER 3

Rachel gaped as she and her pack mates entered the Lloyd mansion the next morning. She'd never been in a place this posh in her life. With its marble floors, crystal chandeliers, and breathtaking view of the Dallas skyline, the immense two-story house looked like it should be on one of those shows on HGTV featuring luxury homes of the rich and famous. It made Rachel wonder why Jennifer was working as an assistant DA. She and her family clearly weren't hurting for cash. And while Rachel completely understood the idea of putting your life on the line for what you believed in because she did it every day, she had a hard time believing a woman who came from this kind of money would risk her life going after people like Alton Marshall.

"You have no idea how glad I am you're here."

Rachel turned to see Dominic Janikowski, the investigator from the DA's office they'd met yesterday, closing the door behind her and the guys. Shorter than any of them, he was a stocky, blond-haired guy with wire-rimmed glasses. "I know the private security Jennifer's husband hired are supposed to be all that and a bag of donuts, but I can't imagine any of them taking a bullet for her."

The man kept his voice low, like he thought the aforementioned security people were going to overhear, which Rachel doubted. Unless they were werewolves, of course.

As Dominic led them from the foyer and through a long hallway to the back of the house, Rachel fell into step beside

Diego while Zane and Trey moved ahead of them, listening to the guy vent about the fancy security guys being more interested in how much they were getting paid than keeping an eye on Jennifer.

"Did you find a sleeping pill that actually works on werewolves or something?" Diego asked softly. "You look more rested than you have in weeks."

Rachel felt more rested, too. To her surprise, she'd fallen asleep on the couch after Knox had left and stayed that way until the alarm clock in her bedroom had gone off. She'd slept deeply and contentedly, free of the nightmares that normally invaded her slumber every time she closed her eyes. While she was grateful for it, she had absolutely no idea why.

"No sleeping pill," she said. "I guess I finally got tired enough."

"That's good."

She nodded in agreement, but at the same time, she found herself wondering if maybe confronting Knox—whom she was convinced was the personification of her inner demon—had somehow helped. After agreeing to help the hunter learn how to be a werewolf, she'd expected to be bouncing off the walls. Instead, she'd felt…calm.

Rachel was still thinking about that when the smell of leather and gun oil hit her. She had a moment to wonder why she'd pick up those scents in the Lloyd home of all places as she and the guys followed Dominic into a library that was bigger than her whole apartment. Floor-to-ceiling bookcases lined all four walls. And above, accessible only by a spiral staircase in one corner, was a catwalk of sorts around the perimeter of the room, so someone could get to the topmost shelves. The only window in the room was up there, too, but it was so big that it let in a tremendous amount of natural light.

The room was dominated by a huge fireplace. With a modern-looking stainless steel chimney that went all the way to the ceiling, it was completely enclosed in glass on the bottom, so you could see though it on all sides, from wherever you were in the library. A reading area made up of comfortable seating was on one side while a large oval table with a dozen chairs took up space on the other.

Jennifer and her husband sat at the table with three men in dark suits—one of whom was none other than former-hunter-turned-werewolf Knox Lawson.

Are you effing kidding me?

Rachel froze halfway into the room, praying he was some kind of delusion, another sign of her impending nervous breakdown. While losing her mind was scary as hell, it was better than Knox really being there. But he *was* there—and he was staring straight at her.

Or more precisely, at her and her three pack mates, who were staring right back at him. Like they knew he was a hunter.

When none of the guys lost it and went into full-on werewolf mode right then and there, Rachel forced herself to take a deep breath and relax. There was no way Diego and her other teammates could know Knox was a hunter. Corporal Jayden Brooks was the only member of her pack who'd actually seen him during the shootout at the SWAT compound, so as long as he never saw Knox face-to-face, everything should be fine.

But while her pack mates might not know Knox was a former hunter, they obviously knew he was a werewolf. The scent was a dead giveaway. Luckily, stumbling across a werewolf in Dallas they didn't know wasn't unusual. The city had become a haven for them since the hunters had become more prevalent.

Rachel followed the guys over to the table, holding out her hand to shake with each of the men on Knox's team. When she got to him, she gave him the same smile she'd given the others, silently screaming at him with her eyes to play along and not say something stupid. Thankfully, he returned her smile and said it was nice to meet her.

Relief surged through her. Thank God the man wasn't an idiot. If Knox started making noise about already knowing her, the questions from her pack mates would never have ended.

Rachel chose a seat on the far side of the table from Knox, going out of her way not to sit directly across from him. That would have been way too distracting and she couldn't be sure she wouldn't give herself away. Out of the corner of her eye, she saw Diego glance her way and prayed he hadn't noticed she was suddenly so discombobulated.

Sitting beside Jennifer at one end of the table, the tall, distinguished-looking Conrad Lloyd didn't seem nearly as thrilled about having Rachel and her teammates there as Dominic. He didn't come right out and say it, but it was obvious he thought his private security would do a much better job of protecting his family than four cops. It was equally clear that his wife preferred to put her faith in the police she worked with every day. As a result, the tension between the two was thick enough to cut with a chainsaw.

Rachel did her best to casually take in the men from Direct Action Personal Security, a task made more difficult by the habit her gaze had of constantly gravitating back to Knox. Dammit, it was like she couldn't take her eyes off the man.

But if she kept staring at Knox, someone was going to notice. Dragging her gaze away from him, she studied each of his coworkers.

In his midforties, curly-haired Theo was the oldest of the three. He sat on the other side of Conrad, and when he wasn't trying to blow sunshine up the rich man's ass, he was making sure they all knew he owned the security company they'd be working with. The other man was a young guy in his midtwenties named Ethan Porter. Like Knox, he seemed to be new at the company and didn't talk much after the introductions had been made. Then again, Theo did enough talking for all of them.

As important as the subject might be, Rachel had to admit she quickly lost interest as Theo and Zane started going into the details of how they planned to protect Jennifer and her family. She couldn't focus on what they were saying, mostly because her head was still spinning over the realization that Knox was working for the security company that was protecting the same Dallas prosecutor as SWAT.

So, instead of worrying about her shift schedule or who she'd be working with, Rachel sat there glancing at Knox out of the corner of her eye and replaying the little she'd learned from him last night.

If Knox was telling the truth about that night at the wedding reception, then she owed him her life. Well, probably not her life, since a random gunshot from a hunter fifty feet away was unlikely to have been fatal. But she doubted Knox would have known that, so he honestly thought he'd saved her life. If nothing else, he'd saved her from a lot of pain. No one enjoyed getting shot, not even a werewolf.

So assuming he was telling the truth, the important question was why would a hunter put himself at risk for a werewolf?

Rachel gave him another covert glance, but other than noting for the second time in two days that Knox was sinfully good-looking, the answer to that question remained elusive. She bit back a growl. What the hell was wrong with her? Knox was a hunter. She should hate his guts. More than that, she should turn him over to Gage and the rest of her pack. But the simple truth was, while she might not entirely trust him, she didn't hate him, either. And the idea of turning him over to the Pack had never entered her mind last night for even a second. Just thinking about it right then made her stomach twist uncomfortably, though she had no idea why.

Great. Another question she couldn't answer.

Nodding now and then to make it seem like she was paying attention to the conversation going on around the table, Rachel continued running through last night's discussion with Knox, realizing maybe she hadn't been truthful about not trusting him. How else could she explain telling him how she'd become a werewolf? No one in the Pack but Gage knew about the clown who'd attacked her.

Then there was the part where she'd agreed to meet with Knox again and give him a chance to explain himself. If that wasn't evidence of some kind of trust, she didn't know what was.

But why the hell would she do that?

There had to be a reason—beyond the fact that Knox

Lawson was ruggedly handsome, smelled delicious, and had a droolworthy body.

Oh. My. God. Had she seriously put the words *drool-worthy* and *former hunter* in the same thought? What was wrong with her?

Rachel was still considering how far around the bend she might have traveled to even think crap like that when Adalynn Lloyd, Jennifer and Conrad's sixteen-year-old daughter, appeared in the doorway. Petite and slender with wavy, dark hair just past her shoulders and blue eyes, she regarded Rachel and the others around the table curiously.

"Mom, Dad," the girl said, sounding more than a little nervous. Rachel didn't blame her. The fact that the family needed private security—and four SWAT cops—to keep them safe had to be terrifying. "Dominic said you wanted to see me?"

Conrad waved her in. "We do. Come in, Addy."

The girl slowly made her way over to the table, still looking a little unsure about this whole thing. Addy seemed to relax after she sat down and her father introduced her to everyone, but Rachel got the feeling it was all an act. The girl's heart still thumped as fast as it had when she'd first walked into the room, and the scent of fear coming off her made it obvious she was scared as hell. It only got worse as Theo went into detail about some of the security measures, like sweeping vehicles for explosive devices three times a day and keeping the curtains closed to reduce the chance of a sniper getting a clean shot. Maybe they thought Addy would be fine with hearing that stuff, but Rachel knew she wasn't. In fact, she was on the verge of hyperventilating. Rachel's heart went out to her. Addy reminded her of

Hannah so much right then, and it hurt to see the girl so anxious.

Since Addy was sitting beside her, it was easy for Rachel to lean over and speak to her without interrupting the conversation the rest of the table were having.

"You want to get out of here and go talk about some of this stuff?" she asked softly. "I promise it isn't as scary as it sounds."

Addy looked at her mom and dad, then at everyone else at the table, before giving Rachel a nod.

The teen led the way over to the spiral staircase and up to the catwalk area, then kept going until she reached the gigantic window with an equally large built-in bench seat. Rachel waited until Addy sat down, then did the same, taking in the picturesque view of the big backyard and woods beyond.

"Wow," Rachel breathed. "It's gorgeous up here."

"I know." Addy smiled. "Besides my room, this is my most favorite place in the house."

"I can see why." Rachel turned back to look at the teen. "So, like I said downstairs, this whole thing isn't as scary as it sounds, and I don't want you to let any of this stuff freak you out, okay? You have my word that we aren't going to let anything happen to you or your parents."

Addy regarded her thoughtfully for a moment, like she'd never had a soul make a promise like that to her. It must have been exactly what she needed to hear, because her heart rate started to slow to normal and the tension began to visibly seep out of her body.

"I'm not naive," the girl said softly. "I know my mom could have been killed in that explosion and that someone I met at last year's Christmas party *was* killed. But to hear you guys talking about searching our cars and having to worry about someone shooting through a window just makes everything so much more..."

"Real?" Rachel asked.

Addy nodded. "Yeah, I think that's the word I'm looking for." She played with the strings on her Dallas Cowboys hoodie, her brow furrowing a little. "Dad said you guys will be around for a while. How long do you think the trial Mom's working will last? I've asked her, but she doesn't want to tell me anything about it."

Rachel shrugged. She hadn't exactly been keeping up-to-date on the Alton Marshall front. Her slowly dissolving sanity had been a bigger concern for her. But Addy deserved at least some kind of answer. It was her life after all.

"I don't know much about the trial but, best case, a couple weeks," she said. "It could drag out for months, though."

Addy's eyes widened, but then her expression changed, taking on a panic-stricken look. "Does this mean I'll be on total lockdown that long? I won't be able to go to school or...date?"

Rachel resisted the urge to laugh. Addy was in danger and she knew it, but she was also a teenager with a social life that was probably more important to her than her *actual* life.

"The plan is to make sure you have as normal of a life as possible," she assured the girl. "That means sending guards with you wherever you go. They'll be discreet when you're at school, so hopefully, no one will even know they're there. And as far as dates, I'm sure we can work something out."

Addy breathed a sigh of relief. "Thank God. The Valentine's Day dance is coming up soon and I can't miss it. Aaron asked me weeks ago to be his date."

The girl's heart began to pitter-patter for a completely different reason now, and Rachel couldn't help but smile at the obvious signs of young love. Or at least what a sixteen-year-old thought was love.

"Aaron?" she prompted.

Addy's eyes took on a dreamy expression. Dang, this girl had it bad.

"He's eighteen, is a senior, and has a motorcycle," she said softly, throwing a glance from the corner of her eye at her parents sitting at the table on the floor below, like they might overhear, then leaned in a little closer to Rachel. "My mom and dad won't let me ride with him, but I've sat on it once. When he asked me to the dance, I seriously thought I was going to pass out!"

Rachel briefly wondered if she'd ever been that dramatic when she was a teen. Man, she hoped not.

"Something tells me he wears a cool leather jacket when he's on his bike, right?" she asked with as much seriousness as she could muster.

"Ermahgerd, yes! He wears it all the time, even when it's not cold. He looks so amazing in it." Addy giggled. "How did you know that?"

Rachel grinned. "Just a guess."

As Addy continued to gush about Aaron and his black leather jacket and how the boy was so gorgeous and smart and funny, Rachel nodded and smiled. While she couldn't remember if she'd ever been as gaga over a boy in high school, she vaguely remembered what it was like to be a teenager, so she knew there was a good chance the girl wouldn't even be interested in Aaron by the end of the school year.

Somewhere in the middle of Addy's soliloquy, Rachel

found her gaze drawn to the floor below and Knox. As if feeling her gaze on him, Knox glanced up at her. Rachel didn't look away but instead locked eyes with him, blatantly studying him.

His face was a bit more rugged, with more scruff, compared to the guys she was normally attracted to, but in Knox's case, she had to admit it worked. Not that she really cared, since he was a former hunter. The guy could be David Boreanaz's twin and she wouldn't have looked at him twice.

Riiiight.

"I think they're finishing up down there," Addy said.

Rachel dragged her gaze away from Knox to look at everyone else at the table and realized Addy was right. By the time she and the teen girl got down to the main floor of the library, Jennifer and Conrad were already heading out the door with Theo and Ethan to show them the room where they could set up the security command post. Addy gave Rachel a wave and raced after her parents, saying something about needing to remind them about the new dress they promised to buy her for the dance.

That left Knox alone with Rachel and her pack mates.

Zane leaned back in his chair and regarded Knox thoughtfully. "You're new in Dallas, aren't you?"

Knox nodded. "I've been in town a few weeks."

"Did you come here looking for protection from the hunters?" Diego asked.

Knox glanced at Rachel and she tensed, suddenly terrified he'd admit he used to be one. No, he couldn't be that dumb. She had no idea if he knew how to lie convincingly, though. Since he was talking to a group of werewolves, he'd better nail it, or he was screwed.

"The hunters did play a big part in my coming here, but I wasn't looking for protection as much as information," Knox said smoothly, looking at Diego. "I wanted to find someone who could help me understand what was happening to me."

"When did you go through your change?" Zane asked.

"A little before Christmas," Knox said. "I ended up in the middle of a shooting, and long story short, I took a bullet in the thigh that hit an artery. I thought for sure I was going to bleed out."

Rachel thought Knox had done an exceptionally good job of lying until she saw the expression on Diego's face change from curious to suspicious. Crap, maybe Knox should have been a little more vague on the details. Something he'd said had obviously caught Diego's attention. But what?

"Wait a minute." Diego's eyes narrowed. "You expect us to believe you turned into a werewolf and were calm enough to not only understand what happened to you but to also figure out you needed help from a pack of werewolves? I've met a lot of new werewolves, and in my experience, most of them were still in denial at the eight-week point, and those who weren't were completely freaking out instead. What's so different about you, and how did you know there was a pack in Dallas?"

Rachel bit back a growl. Diego was like a dog with a bone once he thought something sneaky was going on.

Knox chuckled. "Wish I could take credit for being a genius, but I can't. By pure happenstance I ended up being around some people who knew a thing or two about werewolves. When the bullet wound in my leg healed up on its own, I had a pretty good idea what was going on. I was familiar with the Dallas pack and knew this was the best place to come to find answers. So I came out here and got a job, hoping to run into one of you."

Rachel held her breath as Diego considered that, but luckily, he seemed to accept Knox's story. Zane and Trey continued to ask questions, wanting to know more about him. Knox kept his answers vague, but thankfully, it seemed to satisfy her pack mates' curiosity.

"Why don't you come by the SWAT compound sometime, and we can introduce you to our alpha and commander of our team," Zane suggested. "Gage would like to meet you, and if you want to learn how to be in touch with your inner werewolf, he's the best teacher."

Double crap.

"I could teach him!" Rachel said quickly.

Everyone turned to her in surprise, Knox included. She didn't know why he was so stunned. Maybe because her voice was suddenly so high it practically squeaked. She tried to look relaxed, as if offering to teach Knox how to be a werewolf was the most natural thing in the world, but from the way her pack mates were eyeing her, she was pretty sure she didn't pull it off. Probably because they knew what a train wreck her life currently was.

"What, you don't think I could do it?" she demanded, some of the anger she'd been stuck with for the past few months coming out. She might be a freaking mess, but that didn't mean she wanted her pack mates to treat her like a soup sandwich. They were supposed to support her, dammit.

"Of course we do," Zane said, though he didn't sound convinced.

Diego didn't even bother to hide his concern. It was right there on his face for everyone to see. "You sure about this?"

Rachel wanted to growl at him but couldn't find it in her to be angry with him. Diego wasn't the oldest member of the Pack, but he worried about everyone like a big brother, and since he'd watched her experience those nightmares firsthand in LA, he worried about her constantly.

So instead of biting his head off, she gave him a warm smile. "Yes, I'm sure. I think it would be good for me to focus on someone else's issues for a while instead of mine. And if I run into something I can't handle, you'll be the first one I come to for help."

That seemed to satisfy him and the rest of her SWAT teammates—or at least shut them up—and after another round of handshakes and comments on how much they were looking forward to working together, Diego, Trey, and Zane left to go check out the security command post.

"Well, that went well," Knox murmured the moment they walked out.

Rachel cursed and held a finger up to her lips to shush him before he could say anything else. Only after she was sure her pack mates were out of earshot did she turn and look at him.

"Okay, they're gone," she said. "I'm not sure how well developed your hearing is yet, but werewolves can clearly make out a normal conversation from a block away. It wouldn't be a good idea to have the other members of my pack realize I know you already—or that you're a hunter."

"Ex-hunter," he corrected. "But I get your point. I take it they wouldn't be thrilled to hear about my background?"

Rachel snorted. "They'd be thrilled, all right. Though you wouldn't because they'd probably kill you."

There was a perverse part of her that hoped to get a

reaction out of him with her threat, but she ended up disappointed. He didn't even bat an eye.

"Dead isn't a good look on me," he quipped. "So, thanks for the warning. I'm getting the feeling there's a lot more I'm going to need to learn than I'd realized. I never thought about being able to hear better now that I'm a werewolf."

"Yeah, well, at least you're getting a chance to learn all this from someone else. I had to pick most of it up on my own and it sucked." Knox looked curious, but she waved him off. "Don't worry about it. I'll tell you tonight. You're still coming over, right?"

He nodded. "Yeah. I helped Theo put together the duty roster and made sure I'm on day shift with you."

Huh. That's convenient, she thought as she headed for the door. "Good. I'll see you then."

"It's a date."

She stopped like she'd hit a brick wall, immediately turning halfway around to poke her head back in the door. "No, it's not a date. It's a meeting. It's a training session. It's a chance for us to talk. But it is most definitely not a date."

Rachel left before Knox could reply, but as she walked down the hall, she couldn't miss the amused chuckle he let out. Damn her own werewolf hearing.

CHAPTER 4

The mouthwatering aroma of a home-cooked meal wafting out of Rachel's apartment hit Knox the moment he reached the second-floor landing. He paused, amazed he could possibly discern the smell was coming from her place considering it was all the way down at the end of the hallway. Then again, how did he also know it was something home-made and not takeout? Since getting the answer to questions like those was the reason he was there in the first place, he did his best to ignore his nose as he headed toward Rachel's.

He ran a few opening lines through his head as he went, hoping to come up with something to make up for that lame-ass comment about tonight being a date earlier. He had no idea why he'd even said it. The words had simply slipped out. He was usually smooth with the ladies, but there was something about Rachel that threw him completely off his game.

Knox lifted his hand to rap his knuckles against the door, but she opened it before he could knock. Unfortunately, he still hadn't come up with the line he'd been looking for. Not that it mattered. His mind vapor locked the moment he set eyes on Rachel. *Crap, this is embarrassing.*

Luckily, she didn't notice his mouth was hanging open like he was an oversized carp because she turned away, busy typing something into her phone and motioning him in with a jerk of her chin.

"Addy Lloyd was a little freaked out this morning about

the whole security detail thing, so I gave her my cell phone number in case she needed to talk, but I think that may have been a bad idea," Rachel said as she continued across her small living room toward the kitchen. "She's been texting me nonstop since I got home. I can't believe that girl is worrying about what she's going to wear to a high school dance when there are people out there trying to kill her family."

"It's probably because she doesn't have any idea how much danger she's in." Knox closed the door behind him. "Or she does realize and is using the dance as a way to cope with the fear."

She kept tapping on her phone. "Assuming Addy takes after her mother, I'll go with the former. Jennifer is obviously a brilliant woman, but I get the feeling she thinks this whole security detail is a bother."

He couldn't argue with that. "If it wasn't for her daughter and husband, I don't think she would have even accepted the protection."

Rachel nodded in agreement as she sauntered into the kitchen, silky blond hair hanging loose down her back. His gaze lingered on the curve of her butt as she moved. He was a little disappointed she wasn't wearing the same shorts she'd had on last night, but the jeans she wore looked damn good, too. He also loved the way her snug T-shirt had a tendency to ride up as she walked, showing off a little glimpse of skin above the waist of her jeans. He had a crazy urge to run his fingers across all that exposed perfection to see if she was ticklish.

He forced his attention away from the distraction that was her body and looked around the apartment as he tossed his leather jacket over the back of the couch. He'd been too keyed up last night to notice much beyond the superficial. He hadn't even gotten a good look at any of the framed photos she had on display. There were pictures of her with an older couple who had to be her mom and dad, and some with a tall guy and two women who looked enough like her to be her siblings, as well as some fellow cops. And if her southern accent hadn't already given her away, the apartment's decor definitely betrayed her country roots. There was a homey feel to the place, with pictures of old barns, tree-covered mountains, and crystal-clear lakes. The banner from the University of Tennessee on the wall over the TV as well as the orange-and-white fleece blanket with the signature checkered pattern on either end, along with a bold T in the center, thrown over the back of the love seat were sort of a dead giveaway, too. He wasn't a fan of the Volunteers, since he grew up in Kentucky Wildcats country, but he decided not to hold it against her—much.

By the time he wandered into the kitchen, the aroma coming out of the oven was so amazing he almost started to drool. Seriously, he had to swallow twice so he wouldn't drown in the stuff. Great. All this time, he thought his biggest worry was going to be fangs, claws, and maybe a unibrow. Now, he had to add drooling like a bulldog to the list.

Putting her phone in her back pocket, she washed her hands, then opened the oven and took out a large casserole bubbling and steaming with all kinds of yummy goodness. That was when he finally recognized the aroma.

"You made shepherd's pie for me?" he asked.

It was all he could do to stop himself from hopping up and down like a kid. He hadn't had a good shepherd's pie in forever.

Rachel turned to look at him, brow arched. "No. I made shepherd's pie for me. You happen to be the beneficiary of what would have been leftovers for tomorrow night's dinner."

Knox eyed the large casserole again, confident there were three or four dinners in there for a woman Rachel's size, but he was smart enough not to say that out loud. He was outspoken, not stupid.

"Need help with anything?" he asked. She'd already set the table, but he needed to make the offer anyway.

Rachel motioned toward the fridge as she carried the casserole to the small kitchen table. "You can get us something to drink. I usually have milk with dinner, but you're welcome to anything you find in there. Glasses are in the cabinet by the sink."

Milk, huh? He was pretty sure he hadn't touched the stuff since he was in elementary school. He poured a glass for Rachel, then thought *Why the hell not?* and poured one for himself, too.

Knox brought the glasses over to the table to find her spooning huge portions of meat pie onto both their plates. The pile of mashed potatoes, vegetables, and beef almost made him start drooling again.

"I'm not complaining, but is there something about me that makes you think I usually eat this much?" he asked, setting down the glasses.

Rachel snorted as she took a seat. "Are you honestly telling me you haven't noticed how much food you've been eating since you turned into a werewolf?"

Knox opened his mouth to say no, but then hesitated. Now that he thought about it, he supposed his takeout bill had been climbing recently. "I guess I have." Shrugging, he slid into the chair opposite her and picked up his fork. "I just thought it was because I'd been pushing myself so hard lately."

Rachel nodded, scooping up a forkful of casserole. He was about to do the same but got distracted watching her eat. He wasn't sure when chewing had become a sensual act for him, but when it was the beautiful female werewolf across from him doing the eating, it was.

"Your metabolism is a lot higher now," she said, thankfully missing the weird way he was staring at her mouth. "Whether you realize it or not, your body is going through a lot of physical changes right now, so you're putting on more muscle. Those kind of changes require a lot of energy to make happen. That's why you're eating more."

"Huh." He finally took a bite of food, almost groaning at how remarkable it tasted. The beef was spicy, the vegetables tender, and the mashed potatoes that topped the whole thing were creamy and smooth. If he didn't have to share with Rachel, he would eat the whole casserole dish himself. "So that's why I have to keep buying new clothes every week."

"Oh, yeah. You've easily put on twenty pounds of muscle. You're probably a few inches taller, too."

Knox considered that while he ate, wondering how this situation could get any stranger. What the hell was going to happen the next time he went home to visit his family and they noticed he was taller and heavier? Then again, they hadn't seen him much over the past several years, since he'd been deployed so much, so maybe they wouldn't notice. That's when another thought hit him.

"If the guys on my old SEAL team could see me now," he murmured softly, "they'd probably think I'm taking steroids or something."

Rachel reached over to scoop more shepherd's pie onto his plate. He wasn't even sure when he'd finished the first serving, but he was still hungry, so he kept eating.

"You were a Navy SEAL?" she asked.

He nodded. "Eight years."

She sipped her milk. "So how do you go from being a Navy SEAL to a hunter?"

Knox was silent, not sure how to answer because answering meant talking about a part of his past he'd rather leave deeply buried.

Across from him, Rachel stopped eating and looked up at him, her expression partly curious, partly suspicious. "What, was I not supposed to ask about that? Is the issue of how you became a monster off-limits?"

Something told him, when she referred to him being a monster, she wasn't talking about the claws and fangs. No, she was talking about him being a hunter. He forced himself to give her a small smile. "No, not at all. It's just that… well, it's kind of complicated, and I'm sure you don't want to sit around and hear me talk about myself all night."

She gave him a wry look and motioned at her plate. "Unlike you, I don't consume food like it's going out of style, so we're not going anywhere for a while. Besides, if you expect me to teach you about being a werewolf, the least you could do is tell me how you ended up in this situation."

He nodded but still hesitated. There were few subjects he hated talking about more than himself, but at this moment, he couldn't figure out a way around it. Not that he wasn't willing to give it a try. "I'm not sure where to even start."

Rachel snorted and took another sip of milk—she even made snorting sound sexy. "Most people start at the beginning. How'd you end up in the navy? Are you from a military family?"

Knox chuckled despite himself. "That would be an understatement. Dad is retired army and Mom is the epitome of a dedicated army wife. Of course, being in the army meant we moved constantly when I was a kid, so we never lived in any one place for more than three years, four tops, which sucks when you're a kid trying to fit in at school, but my parents were all about that life. My brother, sister, and I are even named after the military bases where we were born."

"No way," Rachel said. "Let me guess, you were named for Fort Knox in Kentucky."

He nodded. "Bingo. My little sister was born at Fort Riley in Kansas. And my brother at Fort Gillem in Georgia. If you ask me, Gil got the short end of the stick on that. I still don't know what my parents were thinking when they named him."

She laughed. "If you come from an army family, how'd you end up in the navy?"

He shrugged. "After being around all that olive drab and living on all those bases in the middle of nowhere, there was no way I was going in the army. Dad had a cow, but the first time I boarded a ship, I knew I'd made the right decision."

That earned him another laugh. Man, he was really starting to like that sound.

"I can definitely understand wanting to go your own

way," she said. "I grew up in an army family, too. My dad is retired, like yours, and my older brother is a major in the Special Forces assigned to Fort Campbell, which now that I think about it, would suck as a first name, so I'm glad he and his wife didn't go that route when they named my nephew."

"Big time," he agreed, helping himself to another serving of casserole. "Did your family have a problem with you becoming a cop instead of going in the military?"

Rachel shook her head. "Not really. Law enforcement is an acceptable alternative in the Bennett family. Although my two sisters didn't go in the military or become cops." She glanced at him as she spooned some more pie onto her plate. "Now I know why you joined the navy. What made you become a SEAL?"

He grimaced. "You'll probably pick up on this as a recurring theme soon enough with me, but it turns out I have a habit of making impulsive decisions. In this case, I saw a video at the recruiting center about SEALs doing all this badass stuff and decided that was the job for me. The recruiter tried to talk me out of it, saying the SEALs weren't something to jump into on a whim, but I told him it was the SEALs or nothing."

"Ever regret that impulsive decision?"

He grimaced. "I have to admit, there were a few times during training when I was so exhausted I wasn't sure I'd ever be able to move again and thought for sure I'd gotten in over my head, but I kept going. I'm stubborn that way."

"And then after eight years, you decided you didn't like it?" she asked. "What, are you a slow learner or simply a glutton for punishment?"

Knox laughed, loving her sharp tongue and even sharper

wit. "Neither, I hope. Honestly, I loved the job, even if the nonstop deployments didn't leave me much time for a life."

"But?" she prompted.

He cursed silently. Sometimes, it seemed like he had a sign stuck on his forehead that read *I have a screwed-up backstory. Ask me about it!* But the day he'd walked away from the SEALs, he'd made the decision to leave all that shit behind. He hadn't talked about it with anyone, not even friends or family. He didn't want to dredge it up for Rachel, either.

"But," he said, taking a deep breath, "things happened, and suddenly, my perspective on life changed. So, I made another of my famous impulsive decisions and got out of the navy. It was as simple as that."

On the other side of the table, Rachel studied him like she didn't believe a single word he'd just said. He braced himself, expecting her to press for more information, but instead, she took another small bite of food.

"Okay, so you bailed on the SEALs and then what? Stumbled across a recruitment poster for the hunters?" she asked, her voice suddenly sharp. "Let me guess—the offer of all the werewolves you could slaughter was too much to resist."

Knox's first instinct was to defend himself, but he stuck a sock in the urge. While the details might be a little off, Rachel was fairly close to the truth. Yeah, he'd been played for a sucker, but he was still the guy who'd fallen for the lies. What he'd done was his responsibility and no one else's.

"I was in a bar in Tulsa," he said, looking down at his empty plate and wondering when he'd finished the food on it. "I'd been out of the navy for nearly five months by then with no job prospects and no idea what the hell I was supposed to do with myself. After a few beers and a couple of shots, I struck up a conversation with the bartender. I mentioned I used to be a SEAL and was looking for work, and this guy a few barstools down came over and started chatting me up."

"He was a hunter?"

"Yeah." Knox grabbed his glass of milk and downed half of it. The stuff still tasted as good as he remembered. "The guy was prior military, and we did shots and talked until the bar closed, sharing stories about combat we'd been in and people we'd lost."

He swallowed hard, remembering how close he'd come to telling a complete stranger about why he'd gotten out of the navy. He blamed the alcohol and the isolation of having spent months on his own with nothing but nightmares for company. He still wasn't sure why he'd held his tongue, but he had and he was glad.

"As we were leaving the bar, he told me about some people he worked for," Knox continued. "At first, he made it sound like he was hunting down terrorists for a secret branch of the government, but then he started talking weird about fighting an enemy no one else knew about—'a threat to the existence of the human race' was the way he put it."

Rachel let out another snort. Knox silently agreed. He remembered thinking the same thing that night and that maybe he should get the hell out of there before it got any weirder.

"The guy pulled out his phone and showed me pictures of bodies torn apart—violence that even I hadn't seen before. And trust me, I've seen a lot," Knox said. "Then he showed me a photo of a man with glowing blue eyes and fangs and told me monsters really existed and that they were trying to wipe the rest of us out."

Knox didn't dare look at Rachel on the other side of the table, not wanting to see the revulsion he knew was on her face. It was one he was familiar with. He'd seen it reflected in the mirror too many times to count.

"I agreed to help right on the spot," he whispered, staring down at his plate. "I thought I'd be saving the world from monsters. It wasn't until a month later, after being pulled fully into the operation, that I saw my first real werewolf—and what the other hunters did to him. I tried to stop it, but I was too late. That's when I knew I'd made the biggest mistake of my life."

Rachel was silent for so long he almost thought she'd gotten up and left the kitchen table without him realizing it, but when he lifted his head, she was still sitting there, staring at him with a flat, unreadable expression on her face that made him wonder if she might actually try to kill him.

"How many werewolves died while you stood by and watched?" she asked softly.

A stab of pain so intense pierced his chest it felt like someone had plunged a blade into his heart. But no, it was only Rachel's expression of disapproval cutting through him like a knife.

"Just that one," he told her solemnly. "If I close my eyes, I can still see his face at that moment right before they killed him. I can't tell you how many times I've prayed to go back and fix it, even though I know I can't. The best I can do is make sure it never happens again. That's why when I saw you at the wedding reception, I jumped in front of that asshole hunter and took the bullet meant for you. I didn't want another death on my hands. There are way too many already."

Rachel gazed at him for a long moment before she pushed back her chair and stood. "I've got a quart of chocolate chunk ice cream in the fridge. Do you want some?"

The sudden change of subject caught him off guard, but he wasn't going to ignore an olive branch when it was offered.

"Yeah, ice cream sounds good."

"What happened after you were shot?" Rachel asked, smashing the chocolate chunk ice cream in her bowl with the spoon to make it softer. Not only did she love her ice cream that way, but it gave her something to do so she wouldn't have to look at the handsome werewolf sitting across the table from her.

Rachel knew she should absolutely despise everything about Knox. He was a hunter, and even if she took him at his word that he'd made a mistake by joining them, he was still partially responsible for the death of at least one innocent werewolf. Moreover, he'd come to Max and Lana's reception at the compound with the intention of killing more.

But for reasons she couldn't quite get her head around, she was having a hard time finding it in herself to hate him. Hell, she was having a problem churning up enough energy to even dislike him. The more she thought about that, the more it worried her. If she couldn't hate a man like Knox after all the reasons he'd given her, what the hell did that say about her sanity?

Knox dipped his spoon in his ice cream, mouth quirking. "You mean after you let me get away?"

She didn't say anything. She honestly didn't want to talk about why she hadn't shot him when she'd had the chance. She might not hate him, but she still couldn't shake the feeling she'd somehow failed her pack by letting Knox get away.

"I drove back to LA with the three other hunters and your jackass of a police chief—former police chief now, I guess I should say," he explained. "They were all sure I was going to die from blood loss. Hell, so was I. But by the time we got there, the bullet wound looked like it was weeks old. I might not have realized I was a werewolf, but I knew something was weird."

She stuck a big spoonful of ice cream in her mouth, almost moaning as her taste buds did a little happy dance at the rich chocolate flavor. "What did the hunters think?"

"I refused to let anyone see the injury. I made it sound like it hadn't been as bad as everyone thought."

"That was smart," she said. "Then again, I'm not sure the hunters know how werewolves are created, so you probably would have been safe. And the vampires wouldn't have realized you're a werewolf because you didn't smell like one yet."

"Good to know." He shrugged. "But I didn't want to take that chance."

"So, you left?"

"Not right away," he admitted. "When you work for vampires, you don't just quit. Apparently, the coven thought I'd make a good addition to their security team, so they gave me a promotion. On the downside, it meant spending most of my time in their damn nest. But on the upside, it gave me the freedom to finally get the hell away from them."

Knox dug more ice cream out of his bowl, his brow suddenly furrowing as if something just dawned on him. "I'll be damned."

"What?" she asked.

He shook his head. "The night I was bailing on LA, I picked up the scent of cinnamon and licorice jelly beans. I didn't think about it until now, but I smelled the same thing when I was here last night. And again when I first walked in tonight."

Rachel stared at him, spoonful of ice cream halfway to her mouth. "You did?"

"Yeah. I thought it must be potpourri or something, but now I realize it wasn't that at all."

"What was it?" she asked, not sure she wanted to know.

He spooned a big scoop of ice cream into his mouth before answering her, his gaze locked on hers as he let the dessert melt a little before swallowing. She'd never paid so much attention to a man eating before, but there was something about the way Knox did it that worked for her. It wasn't exactly sensual—he was too rough around the edges for anything he did to be described in that manner—but it mesmerized her all the same.

"You," he finally said, the word soft.

Her pulse skipped a little, and she tried ignoring how interested her inner wolf had suddenly become in the conversation. She didn't even like licorice jelly beans. "Me?"

He nodded, busying himself with another bite of ice cream. She marveled at how agile his tongue was as he licked the dark chocolate bits from the spoon, having to work extra hard to shove her dirty mind away from the gutter it was heading for.

"I tracked the scent for nearly ten blocks that night in LA, all the way to a dance club," he said. "You were there with Diego and Zane. It was obvious you were searching for something—or someone. I got curious, so instead of leaving like I planned, I hung around so I could see what you were up to and ended up following you all over town."

She cursed. Thank God she was too angry right then to examine why a new werewolf like him had been able to track her so easily. The reason behind it was too far-fetched to even consider. "You're the one who was stalking me the whole time I was out there. You're the shadow I kept seeing out of the corner of my eye and the scent I kept picking up all the time."

"You picked up my scent?" He grinned. "What do I smell like?"

"What you smell like isn't important right now," she snapped, dropping her spoon into her bowl and refusing to even think about the subject. "What's important is that I smelled you everywhere but I never saw you. I thought I was losing my frigging mind, you jerk, that you were another shadow sent to drive me insane."

Rachel was hyperventilating by the time she finished. One moment, she was simply upset, and the next, it was like she was in one of her darkest dreams as she remembered what it had been like for her in LA when she'd been surrounded by all the scents and visions she hadn't been able to understand.

Then the darkness that had been her near-constant companion for months once again threatened to overwhelm her. She gripped the edge of the table as her fangs and claws came out, the tips of the latter digging into the wood.

She needed to get out of here before she completely lost it and began screaming in terror right there at the kitchen table.

Before she could get her feet under her, two large hands covered hers. Just like that, her claws unclenched.

"Relax, Rachel. Just breathe," Knox said softly.

That advice didn't do crap for her. The problem wasn't lack of air—it was an excess of it. But the warm hands on hers combined with his gentle voice helped more than she could have ever imagined. A calmness enveloped her that was unlike anything she'd ever experienced, and she felt her breathing and heart rate slowing down and returning to normal. As fast as they'd extended, her fangs and claws retracted completely.

She wasn't sure how much time passed, but when she finally lifted her head, it was to see Knox eyeing her in concern. It was a disconcerting expression to see on his face, especially when she was trying so hard to convince herself that he couldn't be trusted.

"You okay?" he asked.

Rachel slowly pulled her hands out from under his, thankful he didn't do anything freaky like try to hold on to them. Taking a deep breath, she nodded. "I'm good. I had a moment there, but I'm good now."

He regarded her thoughtfully. "What happened? Your eyes went bright neon green, and then it seemed like you weren't here anymore."

She opened her mouth to lie—something she'd gotten extremely good at doing lately—but when the words came out, they were a whole lot closer to the truth than she'd intended.

"Sometimes I have dreams about the night that clown attacked me and I became a werewolf." She dropped her gaze, staring unseeingly at the empty bowl in front of her. "When I was out in LA, I experienced some flashbacks related to that. Talking to you about what happened out there brought everything rushing back."

An uncomfortable silence filled the kitchen, and Rachel felt her face heat, shocked she'd been so forthcoming. She wasn't sure what the hell had come over her. She wasn't sure how her mental health—or lack thereof—had become the focus of the conversation, but she definitely didn't like it.

She cleared her throat. "What do you say we move this to the living room, so I can start teaching you how to be a werewolf?"

Knox took their bowls to the sink without being asked. Heck, he even rinsed them out and put them in the dishwasher. Not the right way, but it was the thought that counted, right?

Opening the fridge, she took out two bottles of craft beer from a local Dallas brewery she loved, handed him one, then led the way to the living room. She curled up on the love seat, tucking her feet under her as she sipped the smooth beer.

"I wasn't stalking you back in LA," Knox said quietly from the other couch. "I only wanted to talk to you. I tried to approach you a few times, but Zane or Diego were always with you—sometimes both." He took a swallow of beer. "If you want to label someone a stalker, they fit the bill. They never left your side for a second."

Rachel didn't want to mention her pack mates had been so obsessive about sticking close to her because they weren't sure if she could be trusted. "We were out there searching for hunters. None of us liked any of the others to be on their own."

"Hey, I get it. It makes complete sense," he said, even though he didn't look like he was buying the lie at all. "Regardless, I was still trying to figure out how to get close to you when you guys attacked the vampire nest. The last thing I wanted to do was go back to that place, but once I knew that's where you were going, I tried to help any way I could, as much as I could."

Rachel thought back to the morning she and her pack mates assaulted the nest. They hadn't been sure what they were up against and even less sure if any of them would make it out alive. It had been pure insanity in that dimly lit labyrinth of corridors and rooms, flames roaring across the ceilings as the whole place went up. Even with the acrid smoke filling the air, she remembered picking up that oh-so-familiar scent combination of leather and gun oil. She'd been too busy fighting for her life to pay any attention to it, but now that she knew Knox had been there, it took on a whole new meaning.

"Do I need to ask which side you were fighting for?" she asked.

"Yours, of course," he snapped. "I didn't go to all the trouble of taking a bullet for you in Dallas only to have some bloodsucker do you in. I covered your cute ass the whole time you were in there, then followed you back to Dallas when you left."

Her *cute* ass? Normally she would have ripped him a new one for even going there, but for some reason, she decided she'd let it slip this once. There was something she couldn't let him wiggle free on, though.

"Why do all this?" she asked. "Taking a bullet for me. Staying to fight in that coven nest when you could have easily have gotten killed. Following me halfway across the country. Moving to a city just to be near me. Why would you do all that? You don't even know me."

Knox gazed at her for so long she wasn't sure he was going to answer. And from the expression on his face, it was like she'd just asked him to do a complicated math problem in his head. She held her breath, bracing herself, afraid that when he did reply, he'd confirm her worst fear.

"To be honest, I'm not sure," he finally admitted. "Like I said, lately it seems like my life is a series of one impulsive decision after the next. I can't even tell you what I was thinking right before I took that bullet for you. And if you're looking for why I stayed in LA instead of leaving when I had the chance, I've got nothing for you. I'm not even clear on what I expected when I followed you back here. Yeah, I'd hoped to get your help figuring out this werewolf thing, but I don't know why I thought you'd be the best one to ask."

There were werewolves in the Pack who were walking, talking, growling lie detectors. Unfortunately, Rachel wasn't one of them. Yet somehow, she instinctively knew Knox was telling the truth.

"Are we going to talk about me the whole night?" he asked. "Don't get me wrong. I usually love talking about myself, but I thought I was here tonight to learn about how to be a werewolf. At least, that's what you said."

A small part of her didn't want to stop questioning him. He'd risked his life for her multiple times. There had to be some reason for that beyond the obvious answer she refused to even consider, something that would make sense if she kept digging long enough. But if there was one thing she knew about Knox, it was that he wasn't the kind of man who stayed in any one place for very long. He'd be here long enough to learn what he thought he needed to know about being a werewolf, then another impulsive decision would have him moving on to the next thing in the next town. What did his motivation for saving her and following her back to Dallas matter?

She set her beer on the coffee table. "Okay, what do you want to know first?"

He leaned back on the couch, arms outstretched along the top to either side of him, beer bottle still in one hand. "How does this whole pack thing work? Is it necessary for a werewolf to be in one, and what happens if no one lets me in their club?"

Rachel laughed at his choice of words but sobered quickly when she realized Knox might actually be serious. "You're an alpha werewolf like my pack mates and I. While being around other werewolves is good for us—especially right after going through our change—it's not completely necessary. In fact, I was on my own for almost a year before moving down here and I handled it all right. That said, I didn't feel comfortable in my own skin until I was around my pack mates because I didn't have to hide what I am from them. It was like finding a whole new family of brothers and sisters."

"Brothers and sisters?" he echoed. "Does that include Diego? Because when I was following you around in LA, I couldn't miss the fact that you two were sharing a hotel room."

Rachel did a double take. That wasn't jealousy in Knox's voice, was it? "Yes, brothers and sisters. And Diego is the biggest brother of all of them, meaning he's as overprotective as they come."

"Huh. I guess that explains why he wasn't thrilled when you volunteered to help me out."

She almost groaned at the reminder. "Exactly. I don't think he trusts you. And if he picks up on the fact that you used to be a hunter, there's going to be trouble. I doubt my pack would kill you outright, but if they knew you were at the wedding reception, jail might be the least of your problems."

"I figured as much. Don't worry. They won't hear it from me." Knox sipped his beer. "You said I'm an alpha werewolf, right?"

She nodded.

"Well, if I'm this large-and-in-charge alpha, why the hell am I a frigging mess when it comes to the werewolf stuff? My damn claws pop out whenever they feel like it and never when I want them to. I wake up almost every morning with blood in my mouth from these stupid fangs. And I have random episodes where I get pissed for no reason at all. On the drive over here, someone cut me off on the 635 loop, and the next thing I know, I'm snarling, growling, and this close to going all road rage on them. I think there's something wrong with me."

Rachel knew exactly what Knox was going through because she'd gone through the same ordeal. After her change, the shifts occurred at random—while she was sleeping, while on patrol, even while taking a shower. It didn't help that she hadn't been able to talk to anyone. Police psychologists weren't the people you consulted when you were on your way to becoming a monster.

But it had gotten better, especially after getting to Dallas and joining the Pack. They'd taught her so much about what it meant to be a werewolf and how to accept what she was. Sometimes, she wondered how much easier her transition would have been if she'd had access to that kind of guidance right after she'd changed.

Fortunately, Knox wouldn't have to deal with the situation on his own like she had. He had her to teach him everything he needed to know.

"There's nothing wrong with you," she said, giving him a smile. "All werewolves go through a period of instability after their change. It's your inner werewolf trying to find its way while your human side figures out how to accommodate the changes. Everything will calm down once you learn a little control."

"So, how do I learn to control my inner werewolf?"

She almost laughed at the wary expression on his face. What did he think, that she was going to have him walk over a bed of glowing coals?

"Nothing too drastic, I promise." Climbing off the love seat, she walked around to sit down on the couch beside him, turning his way and crisscrossing her legs. This close to him, the scent of leather and gun oil was stronger and even more comforting, not to mention distracting. "Let's start with a simple exercise. Give me your hands."

Knox placed his beer bottle on the table and turned toward her, holding his hands out. She took them in hers, forcing herself to ignore how big, strong, and work-roughened they were, not to mention the little tingle that spiraled through her on contact.

"Okay, now close your eyes and relax," she said softly. "And before you ask, no, I'm not going to ask you to do the whole wax-on-wax-off thing or anything like that."

Knox snorted, the tension disappearing from his broad shoulders, a slow smile spreading across his face. Score one for movies and their cultural references.

"We're going to do a visualization exercise," she explained, trying to speak in the same calm, soothing voice that Gage had used with her when she'd first done this. "The theory is that it will put you in a relaxed state and allow your inner wolf to come out naturally."

"Doesn't sound too difficult," he said, keeping his eyes closed even as the grin broadened. "But if you start talking like Yoda, I won't be held responsible for what happens next."

"Yeah, right. Worried I am," she said in her best Yoda imitation, closing her eyes and trying to center herself. She wasn't exactly great at this stuff yet and only hoped she didn't make a fool of herself. "Now take a deep breath and visualize yourself standing in a tropical rain forest."

"Which one?"

She peeked one eye open to see if he was messing with her to find him sitting there with his eyes closed, a slightly confused expression on his face. "It doesn't matter. They're all the same—calm and tranquil."

Knox snorted. "Says the woman who's obviously never spent any time in a tropical rain forest. You try walking around in a soaking wet uniform for two weeks, getting rashes in places you didn't even know you had, and then tell me how calm and tranquil you feel."

"Are you screwing with me?" she asked, her gums and fingertips starting to tingle in aggravation. "Because if you don't want to do this, just tell me."

He opened his eyes, looking a little chagrined. "I do want

to do this. Really. It's just...well, rain forests aren't exactly a calming place for me."

She sighed. "Fine. Would you prefer a hardwood forest in the mountains instead? Maybe in early fall, before the leaves have all changed colors and the air is starting to get cooler?"

"That works."

"Good. Then close your eyes again."

Once he did, she followed suit.

"Now picture yourself in the forest," she instructed. "Feel the slight breeze on your skin, hear it rustling the leaves in the trees as you walk barefoot along a smooth dirt path, the soft earth warm between your toes."

"Why am I barefoot?" he asked. "Did I lose my shoes?"

She took a deep breath, biting down on the snarl that threatened to slip out. "You're walking barefoot because you want to. You're comfortable and relaxed, remember?"

"Comfortable, relaxed, and barefoot. Got it."

"Now, I want you to feel the ground under your feet and the breeze on your skin," she said. "Take deep breaths, inhaling the scent of the clean mountain air, the various trees, and the rich brown soil."

She continued to set the scene for him, listening as his heart rate and his breathing slowed. On the couch, his knee pressed against hers, and she took a quick peek to see that he looked completely relaxed.

"The feel of the ground beneath your feet and the breeze on your face is so exhilarating you can't resist the temptation to let go and be free," she said. "Now, take a deep breath and start running. Your toes are digging into the soft ground, propelling you forward faster than the wind. It feels so incredible you can't help but laugh."

Rachel opened her eyes to see Knox grinning, the muscles in his arms and legs tensing and relaxing. Like he was actually running.

"Push yourself to run faster," she urged. "Feel every muscle in your body straining and reaching for more. The wind is whipping your face and running its fingers through your hair."

The muscles of his forearms were visibly twisting as his body started to partially shift. Now came the crucial moment where she was either going to get him to let loose a little, or he'd completely rebel against the animal inside him.

"You know you can run faster if you drop down on all fours so you do it without thinking, your fingers digging into the dirt and leaves, flinging you forward in leaps and bounds."

She held her breath, waiting for him to resist, but instead, the muscles of his forearms continued to twist and shift even as his claws extended.

"Feel the tingling in your fingertips as your claws tear into the dirt," she whispered, closing her eyes and leaning in a little closer to him. "Push harder, dig them into the ground. Just let go and let it happen."

His heart beat faster, and she leaned in so close she could feel his breath blowing gently across her face. She gently slipped her hand out of his and carefully rested it on his jean-clad thigh. The muscles quivered under her touch. The exercise was working. His inner wolf was coming out.

Rachel was so elated her plan was actually working—because seriously, she'd been more than ready for failure the first time out of the gate—she didn't realize that her breathing and heartbeat had perfectly synced up with his until his scent registered, even more powerful than before, almost overwhelming her with its heat and wild energy.

She inhaled deeply, trying to draw in even more of the enticing scent. While it was the same scent she'd grown used to, at the same time, there was an edge and a rawness to it that hadn't been there before. It was his inner wolf in all its glory. And one whiff was enough to make her whole body tingle.

Rachel opened her eyes to see that Knox's claws were fully extended now and his upper fangs were long enough to protrude over his lower lip. He looked dangerous and unbelievably hot.

"Knox, I want you to come back now," she said softly. "Slow down and leave the forest behind. All you have to do is follow my voice back here."

It took a few moments, and when he finally opened his eyes, Rachel was stunned speechless. They were glowing the brightest yellow gold she'd ever seen. Those amazing eyes widened when he lifted his hand and saw the extended claws, but then he quickly seemed to lose interest in his claws as his gaze met hers again. His nose lifted slightly as he tested the air, then his eyes darkened, smoldering and intense, and her heart beat faster at the heat in their depths.

Rachel didn't even realize what she was doing until she felt her claws digging into solid muscle. Startled, she glanced down and realized her own claws were out, kneading his legs like a cat with a fuzzy blanket. She ran her tongue over her teeth to find that her fangs were extended, too. When had she shifted?

She lifted her gaze to look Knox deep in the eyes and stopped thinking about her fangs and claws and instead focused on the lips mere inches from hers. He was going to kiss her. There was a small part of her mind telling her that she shouldn't let him. He was a hunter, one of the bad guys.

But damn, he smelled so delicious. Something told her that he'd taste even better.

Knowing it was probably the dumbest thing she'd ever do, she leaned in, closing her eyes as their lips touched.

Rachel wasn't sure if she pulled back or if it was Knox. Regardless, one moment they were about to lock lips, and the next they were sitting at either end of the couch looking in any direction but at each other and failing miserably.

"So, um…wow…you got my claws to come out," Knox said, his voice almost casual as he stared at the claws extending from the tips of his fingers. "That's pretty amazing."

She shook her head, knowing she was probably blushing like crazy right then. "It wasn't me. It was all you. I simply talked you into a place where you let your inner wolf out. In time, your claws and fangs will extend and retract without having to go to that place in your head."

He seemed to consider that for a moment before nodding. "If I kept going, could I turn completely into a wolf? You know, like with four feet and fur?"

Rachel looked at him, her gaze locking on his sensuous mouth, and for a moment, she found herself wondering what it would be like if they kissed for real. Was he thinking the same thing?

She ran her hand through her hair and cleared her throat, forcing herself to focus on his question. "Some of us can, yeah."

"Can you?"

"No." She gave him a small smile. "You have to be in

complete harmony with your inner wolf. Apparently, I'm not there yet."

He held her gaze. "Maybe we can both get there if we work on it together?"

"Maybe," she murmured, wondering if he was still talking about shifting into a wolf or this thing that was building between them.

CHAPTER 5

"Do you think this dress makes me look grown-up?" Addy asked, twirling back and forth to see herself from the various angles provided by the trio of full-length mirrors mounted on the store's dressing room walls in the alcove in front of her.

Rachel frowned at the slit running up the side of the black gown, flashing skin three-quarters of the way up the girl's thigh, as well as the plunging neckline that didn't belong in the same frigging zip code as a sixteen-year-old. *Grown-up* definitely wasn't the word she'd use to the describe the dress.

She wondered if it was too late to join Knox. After the tenth different gown Addy had tried on, Rachel's partner for this evening's security detail had disappeared, saying he'd rather stand guard in front of the mall's upscale boutique. That was probably good, considering things had gotten a little strained between them ever since they'd almost kissed.

That had been three days ago. Since then, they hadn't talked much or set up another training session. Apparently, Knox had decided he didn't need any more werewolf lessons from her. For some ridiculous reason, that bummed her out.

Pushing thoughts of Knox aside, Rachel glanced at Addy's mom, hoping she would handle the situation regarding the revealing gown. Unfortunately, Jennifer still had her nose stuck in her cell phone, a yellow notepad balanced on her knees. From what Rachel had been able to overhear of the conversation, the prosecutor was talking to one of her investigators concerning new evidence on Marshall that had been uncovered earlier today. It sounded like it was something big, too. At least Rachel hoped it was something big, since Jennifer had ignored her daughter the whole time.

When Jennifer didn't even bother looking up to see what kind of dress Addy wanted to buy, Rachel sighed. It appeared she'd have to be the one to give the girl some guidance. That was damn scary considering she wasn't sure she should be giving herself clothing advice most of the time. Fashion wasn't her thing.

"How about we go for something a little less daring?" Rachel suggested with a smile. "Maybe something more like these."

Grabbing as many dresses from the nearest rack as she could get her hands around, Rachel nudged Addy toward the dressing room. She wasn't sure what most of the gowns looked like, but honestly, almost anything would be better than the one the girl had on now.

Addy dug in her heels, looking down at herself with a frown. "What's wrong with this dress? I think it's perfect. Don't you, Ben?"

Rachel almost groaned out loud, wishing they could have avoided pulling a teenage boy's opinion into this situation. But that was why Addy had dragged her best friend since kindergarten, Ben Sullivan, along on this shopping trip—for his valuable insight on the latest in Valentine's Day teen fashion.

At the sound of his name, the dark-haired teen boy who'd been sitting quietly on the far side of the fitting area jerked as if startled, staring slack jawed at his friend from behind his hipster glasses while trying his best to make it seem like he wasn't looking at all. Because while Addy and Ben were supposedly *just friends*, it was obvious from the way the boy was sweating right then that he'd really rather be anywhere but in the friend zone.

"I think you look amazing," Ben breathed, clearly not helping the situation at all.

Addy smiled and turned to give Rachel a superior look. Without a word, Rachel shoved the dresses into the girl's arms and nudged her toward the dressing rooms again.

"I know you think the gown you have on is beautiful, but I think we can find one even better if we keep looking," Rachel said as she followed the teen to the changing rooms. "One that suits your personality a little better."

Addy regarded her silently for a moment, then sighed and slipped into one of the small alcoves, closing the saloon-style door behind her. "I know you think the dresses I've been trying on are a little racy, and maybe they are. But Aaron is a senior, and I have to look the part if I'm going to date him."

Rachel leaned her shoulder against the wall beside the dressing room. "I know he's a senior, but is going out with him worth it if you have to wear a dress that really isn't you just to impress him?"

"Well, yeah. Duh," Addy said. "Did I mention he's a senior? And gorgeous? And has a motorcycle and a leather jacket? *And* can text with one hand behind his back while taking notes with the other one in class? I mean, who else would I want to go to the dance with?"

Opening the door, Addy stepped out to show off a dress

with a demure neckline and hem that was perfect in every way but the color. Yellow that bright didn't work for anybody but Belle from *Beauty and the Beast.*

Rachel shook her head and motioned Addy back into the dressing room. "You could always go to the dance with Ben. He seems nice."

"Ben?" Addy laughed as if that was the funniest thing ever. Rachel was glad Ben didn't have the hearing of a werewolf. A laugh like that would have scarred the kid for life. "I can't go to the Valentine's Day dance with him. He's my best friend. Besides, he doesn't even like girls."

Rachel did a double take. Could the girl be any more clueless? Ben gazed at Addy like she was the most beautiful girl in the world. How could she have missed that?

"What makes you think he doesn't like girls?" Rachel asked curiously.

Addy stood on her toes to peek over the top of the changing room door. "I've known him since we were five years old, and in all that time, I'm the only girl he's ever hung out with."

Rachel rolled her eyes, wanting to tell Addy how stupid she was being. But then she realized that would have been a waste of time. There wasn't a sixteen-year-old girl on the planet who could ignore a mysterious bad boy like Aaron.

Addy stepped out of the dressing room, modeling another age-appropriate dress. At least, there wasn't a thigh-high slit or boob-baring neckline. Unfortunately, it was red, which still made it too racy in Rachel's opinion. From the expression on Addy's face, she was seriously impressed.

"What do you think?" she asked, twirling around.

"I think we're onto something with this one," Rachel

murmured. "Aaron is going to go absolutely crazy when he sees you in it."

Addy looked down at herself, then back up at Rachel, her blue eyes shining. "He is?"

Rachel nodded. If she was going to talk the girl into buying a different dress, she was going to have to be sneaky about it this time. "Oh yeah. You're going to look like you should be walking on the red carpet—sophisticated... classy...mysterious. Trust me, he won't be able to take his eyes off of you. I just wish..."

"What do you wish?" Addy asked almost breathlessly.

"Well, red isn't really your color." Rachel put on her best disappointed look. "Too bad that same dress doesn't come in another one."

Addy immediately darted into the dressing room, flipping through the gowns on the hangers. A moment later, she came back out with the same dress in a pretty pastel blue. "How about this one?"

"Perfect. Try it on."

As she ducked inside to change, Addy chatted about never even considering a dress like this, whether Rachel really thought Aaron would flip out over it, and what kind of shoes would go best with the gown.

The questions came so fast it was impossible to reply to them. That was okay because Addy answered them for her. Rachel leaned against the wall again and smiled, listening to the endless monologue. Right up until Addy asked a question that simply couldn't be ignored.

"What are you going to wear to the dance?" the teenager asked, poking her head over the top of the door, eagerly awaiting the answer.

Rachel was about to point out that she probably wouldn't be at the dance since she worked the day shift, but the look on Addy's face was so precious she couldn't disappoint the girl.

"I was hoping I could get away with wearing my uniform," she said. "What do you think?"

Addy giggled. "I think that might make you stand out a little, don't you? All the other regular security guys at our school have to dress to blend in, so you probably will, too. You probably have lots of fancy dresses, though."

"Not really. I don't wear dresses very much."

"Seriously?" Addy blinked. "If I was tall like you with legs as long as yours, I'd wear dresses every day and make every boy in school drool all over themselves."

Rachel couldn't help but laugh as the girl disappeared behind the door and went back to trying on dresses. "There's a lot more to life than worrying about what men think about your legs, you know. Trust me, when you grow up, you'll start wanting guys to notice you for more than your body."

Addy came out of the dressing room, looking absolutely perfect in the blue dress. Her normal enthusiasm was somewhat dampened though. "You sound exactly like my mom."

Rachel didn't bother commenting on the dress, since it was obviously the right one. Instead, she focused on the suddenly serious expression on the girl's face. Addy didn't seem like she did serious very often. "Like your mom, huh? Is that a bad thing?"

Addy didn't answer right away, instead moving to sit on the cushioned sofa to one side of the dressing area. Figuring the girl needed to talk, Rachel joined her.

"I haven't been getting along with her lately," Addy said quietly.

"Why's that?" Rachel prompted when the teen didn't elaborate.

Addy shrugged. "Mom's always been focused on work, but it's gotten really bad the past year or so. She told me she got a promotion at the DA's office, but what she really meant is that her boss is giving her all the cases no one else wants. Ever since, it's like we stopped being a family."

Rachel let out a sigh. "I know it's tough on you, but your mom is doing a really important job—one that takes a brave, strong person to handle. You mom is that brave, strong person."

Addy took a deep breath and nodded. "I know what she's doing is important and I'm really proud of her for doing it, but since this trial started, I barely see her anymore. And when she is home, she and Dad spend most of their time arguing. They probably think I don't hear them, but it's hard not to with the way they fight." Eyes glistening with unshed tears, she turned to Rachel. "I think Mom and Dad are getting a divorce."

When she and Addy had started this conversation, Rachel had no idea it would head in this direction. Now that it had, she didn't know what to say. She was absolutely crappy at this kind of stuff. She'd rather deal with a blood-sucking vampire than a scared kid. Especially a girl who reminded her so much of Hannah.

Not knowing what else to do, she wrapped an arm around Addy's shoulders. "I won't try and tell you everything is going to work out okay because I don't know that, but I can promise I'll be there for you, no matter how things turn out."

Addy didn't say anything but instead turned and threw her arms around Rachel's waist, hugging her tightly. Rachel returned the hug, and for what it was worth, it seemed to help. At least Addy was smiling again when she pulled away.

"Now that we've found a dress, I guess I should probably change." Addy stood up. "We've been in here long enough that even my mom might have noticed."

Addy disappeared into the dressing room, returning a few minutes later wearing jeans and a T-shirt, the blue gown draped over an arm. "Your boyfriend will be coming to the dance with you, right?"

Rachel frowned. "I don't have a boyfriend."

Addy looked puzzled for a moment, but then smiled as if she'd just figured something out. "Oh, I get it. You two work together, so you aren't supposed to let anyone know you're dating. That's so romantic."

Rachel knew she probably looked like a fish out of water standing there with her mouth hanging open. "Okay, I think we need to stop and back up because I don't have a clue what you're talking about."

"I'm talking about you and Knox." Addy grinned. "It's obvious you two are together. I see the way you're always looking at him when you think no one is watching. Then there's the expression he gets on his face when he gazes at you, like you're the only person in the world he even sees."

Rachel was so flabbergasted all she could do was stand there continuing her impression of a carp.

"You two are dating, right?" Addy asked, the expression on her face changing back from amused to confused. "I mean, you guys are perfect together."

Rachel almost laughed at the idea that she and Knox

were perfect together. He was a former hunter and she was a werewolf. There was too much that separated them—not that she cared, of course.

"It's not like that, even if Knox and I did have dinner at my apartment the other night," she said, wondering who she was trying to convince.

"You are dating!" Addy said, all smiles again. "I knew it!"

"We aren't dating," Rachel insisted. "He came over so we could discuss some training techniques. It was nothing more than that."

"'Training techniques'?" Addy mimicked with air quotes. "Is that what adults are calling it these days?"

Rachel made a face. "Very funny. Get your teenage mind out of the gutter. Knox came over to my place. We had dinner. We talked. Then he left. That's it."

"What'd you talk about?"

"Normal stuff. Family. Work. The fact that both of us happened to be in LA at the same time recently and the odd turns that life can sometimes take."

Addy nodded, a very knowing look on her face. "Let me get this straight. He came to your apartment. You had dinner. And you talked about personal stuff. I know I'm only sixteen and not nearly as experienced with guys as you are, but that sounds like a date to me."

Rachel opened her mouth to deny it, but Addy cut her off.

"I know, I know. It wasn't a date. But why wouldn't you want to date him? He's cute even if he is almost old enough to be my dad. And he seems really nice. He even played video games with Ben and me the other day."

Rachel was pretty sure Knox wasn't nearly old enough to

have a sixteen-year-old daughter, but she didn't point that out. Mostly because she was too busy trying to come up with an answer to Addy's question.

If Rachel were simply judging Knox on looks, then she'd agree he'd be a catch for anyone. But while she'd enjoyed their dinner together—and yeah that kiss that almost happened had her more than a little curious—she simply couldn't let herself trust the man. She had no idea if it was because she didn't have faith in her own judgment or if it was her instincts screaming at her to stay away from a guy who was a former hunter.

Regardless, the sensation had been strong enough for her to run a background check on Knox. Yeah, it was horrible, but hey, he'd been the one who'd assaulted the SWAT compound with his hunter buddies, then he'd stalked her halfway across the country. In her opinion, that was good justification for snooping.

In the end, Rachel hadn't found anything to justify her suspicions—not in the normal criminal check through the DPD or through the deeper federal scrub her STAT friend, Alyssa, had done for her. According to everything she'd found, Knox had told her the complete truth about his life. Not that it helped. She still couldn't ignore that sensation inside telling her to stay away from him.

"It's complicated, that's all," she finally said.

Rachel expected Addy to tell her it wasn't complicated at all, but instead the girl gave her a knowing look and reached out to squeeze her hand. "Aaron and I have a very complicated relationship, too. For one thing, he's older. Then there's the part about my mom positively hating him." She sighed. "I so completely feel you on this."

Rachel didn't know if she wanted to laugh or simply hug the hell out of the kid. So she did both. "Come on, we've been in this store for more than an hour and we still have to find a pair of shoes to go with your dress."

Thankfully, the mention of shoes was all it took to focus Addy's attention on something other than Rachel's messed-up life.

Knox glanced at his watch. How long did it take to shop for a dress? You went to the store, saw one you liked, and bought it, right? Apparently not because Rachel and Addy had been in the upscale boutique full of wedding and prom dresses for almost an hour and a half.

Thinking he should probably check to make sure they didn't get sucked through a mirror into an alternate dimension, he left his post by the entrance where he'd been standing guard and walked into the store.

Rachel and Addy were just stepping out of the dressing room, and he let out a sigh of relief at the sight of the gown draped over the girl's arm. *Finally*.

He was about to round everyone up so they could get out of there when Rachel and Addy hurried over to a wall filled with more shoes than he'd ever seen in his life. The teen girl looked like she'd found nirvana as she eyed all the colorful footwear.

Knox groaned silently. They were nowhere near done, were they?

Despite the reality of being subjected to more shopping, he couldn't help laughing as Rachel casually steered Addy away from the four- and five-inch stilettos, instead planting her firmly in front of ones with more manageable heels.

Knox considered asking if they needed help—just for the fun of it—when he caught sight of Addy's mother sitting off to the side, not paying any attention to her daughter at all. Instead, she was staring at the blue gown Ben had quickly moved over to hold so Addy could check out the shoes, a disappointed look on her face.

He frowned, not sure why she was upset. Then again, he rarely understood women at the best of times. But as Jennifer's gaze darted back and forth between the dress and her daughter, then the notepad and the cell phone on her lap, the picture started coming into focus.

While Addy had been shopping for her dress with Rachel, her mom had been sitting there working on her case. Maybe Jennifer hadn't been aware how big a deal buying a gown with her daughter would be, but from the expression on her face, it seemed like she finally realized now what she'd missed out on.

Setting her notepad and cell phone on the table beside her, Jennifer stood and cautiously walked over to where Addy stood gushing about shoes, like she thought her daughter might rebuff her.

Rachel must have noticed the ADA's hesitance because she gave Jennifer a smile and motioned her forward. Grabbing a pair of blue, low-heeled sandals, she handed them to Jennifer, then tugged Addy closer. The teenager laughed, and just like that, the gulf separating mother and daughter lessened a little.

As Addy and Jennifer *ooh*ed and *aah*ed over the shoes, Ben handed Rachel the dress and smoothly extricated himself from the situation—well, as smoothly as a sixteen-year-old boy terrified of letting his best friend know he had a thing for her could do.

The kid wandered over to Knox with a look on his face that seemed to indicate he was glad he didn't have to be responsible for the dress anymore.

"I think they're almost done," Ben said, clearly relieved.

Knox snorted. "Sorry, kid, but there's a good chance they're just getting started. Once Addy tries on a dozen or so pairs of shoes, going back and forth between the same ones over and over, they still have to find a purse that matches the whole outfit. Then there's the endless jewelry and a wrap to keep her warm, of course."

Ben stared at him like a pig checking out a Rolex. "A wrap?"

"Yeah. Like a coat but without sleeves."

Ben looked even more confused. "Um. Do you think it will take them much longer to finish shopping? Seriously, when Addy invited me, I thought we'd be done in thirty minutes. I didn't know buying a dress could take this long."

Knox laughed. "You ever hear that old line about it's not the destination that matters, it's the journey? Well, for some women, shopping is like that. They enjoy the process of the shopping more than buying. It gives them an endorphin rush or something. Regardless, guys don't need to understand it. We just need to stand around patiently and carry the bags afterward."

Ben nodded, quiet for a while, like he was considering what Knox had said. "I guess you'd have to know a lot about women since you're dating someone like Officer Bennett."

Knox was about to agree, until he realized exactly what

the kid had said. "Wait a minute. Dating? I'm not dating Rachel."

Rachel suddenly turned, throwing him a curious look from the far side of the room, and he lowered his voice as he spoke, just in case she could hear him. He remembered her saying something about werewolves having better hearing than regular people. His wasn't any better than before he'd turned, but she'd done this werewolf thing longer, so hers might be.

"Okay, whatever you say," Ben said, though he didn't look convinced. "It's just that I see the way you look at her. I might be in high school, but I'm smart enough to know that's not the way a guy looks at someone they work with. I just assumed..."

Knox opened his mouth to tell the kid he was wrong, but right then he caught sight of Rachel reaching over to grab another pair of sandals to show Addy. The girl snatched them up and let out a squeal, making Rachel laugh. Knox couldn't help but smile. He liked hearing her laugh.

He realized then that he hadn't seen Rachel laugh much over the past few days, but truthfully, he didn't know her well enough yet to say if that was normal for her. For all he knew, she was always this serious and withdrawn. Something told him that wasn't the case, though. He hated to think he was the reason for it.

Unfortunately, he was pretty damn sure it was his fault. All because he'd tried to kiss her the other night. The worst part was he could barely understand why the hell he'd done it.

The relaxation exercise they'd done had been amazing. He'd felt more alive than he'd ever felt in his life, his whole body tingling as his inner wolf emerged. But when he'd opened his eyes and found Rachel sitting so close he could feel the heat coming off her, he forgot about his claws and his fangs and focused completely on her.

Her eyes had been glowing the most vivid and beautiful green he'd ever seen, and it had been impossible to look away, almost like she'd hypnotized him. Then her scent hit him, surrounding him in licorice jelly beans and cinnamon and something else he couldn't put a name to—something so tempting and feminine it had taken everything he had not to reach out and yank her body closer to his.

Knox hadn't realized he'd moved to kiss her until their mouths were almost touching, but when her tongue slipped out to wet her lips, he'd about lost it. It had probably been a completely subconscious gesture on her part, but damn, he'd wanted to eat her up.

The mere touch of her lips to his had been like heaven, but then she suddenly jerked away. Or maybe he had. Either way, it felt like a chain linking them together had snapped, leaving him to float weightless for a moment before slamming back into reality with an impact that left him gasping for air.

He'd wanted to apologize, but before he could get the words out, everything had gone downhill and Rachel had told him without saying the actual words that what had happened would never happen again. Since then, she'd barely looked at him. And yeah, that werewolf training he'd been hoping she'd provide had come to a screeching halt, too. He'd tried to talk to her a few times since then, but each time, she'd refused to engage, her expression making him think she was a hundred miles away.

"So, what do we do now?" Ben asked softly, interrupting

his musings. "Just stand around and wait for them to tell us what to do next?"

"That's pretty much all we can do." Knox sighed, knowing the words applied to this shopping marathon they were on as well as to the situation he found himself in with Rachel. "Hate to break this to you, kid, but women generally hold all the cards. Guys just have to sit back and see how everything plays out."

CHAPTER 6

"We're on the move, Ethan," Knox said into the miniature radio mic attached to the cuff of his suit jacket. "We'll be at the service entrance in three minutes. Have the vehicles waiting for us."

"About damn time," his coworker from the security company said with a groan. "My butt's numb from sitting out here so long."

"I hear you, dude."

Knox chuckled as he followed Rachel, Jennifer, and the kids along the first floor of the Galleria Mall toward the service corridor that would get them out of there quickly without having to mess with the crowds. Theo had arranged the clandestine route with mall security, ensuring there'd be no one back there.

"Anything outside we need to worry about?" Knox asked over the radio.

He wasn't too concerned someone would try anything out in public like this, but he wanted to be sure.

"Negative," Ethan said. "All clear out here. We'll be waiting at the door for you."

Since Alton Marshall had already shown a willingness to deploy bombs in an attempt to get to the ADA, Ethan had been waiting outside with another teammate from DAPS, keeping an eye on their vehicles. It was a threat they all took seriously, which meant vehicles carrying members of the Lloyd family were never left unguarded *ever*.

The entrance to the service corridor was only a thirty-second walk from the dress boutique, and because there were restrooms in the same hallway, few people looked at them twice when they all turned that way.

Knox moved up to join Rachel at the front of the group as they walked through a door at the end of the corridor and slipped into the part of the mall few paying customers probably ever saw, and for good reason. While the rest of the Galleria was all glitz and polish, the behind-the-scenes part was a maze of boring passageways.

When Theo had mentioned using the service corridors to get in and out of the mall faster, Knox had pictured a few narrow hallways, but his imagination had been sorely lacking. The place was a combination of storerooms, service elevators, stairwells, catwalks, and doors leading to who the hell knew where. If Theo hadn't provided a floor plan for them, they would have gotten lost in here for sure.

Knox led the way through the labyrinth, Addy and Ben several paces back babbling about something on Netflix they wanted to see when they got back, while Mrs. Lloyd brought up the rear, cell phone shoved against her ear again.

The silence between him and Rachel became hard to ignore, even with their footsteps echoing along the hallway, the near-constant conversation between the two teens, and the ADA snapping random questions into her phone. But since they were only a few minutes from the exit, he wasn't sure what he could possibly say, especially in front of everyone.

But he had to say something.

"You got any plans for dinner later? I thought we could get together and talk a little more about...stuff." He almost rolled his eyes at how unsmooth that sounded, but he was too late to take it back now. So, he doubled down. "My treat in repayment for the shepherd's pie."

Rachel gave him a sidelong glance. "I was planning to grab some pizza later with Diego."

Knox bit back a growl. She'd said she and Diego were friends, but that didn't stop the insane twinge of jealousy from surging through him. He fought it down and turned to ask if maybe they could try it again later in the week, but beside him, Rachel slowed, her eyes swirling with bright-green color.

He slowed, too, a strange tingle running up and down his spine, making the hair on the back of his neck stand on end.

"It's an ambush!" Rachel shouted.

Spinning around, she lunged for Addy and Ben, then slammed her shoulder into the first door she reached, dragging the two teens inside the room. Knox didn't hesitate. Turning, he launched himself at Jennifer just as automatic weapon fire ripped through the silence of the passageway.

He took the ADA down as carefully as he could, twisting while still in midair so he landed on his shoulder with most of her weight on top of him. But there was only so much he could do to be gentle when bullets were chewing up the wall and floor around them.

Still lying down, Knox used one arm and his feet to scramble backward with Jennifer, pieces of Sheetrock and tile raining down on both of them as he propelled them into a storage room across from Rachel and the kids. Ben had his body draped protectively over his friend's, and Knox absently wondered how the girl could possibly miss how much the boy cared for her.

Knox got on the radio and let Ethan know what was happening while Rachel did the same over her DPD channel. Backup would be there soon, but they'd have to keep themselves alive until it arrived.

"There are two in the stairwell to the right and another one on the catwalk directly across from them," Rachel yelled as they both moved to their respective doorways and began to return fire. "You deal with the one up high. I'll keep the others occupied."

Knox pondered the intelligence of charging straight at three men armed with automatic weapons, but Rachel was already moving, and he sure as hell wasn't letting her go alone.

As Knox drew his Glock and stepped out to follow, a voice in the back of his head reminded him that he'd been in a situation like this before and it hadn't ended well. He resolutely pushed those warnings aside and forced himself to stop thinking and instead move and react.

Rachel darted down the wide corridor, heading toward a three-way intersection at the end, avoiding the incoming rounds like she somehow knew exactly where they were going to land. That didn't keep Knox from trying to rush ahead of her, unable to ignore the protective instinct threatening to overwhelm him.

The guy up on the catwalk emptied a full magazine from an MP5 while his buddies hidden on the stairwell did the same. If he and Rachel hadn't been moving so fast, they probably would have been filled full of holes. But while the rational part of his mind told him this was insane, another part—the part that wanted to rip the men limb from limb—assured him this was completely normal.

Knox didn't think as he snapped his Glock into position out of pure instinct and put three rounds into the chest of the guy on the catwalk. He was already turning his attention to the stairwell and the other two attackers there before the first man tumbled to the floor of the hallway with a heavy thud.

For a moment, it looked like both he and Rachel were going to go down in the storm of bullets coming from the stairwell. Hell, the rounds were so close he felt a few of them tug at the material of his suit. But the remaining two bad guys must have realized this whole thing wasn't going to end well for them because they turned and bailed up the stairs.

"Stay with Jennifer and the kids!" Rachel yelled over her shoulder before charging up the steps after the escaping men.

Knox growled in frustration and started to go after her only to stop when he realized he couldn't leave the ADA and two teenagers alone. There could still be other hired killers lurking around the service area waiting for an opening to make their move.

So he was forced to stay where he was and stand guard, the seconds ticking down as Rachel moved farther away. Heart beating fast, gums and fingertips on fire, it was all he could do not to shift. He was so freaked out he nearly shot Ethan when the other man came running up from the third passageway near the stairwell. Ethan had his weapon drawn and his eyes widened when he saw the dead body on the floor.

"Mrs. Lloyd and the kids are in there," Knox shouted, pointing with his free hand as he ran past Ethan. "Stay with them. I'm going after the two that got away."

Knox raced up the steps, desperate to catch up to Rachel and the men she was chasing. But she had a good thirty-second head start, and as fast as she'd been moving, he wasn't sure he could get to her in time.

When he reached the third-floor landing, he yanked open the door, then sprinted down the hall. He took the first left-hand turn followed by a right, then another right. He had no idea where the hell he was headed, but everything inside him told him to keep going, so he did.

He was sure he was completely lost when he heard shooting from up ahead. Snarling, he ran faster.

Knox finally caught up to Rachel as she opened a heavy steel door to another stairwell. She glanced over her shoulder as she led the way down the steps, taking them three and four at a time. Damn, she was so graceful it was difficult not to stop and stare.

"Is someone guarding Jennifer and the kids?" she asked.

Below, Knox heard heavy footsteps, then the clanging of a door. "Ethan is with them."

When they got to the first floor, Rachel yanked open the door and rushed out of the building. Knox had enough time to realize they were in the parking garage before a burst of automatic weapon fire sent both of them diving for the pavement. He didn't get hit, but Knox's heart slammed into his ribs when he heard Rachel grunt in pain. But before he could even see where she'd been shot, she was up and running after the bad guys again.

He raced after her to see a black SUV with heavily tinted windows speed up to the curb, where the two would-be assassins were waiting. The moment the men jumped in, the vehicle squealed away. He and Rachel put round after round of bullets through the back window, but while the glass shattered, the big SUV didn't slow.

Knox cursed and lowered his weapon, knowing there was no chance they could catch them. The vehicle was already racing out of the garage and gaining speed.

Beside him, Rachel growled and took off running so fast she was almost a blur. He automatically followed, stunned when they started to catch up to the vehicle. The bad guys must have realized he and Rachel were chasing them because the SUV turned onto the exit road so fast it almost flipped. Rachel jumped a row of hedges and took off cross-country to cut them off.

Knox did the same, throwing a quick glance left and right, praying no one saw them. He couldn't imagine explaining how they were able to chase down a speeding vehicle. Thankfully, it was poorly lit and no one else was around.

He knew Rachel was better at this werewolf thing than he was, but he was still shocked at how fast she could run, and it was all he could do not to get left behind. She snarled at him over her shoulder, her eyes glowing red instead of their usual green when she shifted.

Okay, that's different.

Knox pushed harder to catch up to her, but no matter how fast he ran, she stayed ahead of him.

As they reached the access road that led toward the toll-way, Knox opened his mouth to call out to her, but his head abruptly stopped working when he caught a scent he didn't recognize. The werewolf inside him did, though.

It was blood.

Rachel's blood.

Panic like he'd never felt before overwhelmed him. Rachel had been shot and the smell of her blood was driving his inner wolf insane with fear.

Knox ran faster, and when he demanded more speed from his body, this time it delivered. He vaguely felt the muscles of his legs and back twisting and tearing as they changed into a different, more powerful shape. He leaned forward so far he was damn near close to dropping down on all fours. He didn't know what was happening—and he didn't care—as long as he caught up to Rachel. As his concern for her grew, so did the need to punish the men who'd hurt her.

He didn't even realize he was growling until Rachel snapped her head around to look at him again. All at once, the red glow in her eyes faded and she slid to a stop in front of him, her hands coming up to his chest to halt him.

"Knox, calm down," she said. "You're losing control."

He had no clue what the hell she was talking about. In fact, he was having a hard time thinking at all. Then he lifted a hand and saw that his claws were extended even farther than they'd been the other night at her apartment. He carefully lifted his hand to his face and confirmed his fangs were out, too. Hell, his whole jawline had changed shape to fit all the teeth he'd suddenly sprouted.

He glanced at the SUV that was getting away, the urge to chase it down and kill the men who'd shot her impossible to ignore. But Rachel's hand on his chest kept him where he was.

"Let them go," she said firmly. "You can't chase after them when you're so out of control. If you do, you'll probably end up tearing them apart right in the middle of Interstate 635.

The cops are already on their way, and we can't have anyone seeing you like this."

Knox watched the taillights of the SUV disappear around a corner. They were gone, and he knew there was no way to catch them now. Besides, Rachel was right about the cops. He could already see the glow of flashing lights strobing against the night sky.

He took a deep breath, hoping it might calm him down enough to lose the werewolf accessories. But the extra air only made his inner wolf howl more when all he could smell was the scent of Rachel's blood.

"You're bleeding!" he said, running his hands down her body, trying to find the wound and see how bad it was.

"No duh." She backed up. "And you'll be bleeding too if you try to grope me while your claws are out."

He was smart enough not to touch her again, but he continued to visually search her body in the dark, smelling the blood but still unable to pinpoint the source. And his damn nose wasn't helping him at all. Not being able to see how badly Rachel was hurt pushed his shift even further. His claws and fangs extended so far so fast it plain hurt.

And the lights and sirens were getting closer by the second. The cops were going to be there any minute.

Shit.

Realizing he was never going to be able to change back in time, Knox threw a quick glance over his shoulder. Maybe he could find a place to hide in the parking garage.

Rachel must have realized what he was thinking because she reached up and grabbed him by the shoulders. "Relax," she said, her voice gentle. "Trust me and I'll get you through this, okay?"

He didn't know how he could feel the warmth of her hands through his suit, but he could, and they were the most comforting thing he'd ever felt. But even that couldn't compare to the serene expression in her eyes. He expected her to start talking about running through the mountains or some crap like that, but instead, she grabbed the bottom of her uniform T-shirt with one hand and yanked the material out from under her equipment belt, pulling it up until he could see several inches of perfectly toned stomach…along with the blood marring that perfection.

He growled again.

"It's okay," she said, wiping away the blood between her waistline and lowest rib. "The bullet punched through the muscle below my ribs, so it didn't hit anything important and barely hurt at all. See? It's healing up already. In a few hours, it will be completely sealed, and nothing more than a slight scar in a week or so."

Knox let out a breath, more relieved than he'd expected.

Rachel lowered her shirt and wiped her bloody palm on the leg of her pants, then took his hands in hers. "I'm okay, so let's get you to shift back now. Because I have no idea how I'd explain this if someone saw."

It took a little while. In fact, the emergency vehicles were already moving around the mall parking garage by the time they were done. But Rachel finally got him tucked back into his normal form, no claws or fangs in sight.

"Come on," she said. "We need to get back in there before the DPD shuts down the entire Galleria and blames it on us."

Knox nodded, and together, they jogged through the parking garage and the stairwell they'd come out of. While he should have been trying to remember the twists and turns they'd taken on their run through the service corridors of the mall, instead, all he could think about was Rachel—the grace she'd displayed as she ran, the way her eyes glowed red in apparent anger, the scent of her blood and how it had made him completely lose his mind. But more than anything, he thought about how much it had disturbed him when he'd seen all that blood smeared across the perfect skin of her stomach.

What was this woman doing to him?

CHAPTER 7

"Sorry about all that crap back at the mall."

Rachel slid into the restaurant booth across from Knox and ran her fingers through her hair, trying to overcome the worst case of helmet head she'd ever had. Well, technically it was the only case of helmet head she'd ever had, since she'd never ridden on a motorcycle before. Still, it made her understand why Knox had been so quick to let her use his helmet while he went without. When he'd offered, she'd thought he was simply being a gentleman. Now, she wasn't so sure. Maybe he simply didn't like the way it messed up his hair. On the other hand, she was thrilled with how much fun it had been to ride on the back of his bike. Finally giving up on her hair, she dug a ponytail holder out of her pocket and put it up.

"I don't know what they were thinking, blaming you and the DAPS guys for the ambush. They were out of line," she added as she skimmed the menu. She probably shouldn't waste her time. They were at a pizza place. What else would they order?

Out of line was putting it nicely. Both Gage and Chief Leclair had shown up at the mall, furious when they found out the hired killers had known the exact route the family would be taking through the mall's service corridors—information they could only have gotten from an inside source. They'd immediately thought someone at DAPS was responsible for the leak, even though Theo insisted the mole must be in the DPD or someone in mall security.

At least no one suggested Knox was involved. Not only had he almost gotten killed, but he'd also been the one responsible for the dead bad guy they were still trying to identify. All in all, the scene had been tense and had only gotten worse when Diego, Trey, and Zane had arrived. Diego lost his mind when he realized she'd been shot, immediately blaming Knox, saying it wouldn't have happened if he'd been there. Knox and Diego had damn near come to blows before Gage and Rachel had stepped in to separate them.

"Don't worry about it," Knox murmured, reading his own menu for all of three seconds before setting it on the table. "Everyone was heated up over the attack on the prosecutor and looking to vent. Thanks for sticking up for me, though. I'm pretty sure your pack mates weren't too thrilled about it."

Understatement there. Taking Knox's side in the ensuing argument had thrown her pack mates—especially Diego—for a loop. When she'd told him she was blowing off dinner with him to go out with Knox instead, he'd almost blown a gasket. She'd owe him a big apology later…with donuts. Putting an outsider before the Pack was going to rankle for a while. But Knox had saved her life, dammit.

"They'll get over it," she said with a shrug, not sure if that was true.

Diego had actually pulled her off to the side, wanting to know if she was sure about what she was doing. He thought she was overreacting to the intense situation they'd just gone through together, warning her that Knox was a player only interested in one thing and couldn't be trusted. She told her pack mate it wasn't like that, insisting Knox was simply a new werewolf she was trying to help out. Diego didn't look like he believed her.

Truthfully, she wasn't sure what to believe herself. So many things had happened over the past few hours that her head was still spinning.

She was distracted from deeper contemplation on how screwed up her life was at the moment by the arrival of their server, a thin teenager with glasses and a bored expression who looked like he'd rather be anywhere in the world but here.

"What can I get you?" he asked, not bothering to look up from his notepad. If the guy were any less engaged in his job, he'd be a zombie.

She glanced at Knox. "Pepperoni good for you?"

When Knox nodded, she turned back to the waiter and ordered two medium pepperoni pies and breadsticks to hold them over until the pizza got there.

"And unsweetened iced tea for me—no lemon," she added. Asking for anything but sweet tea was practically a crime back in Tennessee, but in Dallas no one batted an eye.

"Make that two," Knox said.

The kid walked away without a word, making Rachel wonder if there was any chance of getting what they'd asked for. In the server's sudden absence, silence descended over the table. But it wasn't the uncomfortable kind. At least not as uncomfortable as it could have been, she guessed.

It was well after eight o'clock, so the dinner rush was mostly over and there were only half a dozen customers in the restaurant. With an open kitchen so diners could watch pizzas being made in the brick ovens and framed photos of Italy on the walls, the place was seriously quaint.

The red-and-white-checked tablecloths only added to the charm. But it was the aroma filling the dining room that was the real treat. She hadn't realized how hungry she was, but now she couldn't wait for the food to get here.

"Are we going to talk about what happened earlier?" Knox asked quietly.

Rachel tensed. She wasn't sure where Knox was going with this but was afraid she might have an idea. Of all the stuff that had happened during the ambush and in the chase that had followed, the only thing that had freaked her out was the one part she couldn't remember.

She couldn't explain it, but she couldn't recall anything from the moment she'd run out of the stairwell into the parking garage to when she'd found herself standing in the middle of the highway access road with her hands on Knox's chest. She vaguely remembered being angry, but then it was a complete blank—like an alcoholic blackout without the entertainment value of the booze. And it was scaring the hell out of her. She didn't know much about PTSD, but losing time had to be bad.

"What do you want to talk about?" She met his gaze, hoping she sounded calmer than she felt. "We were ambushed. We chased the bad guys. They got away. What's to talk about?"

Before Knox could say anything, their nameless server reappeared carrying a serving tray with a pitcher of tea, two glasses with ice, breadsticks, marinara dipping sauce, and a little bowl of sweetener packs. Dang, the kid had actually paid attention. He still didn't acknowledge their existence as he placed the stuff on the table and left, but maybe that was asking too much.

As Knox poured tea into the glasses, Rachel pounced on the still-warm breadsticks. Partly because she was hungry, but mostly to put off answering any questions for as long as possible. The breadsticks were crunchy on the outside, soft on the inside, and perfectly seasoned. Good thing she was a werewolf and could eat anything she wanted or this particular avoidance technique would have required one hell of an exercise program.

"There are a few things I've been wanting to ask you, but I'll start with the easy stuff first," Knox said, obviously missing the part where she was stuffing her face to avoid talking. "Like how you knew about the ambush. I've spent years in combat and didn't have any idea it was coming until the shooting started. I mean, I felt this weird tingle on the back of my neck, but I didn't know why."

"That was your inner wolf telling you something was up," Rachel said.

She paused to take another bite of garlic-flavored breadstick, following it with a big sip of tea. Then she delayed a little longer by adding a few packets of sweetener to the drink.

"I picked up their scents the moment we entered that hallway," she added. "It wasn't until I smelled the gun oil on their weapons that I realized we were walking into an ambush."

She couldn't bring herself to admit she'd nearly gotten them killed by confusing the scent coming off the assassin's weapons with the pheromones Knox put off on a nearly constant basis. That was a secret she'd keep to herself for a while. Like forever. She didn't plan to ever let him know he smelled like her favorite scent. She felt her face heat just thinking about it.

Knox stared at her incredulously. "Damn, it would have been nice to have a talent like that back when I was still in the SEALs." He reached for a breadstick and dipped it in the sauce. "So, what about after the ambush? I tried to get your attention when you were running down that SUV, but you turned and snarled at me. And the way your eyes were glowing, it was like you'd completely lost it. What was that about? And is that something else I have to worry about happening to me?"

Rachel almost groaned. So that was what happened during her blackout. She'd lost her mind and gone feral. *Great.*

"You already know from experience that we lose it now and then," she said. "The newer you are to the whole werewolf thing, the more likely you are to lose control. But no, I don't think you need to worry about having an episode like I did. I think what you saw might be a problem unique to me."

He snorted. "I don't know about that. I lost control when I smelled your blood and realized you got shot."

Rachel took another bite of breadstick, without the dipping sauce this time. She didn't know what to think about what he'd just admitted. That he'd lost control when he smelled her blood probably meant something significant, but she didn't want to ponder that now. She was too worried about her own problems.

"But you remember losing control. I don't," she explained. "I've talked to enough of my pack mates to know that's not normal. I think maybe I kind of black out a little."

He regarded her thoughtfully, but before he could say anything, their server was back with the pepperoni pizzas they'd ordered. They were large instead of medium, but she wasn't going to complain. She was starving.

After the kid left, Knox topped off their teas, then grabbed a slice of pizza. Rachel did the same, adding parmesan cheese to hers before handing the shaker to Knox.

"Are you honestly saying you don't remember chasing the SUV through the parking garage and halfway to the interstate while blood was leaking out of you?" he asked.

She took a big bite of pizza. The crust wasn't too thick or too thin, but somewhere perfectly in between, while the marinara sauce was spicy yet sweet, the mozzarella cheese was gooey and delicious, and the ratio of pepperoni per slice was perfect. She was even more glad now the kid had messed up and brought them large pies.

"I know it's bizarre, but it's the truth," she said. "I remember the ambush and running through the hall while tracking their scents. The next thing I can recall was standing in the middle of the road with my hands on your chest. I don't remember getting shot or running after the SUV or anything in between."

"Has this happened to you before?" he asked, picking up another slice of pizza.

"I've zoned out a few times since coming back from LA, but nothing like this," she admitted. "I thought it was because I've only been getting an hour or two of sleep a night, but now, I'm not so sure."

"A person can't go for very long on a few hours of sleep," he said. "I've done it for prolonged periods a few times on missions and it sucks, but what you're doing sounds worse. If you don't give your body the rest it needs, it's going to shut down."

She finished that slice of pizza and helped herself to another. "It's not like I'm doing it on purpose. I've had a hard time sleeping lately."

"Nightmares?"

She looked up sharply. "How did you know that?"

It was Knox's turn to shrug. "I was outside your apartment the other night, remember? I heard you scream, then saw you walk into the living room. You looked freaked out, and since no one else was in there with you, I figured it must have been a nightmare."

Rachel sat there with a half-eaten slice of pizza in her hand, trying to wrap her head around Knox seeing her after she'd had a nightmare when she was covered in sweat and looking like crap. That thought bothered her for some reason.

"I get nightmares a lot," she admitted, deciding there was nothing to be gained from lying or ragging on him for being a stalker and a Peeping Tom. "They make it hard to sleep."

"How often do you get them?"

"Pretty much every night."

She stared down at her plate so she wouldn't have to see the pity on his face. She didn't want him looking at her that way—like she was broken AF.

"Does this have to do with the clown who attacked you in the graveyard?" Knox asked.

Rachel suddenly wanted to tell him everything. That the clown who'd almost killed her was still haunting her to this day. That he was driving her more insane every day. But she censored herself at the last moment, afraid she'd scare Knox away.

So instead, she nodded. "His name is Horace Watkins, and he worked as a clown of one type or another for most of his adult life. If you ask me, that's what drove him crazy. I mean, it has to be tough making a living being something that freaks everybody out. As far as I'm concerned, that's worse than being a dentist."

Across from her, Knox's mouth edged up.

"Anyway, he went nuts one day and kidnapped a teenager, then dragged her to a nearby graveyard and started carving her up," Rachel continued. "Someone called 911 saying they'd heard screaming coming from the cemetery, so since the place was on my beat, I went to check it out. In the interim, Hannah managed to get away from Watkins and hid in the woods. When she saw me, she ran out of the darkness and right into my arms." She shuddered a little at the memory of that night. "I got her back to my patrol car just as Watkins showed up. He did a number on me with the same knife he used on Hannah, then went after her again. I finally took him down and cuffed him, but he damn near killed me. Even before that, I never thought much of clowns. But now, I frigging hate them."

"I don't blame you," Knox said. "I'm guessing he got one hell of a long prison sentence."

"Yeah, but that didn't stop me from being a complete mess for weeks following the attack." She dropped her gaze, finding it easier to talk to her slice of pizza than to the guy across from her. "The trauma of getting stabbed multiple times by a clown was bad enough, but I was also dealing with the whole werewolf thing to boot. One moment, I wanted to hide in a corner, and the next I wanted to rip somebody apart. But even that wasn't as bad as the nightmares."

"Didn't you talk to anyone?" Knox asked. "Police departments offer help for stuff like that, right?"

"They do, but I couldn't bring myself to do it." She shrugged. "I guess part of it was the cop code. You know, never admitting something on the job is bothering you? But part of it was also my own stubborn nature. I was brought up in a tough family to be a tough girl. I refused to let something as stupid as a damn clown in a graveyard get to me. Besides, it wasn't like I could tell the department shrink I'd been waking up in the middle of the night with blood in my mouth because I kept biting myself with my flashy new fangs. I was pretty sure that wouldn't have gone over well."

Knox frowned. "So you've been having these nightmares since your change?"

She shook her head, finishing that slice of pizza and reaching for another before answering. "The nightmares gradually faded over the next several months as I came to grips with everything that'd happened. It also helped that I was able to figure out the whole werewolf thing a little while later. After that, things became almost normal for a while. Then the nightmares started showing up again two months ago. They weren't too bad at first, but they've been getting worse lately."

"Two months ago?" he repeated. "That was around the time I showed up at the wedding reception with the hunters."

She gave him a small smile. "As much as I'd like to blame it all on you, I can't. I thought I'd dealt with my demons, but now I realize I'd simply done a good job of shoving them in a dark closet somewhere. Now those demons are out, and the nightmares are back worse than ever."

Rachel expected Knox to ask what she saw in those nightmares—something she definitely didn't want to get into—so she was extremely grateful when he turned his attention to the pizza. Maybe she'd get out of this dinner without having to reveal how completely screwed up she really was.

"How'd you figure out the whole werewolf thing on your own?" he asked, catching her off guard and with a mouthful of pizza.

She sipped her tea to wash it down. That part of the story she could talk about without breaking into a cold sweat. "I didn't really do it on my own. I was still working street patrol five months after the attack when I responded to a suspicious activity call down near the river. There are a lot of abandoned buildings down there, so it's a prime location for transients to live. As I was searching the area, I picked up a scent that seemed vaguely familiar, so I followed it and found three female beta werewolves hiding out in one of the buildings, terrified and nearly starving to death. Hunters had been tracking them for weeks and had already killed their alpha, so they were beyond relieved to finally see another werewolf. I think they were hoping I'd become their new alpha, while I was just thrilled to realize I wasn't alone in all this."

"What happened?" Knox prompted, transferring another slice of pizza to her plate, then doing the same for himself.

Rachel picked up the cheese shaker and sprinkled some on it. "They lived in my apartment with me for about a month, and it was amazing. They taught me so much about what it means to be a werewolf, and I made sure they had food on the table and kept them safe. Being around other werewolves was calming for me, so that helped, too."

"So, why didn't you want to become their alpha?"

"It wasn't that I didn't want to," she said. "While they were awesome to hang out with, my inner wolf instinctively knew we weren't supposed to become a pack. But with hunters crisscrossing the country, killing every werewolf they could find, I realized it wasn't safe for them to stay in Chattanooga on their own, so when they mentioned hearing about a SWAT team in Dallas made up of a huge pack of alpha werewolves who were offering protection to any werewolf who came to them, I put all three of them on a plane and got them to safety."

He finished that slice and grabbed another. "You didn't come out here at the same time?"

"I was tempted," she admitted. "But I didn't want to show up in their city looking for a handout, so I stayed with the Chattanooga PD for a little while longer, volunteering for SWAT cross-training, so I'd have the résumé of someone they'd want on their team."

Knox snorted. "You're a cop and an alpha werewolf. Why wouldn't they want you?"

"I didn't want to make it because I had claws and fangs," she said. "I wanted to make it because I'm a good cop."

They polished off two more slices of pizza while she told him what it had been like for her to show up at the SWAT compound and ask for a job, as well as how quickly her teammates had accepted her into their pack.

"They're like family now," she added.

"Speaking of family," he said in between bites of pizza. "Does your real family know you're a werewolf?"

Rachel almost snorted iced tea out her nose. She could only imagine how her family would react if she sat them down and announced she was a werewolf. Half of them would hurt themselves laughing, while the other half would probably go for their guns.

"No, they don't know I'm a werewolf," she said. "I love the hell out of my family, but there's no way I could trust them with something like this. If it were just me, I might try it, but there are other werewolves I have to worry about. If I told my family and one of them slipped up and said something they shouldn't at the wrong time to the wrong person, it could mean death and misery for a lot of innocent people."

"Don't you think you're exaggerating a little?" he asked. "I think people can handle the truth better than you think."

She lifted a brow. "You mean like your hunter buddies did? They handled the truth by hunting us down, torturing us, and executing us for fun. You don't think there aren't thousands of other people out there just like them who'd want to kill us simply because we're different? If you don't realize that's how the world works, then you aren't as smart as I gave you credit for."

Knox flushed beneath his tan. "I was being naïve, I know. I guess it's because I was hoping I'd be able to tell someone else about what I am. You've got your pack, but I don't have anyone, and I've already experienced how shitty it is dealing with this on my own." He sighed. "But you're right. Telling people would be risky. For everyone."

He fell silent after that, and Rachel felt kind of crappy for snapping at him. She knew what it was like to go it alone with this werewolf thing. It sucked.

She was about to point out that he wasn't in this thing alone and that she would help him when her phone beeped at her. Wishing she could ignore it but knowing she couldn't, she dug the thing out of the cargo pocket of her uniform pants and checked the screen.

"It's a text from Diego."

Knox's mouth quirked. "Don't tell me he's worried I've kidnapped you already?"

She laughed. She'd kind of thought the same thing. "No. He wanted to let me know they've identified the guy you shot at the mall. His name is Keylor Mora and he's a freelance killer for hire from Costa Rica. They also found the SUV we chased in an alley a few miles from the mall—on fire. No one thinks they're going to find any evidence when they get the thing put out, so no clue yet on who the other two assassins are. The chief is working with the State Department and TSA to see if all three might have flown into Dallas together."

"That's unlikely, especially if they're professionals."

Rachel silently agreed. Alton Marshall hiring outside help made complete sense, but there was nothing to say the three men came from the same part of the world. More likely, they were complete strangers who'd arrived separately. No doubt each one had their own escape plan in place.

"Here's your bill. Thanks for coming."

She looked up to see their server standing at their table. This time he didn't leave but, instead, waited for them to pay. In the kitchen, the remaining members of the restaurant staff were eyeing them with expressions that clearly said they were eager to go home.

Rachel glanced at her watch to see that it was well after midnight. She hadn't even realized until then that both pizzas were gone, along with the breadsticks and iced tea.

She reached for the bill, but Knox got there first. She let him win. While she was all about girl power, she still liked the guy to pay. Besides, he still owed her for being a hunter.

Once outside, they walked over to his bike, a big Harley that made Rachel think of huge guys with long gray beards. Not that Knox fit that image.

Tugging off her ponytail holder, she shoved it in her pocket, then picked up the helmet. She was about to put it on when the look on Knox's face stopped her. "What?"

"Nothing," he said. "I just wanted to tell you that if you ever need someone to talk to about those nightmares, I'm available. I know I'm not a therapist, but I'm a good listener. I also have more than my fair share of experience with nightmares and trying to forget things that keep a person up at night."

Before she could answer, Knox climbed on the bike and started it up, the deep rumble of the engine echoing in the night. Slipping on the helmet, she threw her leg over the seat, climbing on and putting her boots on the rear pegs like he'd taught her. She wrapped her arms around his middle, tucked her hands under his coat to keep them warm, then pressed her bare cheek against his back and held tightly as he applied the gas and they took off.

The bike growled under her like a beast, vibrations spiraling through her body. The sensation was surprisingly relaxing, like the monster they were riding was keeping other more menacing monsters at bay.

As they sped along the street, Rachel thought about Knox's offer to tell him about her nightmares. Her first instinct was to scoff at the idea. If she was going to tell anyone about her dreams, it would be someone in her pack, right?

But then she realized she didn't want to talk to any of her pack mates—not about the nightmares at least. The idea of talking to Knox appealed to her on a level she had a hard time understanding. How could she want to tell her secrets to a guy she barely knew? Especially one who'd wanted to kill people like her only a little while ago?

She didn't have an answer to that question. Luckily, she didn't have to worry about it because the bike was way too noisy to think anyway.

Scooting up closer to Knox's back, Rachel squeezed her arms around him a little more, letting the rumble of the bike and the heat of his body soothe her conflicted soul.

CHAPTER 8

Knox had to force himself not to glance down when a herd of teenage girls walked past him, all of them trying to act as if they weren't looking at him out of the corner of their eyes and failing horribly. When the girls fell apart in a fit of giggles after making it a few feet, he gave up and looked down at himself just to confirm he had, in fact, remembered to put on pants tonight. Yes, he had, and no, that didn't make him feel any better. He'd never been happier in his life than when he'd left the juvenile drama of high school behind, yet here he was, right back in the middle of it and hating it as much as ever. Whose bright idea was it for him to play bodyguard/chaperone at this high school dance anyway?

Then he heard a devious chuckle from beside him and remembered exactly whose fault this was.

"Damn, have you ever seen so much jailbait in your whole life?" Theo murmured, his eyes narrowing as he scanned the crowded gymnasium of kids all dressed in their finery for the Valentine's dance.

Knox tried to decide whether he wanted to slug the asshole or simply throw up. Since the former would almost certainly get him charged with assault and the latter would make a mess all over the place, he went for option three. "I might have said this before, but in case I didn't, I think you're the most disgusting human I've ever met. And trust me when I say this—I've met some people that seriously qualify as scum of the earth."

Theo didn't have enough character to be insulted when someone called him a piece of crap. Instead, the moron laughed like he thought it was the funniest thing in the world.

"You know, that's one of the things I like about you," he said, clapping Knox on the shoulder. "You're willing to say what's on your mind even if it could get you fired."

"Acting first and worrying about the consequences later is the story of my life," Knox said dryly. "Should I go back to the office and turn in my weapon and tactical gear?"

"Yeah right. Like I can do without you right now." Theo let out a snort. "Our dear prosecutor seems to trust you with her daughter's life. After what happened at the mall the other night, I doubt she would have let her kid even come to this dance if you weren't here to protect her. For whatever reason, the woman demanded you and that sexy piece of ass, Rachel, be assigned to protect her kid 24–7."

Knox bit back a growl. Hearing Rachel's name come out of Theo's mouth was enough to make him want to rip out the guy's throat. The thought made his fangs extend half an inch, and this time, he did let out a low growl. Good thing the music in the gym was so loud or there's no way Theo would have missed it. "Maybe it's because Jennifer recognizes we actually care about keeping the kid safe."

"Whatever." Theo shrugged as if he couldn't care less. "Speaking of protecting the brat, I'm going out front to nab Ethan and Gerald and take them back with me to the mansion."

Knox frowned. "The plan was to have two people outside the gym and two inside. If you pull them off the detail, there won't be anyone to guard the perimeter. Officer

Bennett hasn't shown yet, and I can't be in two places at once. What's so important at the mansion anyway? I thought Mrs. Lloyd was working late."

The prosecutor worked late every night. Hell, she hadn't even seen her daughter all dressed up for the dance. The poor girl had to send her mother a selfie. But even if she'd come back early from the DA's office, Theo didn't need to pull assets from the high school because there were more than enough with Jennifer already.

"Don't worry about your cute backup. She's at some meeting at the SWAT compound," Theo said. "And as for moving *my* people around, first rule of the private security biz—always dedicate the most assets to the person paying the bills. Everyone else is secondary."

That was so stupid it took Knox a moment to process it. "I thought Lloyd was paying us to protect his wife and daughter."

"Is that what you think? But since you're so concerned, I'll leave Ethan outside."

Mouth twitching, Theo walked off, leaving Knox standing there wondering what the hell his boss meant by that cryptic comment. Theo was all about the politics of the business—and the money—but that still didn't explain what he'd said.

Knox considered going after the jackass when a familiar and delectable scent smacked him across the face, wiping everything else from his mind.

"Wow, someone certainly cleans up nice."

The warm, sexy voice sent tingles up and down his back and Knox turned to see Rachel standing there looking absolutely mouthwatering in a slightly longer version of the classic little black dress, toned legs sculpted by a pair of black, strappy platform heels, and shoulders left bare of everything but her shiny blond hair.

Knox had to bite his tongue to keep from growling—this time in appreciation. Unfortunately, that plan didn't work so well since the fangs that were still partially extended sliced into either side of his tongue. He grunted and nearly reached up to shove a finger in his mouth to check the damage but stopped himself. Rachel gave him a smile, as if she knew exactly what she was doing to him.

"I was starting to think you weren't going to show up." He stepped close enough to get a good sniff of her—without being too obvious about it. "Theo said something about a meeting with your team at the compound. Are Diego and the rest of your pack still giving you trouble about working with me?"

Rachel laughed and moved even closer. Knox was certain he saw her nose lift a little, like she was trying to get a good whiff of him, too. Maybe it was the strobe lights mounted above the gymnasium, but he thought he saw her eyes flash bright green. He wasn't sure if that was good or bad. What if she didn't like the way he smelled?

"Nothing like that," she said. "Sergeant Dixon normally holds roll call in the morning, but with the four of us working the protective detail, we've missed most of them. He had one this afternoon to catch us up on everything we've missed the past few days."

Knox nodded, remembering what team meetings were like in the SEALs. With the navy deploying them so much, commander's call was the only chance to even see the guys outside his own platoon.

"Anything interesting come up?" he asked, making conversation so he'd have an excuse to stand there and gaze at her.

"One or two things." She glanced around, immediately locking on Addy and Aaron, where they were standing by the refreshment table. She studied them for a few moments before turning back to fix those beautiful eyes on him. "The chief has asked Gage to put some of my pack mates on the jurors in the Marshall trial and a few of the key witnesses."

Knox didn't see anything wrong with that idea.

"Gage also mentioned TSA thinks those other two hired killers have both fled the country. They found the owner of a small single-engine Cessna who confirms taking two guys who match their description across the border to Monterrey hours after the shooting at the mall. They booked the trip a few days in advance, so the pilot didn't even think about it until the cops showed up to talk to him. The reason he remembered them at all was because there was supposed to be a third guy, but he was a no-show."

"That definitely sounds like them," Knox said. "Those guys were hired to come in specifically for this hit and they would have had an evac plan in place before they agreed to the job. They were getting the hell out of here whether they succeeded or not."

"That doesn't mean Marshall didn't hire other assassins as part of a backup plan," Rachel said. "As long as this trial continues to go badly for him, we have to assume Marshall will keep trying."

"No doubt," he replied. "Anything else interesting?"

"Depends."

"On what?"

"On whether you're interested in a job that involves you actually acting like a werewolf."

Well, that was cryptic. "What kind of job?"

"There's a federal agency known as the Special Threat Assessment Team—aka STAT—that knows about werewolves," she explained. "After some of their agents helped us out with the vampires in LA, they realized how beneficial it could be to have people with our talents on their team. They've asked my commander if he could suggest a few possible candidates. Since you were a SEAL, he thought you might be interested."

Knox wasn't sure what stunned him more—that the federal government knew about werewolves or that the SWAT team commander knew about his military background. What else had Rachel told her pack about him?

"And how exactly did your sergeant find out I used to be a SEAL?"

Rachel's oh-so-kissable lips curved. "He had background checks done on every member of DAPS the day he found out my pack mates and I would be working hand in hand with them. He was impressed with you and not simply because you're one of us. Unfortunately, the same can't be said about all the people in your organization. I don't know if you know this, but there are some real dirtbags in that company."

Yeah, he knew. Theo liked to hire prior military, but that didn't mean he hadn't picked up a few bottom-feeders. Even in his short time working there, Knox had already figured that out. But ultimately, he didn't work in human resources and currently had other things to worry about.

"Aren't you the one who said you couldn't tell your

family you're a werewolf because you were concerned about how the world would handle knowing our secret if it got out?" he said. "Isn't that kind of a moot point now that the feds know?"

She regarding him thoughtfully. "Having people in the government know about us isn't something any of us wanted, but they know, so there's nothing we can do about it. We have to trust that the few people who have the knowledge won't abuse it."

Knox wasn't sure if he liked the idea of trusting the government with such sensitive information. They tended to have a way of screwing things up. But like Rachel said, what could they do?

"Is anyone in your pack considering the offer from STAT?" he asked, really only worried about one particular member of the DPD SWAT team leaving for a new job—her.

She shook her head. "No. Being in a pack means we don't walk away from each other. Gage has only been asking alphas who aren't in a pack if they'd be interested."

While Knox understood the concept of approaching werewolves who weren't already in the pack, he couldn't help picking up on the unspoken part of that statement—that Rachel was part of something she'd never walk away from. Something a former hunter like him could never be part of.

Rachel scanned the school gym again, taking in the collection of red, pink, and gold balloons, fresh roses on each table, and dozens of kids on the dance floor moving to the rock beat before looking back at him. "Is a job like that something you'd consider? The pay they're offering is good and you'd get to travel a lot."

He hesitated, trying to figure out why she was asking. Did she want to get rid of him that badly? "Do you think I should consider it?"

Rachel opened her mouth to answer, but something across the room caught her attention and she closed it again. Knox turned to track her line of sight and saw Ben standing on the far side of the gym. He was holding up the wall and trying hard not to look like he was staring at Addy and Aaron. While Aaron was currently standing on the dance floor near his girlfriend, the punk spent more time talking to his other too-cool-for-school friends hanging around them than paying attention to Addy, much less dancing with her.

"That is just sad," Rachel said. "I hope Addy realizes what a big mistake she's making before it's too late."

Knox was pretty sure the girl wouldn't figure it out. He'd been at the Lloyds' when Ben had shown up, wrist corsage in hand. The kid might be firmly in the dreaded friend zone, but that didn't keep him from trying to get out of it. While Addy loved the corsage and immediately put it on, then thanked him with a hug, she was clueless about how much the kid liked her. She also didn't notice that when she met up with Aaron at the dance, the bozo didn't have a corsage or any other gift for her.

Since then, Knox had spent the past thirty minutes keeping an eye on Addy and her date. Knox hadn't talked to Aaron yet, but he'd already decided he didn't like him. Addy was too good for the jerk, but apparently she didn't know that yet.

Knox and Rachel wandered around the perimeter of the dance floor, past the refreshment tables full of punch, sodas, chips, cake, cookies, and nachos, then the crowds of kids too nervous to dance, and finally the other adults there to perform their chaperone duties.

"Man, this brings back memories," Rachel said when they came to a halt on the other side of the dance floor.

"Let me guess," Knox said, knowing the answer to the question before he even asked. "You're one of those bizarre people who actually enjoyed high school, right?"

Rachel grinned. "Heck yeah. I loved it. Didn't you?"

He let out a short laugh. "That would be a no. We moved between my sophomore and junior year, and I never felt like I fit in at either high school. Your dad's military. Didn't you have that same problem?"

"When I was in elementary and middle school, yes. But my dad retired from the army when I was in high school, so I was in the same one all four years."

"That's cool then. Did you play any sports or anything like that?"

She nodded. "Sure did. I was on the softball and volleyball teams, and I was a cheerleader for the football team. Oh, and I was in the science club, too."

He did a double take. He hadn't seen that coming. "You were a girl jock *and* a nerd? I didn't think that was even possible. Isn't that like crossing the streams or something?"

"Crossing the streams?" She looked confused. "I have no idea what the hell that means. And while some people might have described me as a girl jock, I was never a nerd. I just loved biology."

Knox considered providing a quick pop culture lesson on the *Ghostbusters* movie at the same time he glanced at Addy to make sure Aaron wasn't up to anything. They were still standing there talking. Deciding the *Ghostbusters* thing would probably be a waste, he asked a more relevant question.

"You weren't one of those strange kids who actually enjoyed dissecting things, were you?"

She made a face. "No, I didn't enjoy dissecting things. No one but serial killers would. But it was part of the AP class curriculum, so I had to do it."

A big group of kids suddenly decided the part of the gym beside him and Rachel would be a good place to hang out. Unfortunately, they couldn't see Addy and Aaron now.

"We're going to need to find someplace else to stand so we can keep an eye on Addy," Knox said.

Rachel nodded. "Lead the way."

Taking her hand, he weaved his way through the crowd. Addy and her date were still on the dance floor, and the girl only seemed to have eyes for her boyfriend as Knox and Rachel moved into the crowd of teens dancing. He realized then that the dance floor was probably the best place for him and Rachel to keep watch. When they reached an unoccupied corner, he halted and turned to Rachel.

"What do you think about dancing?" he asked. "That way we can blend in a little better."

Knox wasn't sure if she'd be cool with the idea or not, but she smiled, her eyes swirling with that iridescent green color. He had no idea if that meant she was pissed at him or not, but when she began dancing to some pop song he wouldn't have recognized if his life depended on it, he decided she wasn't.

He didn't think much of the fast beat because that meant they had to dance with some distance between them, but at least dancing gave him a valid excuse for staring. That's what people did when they danced, right? Looked at each other?

Knox did his best to keep his eyes focused on Rachel's face, but if they dipped down occasionally to take in the hint of cleavage or the way the dress molded to her hips as she swayed back and forth, he wasn't to blame. It wasn't his fault she was so damn beautiful in the thing.

He caught himself before his eyes wandered too low, but when he forced his gaze back up to her face, he found her looking at him curiously. Crap, had she caught him?

"Is there something wrong with my dress?" she asked.

Knox shook his head, trying to figure out what the hell to say to get himself out of this mess. "No, not at all."

"Okay. Then why are you looking at me like that?"

"I...um...was just wondering about that stuff you said before about taking AP science. If you took classes like that and loved biology that much, how did you end up becoming a cop? Why not go to college and become a world-famous scientist? You know, the next Jacques Cousteau? Or Jackie Cousteau, I guess."

Rachel laughed, her body sinuous and hypnotizing as she moved to the beat. Then her scent hit him, coming off her in waves as her body heated up, and it was all Knox could do to keep from leaning forward to lick her bare skin. He silently groaned, the image of him running his tongue all the way from her cleavage to her neck making him harden immediately.

"I did go to college—the University of Tennessee," she told him. "But it wasn't for biology. I might love that kind of stuff but didn't see myself doing it for a living. Instead, I went with every intention of getting a law degree."

"Law?" Knox was so stunned he stopped dancing. "You

went from wanting to be a lawyer to riding patrol with a gun on your hip?"

"It wasn't anything that monumental," she said. "I took a few classes where we got to spend time in the local station, observing the booking process, how the DUI process works, processing warrants, use of force procedures, stuff like that. It was an unbelievable learning opportunity for me, but it was also the thing that changed my life."

"What do you mean?"

"I got to meet some amazing cops," she explained. "One of them offered to take me out on a ride along and I was hooked. When I finished my prelaw degree, I went to the police academy instead of going to law school. I became a cop, then a werewolf. The rest you pretty much know."

The music slowed, and Rachel stood there, as if waiting for him to slip off the dance floor with her. Suddenly, Knox didn't want the moment to end. Taking her hand, he tugged her close until her body was pressed against his. The feel of her breasts, hips, and thighs touching him made him tingle like he'd just touched an electric fence.

He glanced at Rachel to see her gazing back at him, the green glow in her eyes even more vivid. "I kind of got the feeling dancing wasn't exactly your thing."

He shrugged and slid one hand around her back, finding a nice resting place on the curve above her ass. He told himself to be good and not let his hand wander lower, even though he really, really wanted to. Especially when Rachel wrapped one of her arms around him, gripping his shoulder and pulling him even closer.

Why do we have to be in a high school gym full of teenagers right now?

"I don't mind this kind of dancing," he murmured softly, his mouth mere inches from her ear, her scent enveloping him like a drug.

Knox was ready to lose himself in her—until he saw Addy and Aaron dancing a few feet away. That would have been fine if it wasn't for the direction the boy's hand was moving between their bodies, like he was trying to cop a feel of his girlfriend's chest. As for Addy, her blue eyes were huge. She looked about three seconds from a full-on panic attack.

Aaron must have felt Knox staring at him because the punk jerked his head up, his eyes locking with Knox's. They stared at each other for a few heartbeats before Aaron's face went pale and he dropped his hand away from the place it had no business going. Knox continued to glare at him until Aaron got the idea and took a step back, putting a good six inches of space between him and Addy.

Knox grinned at him, silently promising dismemberment if he caught the twerp doing something like that again, then turned his attention back to Rachel as they moved to the music in their little corner of the floor. He realized then that his whole body was vibrating at the feel of having her in his arms. It must be some crazy werewolf thing because he'd never felt anything like this in his life. Maybe it was like plugging two overcharged batteries together the wrong way, getting instant heat and sparks. Then again, he'd never been around a woman like Rachel, so maybe that was the real reason.

Either way, he didn't miss the easy rhythm they'd fallen into. They moved like they'd been together for years. At least, that's what he told himself when lowered his head to bury his face in the waves of shiny blond hair resting there. Damn, she smelled so frigging good!

It might have been his imagination, but he was sure he felt a shiver run through Rachel's body as she moved there with him. Praying it wasn't a shudder of revulsion but worried it might be, he pulled back a little to check. At first, she didn't seem all that interested in peeling herself off his chest, but when she finally looked up at him, her eyes seemed a little unfocused.

"You okay?" he asked softly. "Was that too close?"

Rachel smiled up at him. "I'm good," she said, her voice rough and husky and so damn sexy.

Knox slid his hand an inch or so lower on Rachel's back and allowed himself to enjoy the moment as she snuggled close to him again.

He had no idea how long they danced. It must have been at least three or four slow songs. All he knew for sure was that his heart was thudding so hard he had no doubt Rachel heard every beat. Not that she seemed to mind. If anything, she seemed to be doing her best right then to wiggle herself farther into his arms. He was good with that.

And yeah, it was doing something for him. Best of all, Rachel didn't seem to mind the thing poking her in the belly any more than she minded his thudding heart.

Knox barely realized it was happening until it was already happening. But when he felt warm soft lips on his, he figured out that Rachel had tilted her face up to his and was kissing him. And he was kissing her back.

"Addy's gone!"

The sound of panic in Ben's voice jerked Knox out of the moment, and he broke the kiss and sprang apart to see the kid standing beside them, looking freaked out.

"What do you mean, Addy is gone?" Knox asked.

Looking around the dance floor, he saw that Aaron and Addy were in fact gone. He wasn't sure for how long, but it couldn't have been more than a song or two.

"Are you sure they didn't go to the restroom?" Rachel asked, while Knox was still trying to figure out how long he'd been mentally absent from the dance. Good thing one of them still had some working brain cells. His had disappeared as soon as her arms had wrapped around him, which was kind of scary when he thought about it.

Ben explained that the teen couple had been missing for at least five minutes, though that sounded like an exaggeration to Knox. Regardless, Ben had already checked the bathrooms, the steps out in front of the gym, and the dark areas behind the building, where the seniors liked to go to make out.

"I even checked the parking lot," the kid added. "Aaron's bike is still here."

Ben was obviously very industrious and perhaps a bit jealous. Maybe more than a bit.

"Where's the last place you saw Addy?" Rachel asked.

The kid led them over to the refreshment table, arms waving as he pointed out the place in line he'd seen Addy and Aaron a while ago, waiting to get some nachos. "They were right here. I swear!"

Rachel glanced left and right, her nose in the air, before she headed for the exit. She moved fast, too. Like she knew exactly where Addy and Aaron had gone. Which she probably did.

"Where's she going?" Ben asked, almost stumbling over his feet to keep up.

Knox didn't answer. Rachel was obviously tracking Addy's scent, but it wasn't like he could tell Ben that.

As they left the gym and hurried along one hallway after another, Knox did his best to find and track Addy's scent. He could definitely pick up a lot of smells, but he couldn't separate them into anything unique to a particular person. In fact, the only scent he was able to lock onto was Rachel's.

Ben babbled nonstop the whole way, sure Aaron had already dragged Addy away somewhere to make out with him.

Knox cursed silently. Why the hell hadn't he been paying attention to the girl he was supposed to be protecting? Oh, yeah. Because he'd been acting like a hormonal teen himself with Rachel.

While most of Rachel's attention was focused on tracking Addy's scent, Knox could tell Ben's words were bothering her, too. Her shoulders were lifting and falling rapidly as she breathed hard, and he'd caught a hint of red glow in her eyes when she glanced over her shoulder at him. Crap, she was about to lose it.

Sprouting fangs and claws in front of the kids definitely wouldn't be good.

When they finally stopped in front of a classroom on the other side of the building and Rachel shoved open the door with a snarl, Knox made sure he was the first one in the room, a hand on Rachel's arm to hopefully keep her from doing anything she'd regret—like ripping Aaron into small, messy chunks of wannabe bad boy.

They found Addy and Aaron at the front of a science classroom, the girl pressed back against the whiteboard, eyes wide in fear as her boyfriend leaned into her personal space. Knox didn't miss the fact that Addy's pink lipstick was smudged.

He felt his gums and fingernails tingle as his inner wolf began salivating at the thought of tearing this punk apart. Then Rachel shoved his arm aside and charged forward, and he realized he probably wouldn't get the chance.

Knox quickly got in front of Rachel, stopping her before she could get more than two steps. "I'll take care of lover boy. You get Addy out of here."

Rachel stared at him as if she wanted to argue, but then the red glow in her eyes disappeared. She looked at him in confusion for a fraction of a second before moving over to put her arm around Addy to lead her out of the room, glaring at Aaron as she went. Ben threw a pissed-off look at Aaron, then followed Rachel and his friend out of the room. Aaron made to follow, but Knox stopped him with a glower.

His fangs were doing their best to push their way out, a sure sign he was close to losing control. He forced himself to calm down, envisioning those peaceful forest scenes Rachel had described that night in her apartment.

It didn't help that Aaron's heart began thumping like a drum. Knox paused. Damn, he could actually hear the kid's heartbeat. This was the first time something like that had happened to him.

"I...um...should get back to the dance," Aaron stuttered.

"Not until we have a little talk," Knox said.

The kid swallowed hard. "About what?"

Knox put his hand on the back of the kid's neck and guided him toward the door. "Consent and what that word means."

"Okay," Aaron said nervously.

He steered the kid into the hallway and started back toward the gym. "Then we'll talk about you finding a girlfriend your own age. And after that, we'll discuss the way you're going to treat women from this day forward for the rest of your life."

Knox was almost at the gym when he heard Rachel and Addy talking just ahead of him. It sounded like they were having a serious conversation, so he stopped where he was in the darkened hallway around the corner to give them a chance to finish. He paced away a bit, but it didn't matter. He could still hear them clear as a bell. He guessed his werewolf ears had finally decided to make a full-time appearance.

He and Aaron had talked for a good fifteen minutes, and Knox liked to think he'd gotten through to the kid—at least it seemed like the teen had been seriously considering what they'd talked about as they walked out to the parking lot. The kid had even given him a look that seemed appreciative as he'd started his small bike to head home.

"Did you really want those nachos, or was that an excuse to get rid of Ben?" he heard Addy ask.

Rachel laughed. "You got me. It was a ploy. I know you said you didn't mind him being there as we talked about what happened with Aaron, but there's something I wanted to say to you without Ben around to overhear."

Addy sighed. "I already know what you're going to say. Now that I'm never going to get within twenty feet of Aaron or anyone like him, you think I should give Ben a chance, right? That he's always been there for me. Risking his life at the mall. Coming to look for me tonight? You think he could be someone I'd get along with better?"

Another musical laugh filled the air. "I was all set to give you this wonderful advice about giving him a shot, but it sounds like you already have all the answers."

There was silence for a moment, then Addy spoke again. "If I had all the answers, I never would have been dumb enough to think that Aaron was the kind of guy I wanted to be with. But I'm ready to give Ben a chance if you do one thing for me."

"What's that?" Rachel asked, amusement filling her voice.

"If I'm going to give Ben a chance, you need to make a move on Knox. I saw the two of you out there on the dance floor, so don't tell me there's nothing between you guys because it's obvious there is. You see it, right?"

Knox was stunned at how badly he wanted to hear Rachel's answer. So badly in fact that he moved closer to hear the conversation. But then, just when it seemed like she was going to reply, he heard footsteps, then Ben announcing he'd gotten two trays of nachos with extra cheese. There was no chance of getting an answer to Addy's question now.

He waited another few moments, then turned the corner, asking if they'd saved any chips for him.

CHAPTER 9

Rachel was still smiling when she walked into her apartment after dropping Addy off at home. Locking the door behind her, she headed straight for the bedroom, where she slipped out of her dress and kicked her heels into the corner of her closet. The little .380 double action pistol that had been tucked into the thigh holster nestled against her leg came off next, then finally her panties. She almost laughed as she tossed her underwear into the hamper. The evening hadn't been anything like she'd expected it to be.

In a word, it had been *ah-mazing.*

While she was thrilled with how the night had ended for Addy and Ben—with the girl promising to talk to her friend soon about how she felt about him—it was spending time with Knox that had her almost...well, *giddy* was about the only word she could come up with to describe it. Normally her name and *giddy* would never exist in the same zip code, but what the hell? It fit now.

Yeah, she was a little bothered she'd lost time again, while trying to find Addy at the high school. That moment of hesitation when she'd asked Knox if he'd be interested in taking a job with STAT had her a bit concerned, too. And there was still the whole former-hunter thing of his to deal with. But she'd worry about all that later. Because seriously, when was the last time she'd been this excited about a man?

That would be never.

She padded barefoot into the bathroom, ignoring the

oversize bath towel she'd draped over the mirror the other day. If she could have figured out how to do it, she'd yank it off the wall and throw it out. But since she couldn't—not without forfeiting a chunk of her security deposit—the towel would have to do. Regardless, she didn't plan to ever look in the damn thing again.

Rachel turned on the water in the shower, letting it heat up as she replayed the evening's highlights. There were so many good moments she had a difficult time focusing on one or two things. Telling Knox about how she became a cop was one thing, but she still couldn't believe she'd admitted she'd been in the science club. No one knew about that part of her life, not even the members of her pack.

She and Knox had fit together like two pieces of a puzzle, his hard body pressing against hers, making her feel like she was standing too close to a fire, his heat threatening to scorch her right through the dress she'd been wearing. And that kiss? She'd never experienced anything like that. If Ben hadn't shown up when he had, they'd probably still be going at it. Unless they'd moved on to something else entirely. She laughed. That would have been one Valentine's dance none of those kids ever forgot. Of course, she and Knox would probably be in jail right now.

It wasn't until steam filled the bathroom that Rachel realized the water had gotten plenty hot while she'd been daydreaming about Knox. She reached in and adjusted the temperature, then stepped into the tub, groaning as the spray poured over her skin.

Squeezing shampoo in the palm of her hand, she began washing her hair. As the bubbles slid down her back, she let her mind run wild, imagining it was Knox's hands gliding down her skin as the lather caught in the curve of her back just above her butt, tickling her there like his fingers had done earlier. Over and over, she replayed the kiss they'd shared, remembering how delicious he'd tasted and reveling in the knowledge that he wanted her as much as she wanted him. For a brief moment, she allowed herself to think there was something more than random attraction going on. But then she stopped herself, refusing to jinx whatever it was that was building between them.

Rachel was so wrapped up in her fantasies of Knox she didn't notice the nasty stench filling the air until she almost gagged on the greasy, rotting smell assaulting her nose. It was like something had died in her apartment. Rinsing the shampoo out of her hair as quickly as she could, Rachel squeezed the excess water from her hair, then turned off the water and scrambled out of the shower. Hastily wrapping a towel around herself, she walked out of the bathroom and into the living room, half expecting to find some kind of dead creature lying on her couch.

But there was nothing on the couch or under it, or even shoved in a corner behind the TV. She attempted to follow the rancid smell to its source, but it faded away completely until she couldn't smell it anymore. She spun around in a circle, confused, trying to find it again. But it was like the smell had never been there at all. That wasn't possible. Odors that strong didn't simply dissipate that quickly or neatly.

She glanced at the central air vents, wondering if maybe something horribly wounded had somehow gotten into the duct work and randomly dragged its rotting ass past her apartment. But she immediately dismissed that thought.

There couldn't be anything like that in the ducts. Not unless it was a zombie rat. Because nothing living could smell that awful.

Deciding the issue was going to remain a mystery, Rachel padded into the bathroom long enough to dry off and grab a fresh towel for her hair. Naked, she headed for the bedroom, toweling her long hair dry and telling herself to forget the phantom smell that had unsettled her so badly.

Rachel slipped into the XXL University of Tennessee T-shirt she sometimes slept in and headed for the kitchen. Taking her electric toothbrush from its recharging station beside the coffeemaker, she squeezed a generous amount of paste on it, then stuck it in her mouth and turned it on. It was a little embarrassing to keep her toothbrush in the kitchen, but she'd been afraid to brush her teeth in the bathroom since the episode with the mirror. The mere thought made her cringe.

Rachel was rinsing the toothpaste from her mouth when a cold breeze blew across her shoulders. It was immediately followed by the creepiest sensation she'd ever felt. She spun around, sure that someone was behind her.

But of course, no one was there. Even so, she couldn't stop herself from glancing around the kitchen again, then the living room, to make sure. Her heart rate that had kicked into overdrive seconds ago slowly started to come back down.

Telling herself to stop being such a fraidycat, she rinsed her mouth again, then put the glass in the dishwasher. She turned to head to bed when she caught her reflection in the dark glass of the cabinet-mounted microwave.

Only it wasn't her reflection.

Rachel stumbled back with a yelp, her butt colliding with the kitchen table as she stared back at the clown from her nightmares. Even in the dull glass of the microwave, it was impossible to miss the white paint covering his face, the permanent smile, and the glowing, red gaze.

She closed her eyes, sure the mirage would go away when she opened them again. But it didn't, and she nearly fell on her ass when the face in the glass turned to continue regarding her as she moved slightly to the side. She got her bare feet under her only to lose them completely when the deep chuckle rumbled around the kitchen.

The last time she'd heard that laugh was over a year ago in a courtroom in Chattanooga.

Rachel knew she was hyperventilating, but she couldn't stop.

This isn't real.

The clown isn't here.

Another chuckle echoed in her apartment, coming from every direction at once. "Oh yes, dear Rachel, this is very real and I'm most definitely here. As for losing your mind, you are indeed going insane. Of that, you can be quite sure."

The voice was so calm yet so evil it made her skin crawl. And it was so close she swore she could feel the clown's warm breath on her neck.

Rachel looked around wildly, trying to locate the creature who'd tried to kill her. To her horror, she found his face in every reflective surface—the toaster, the coffeepot, even the stainless refrigerator and dishwasher.

The clown's lips pulled back in a sham of a grin, his eyes full of amusement as they bore into hers. He was stalking her. Toying with her.

She retreated, putting her back to the wall, shoving her kitchen table aside to make room. Even though she was still gasping for breath, her heart thundering in her ears, self-preservation instincts demanded she protect herself, but both the .380 and the larger .45 were in her bedroom. The thought of turning her back on the faces all around her was too terrifying to consider.

So, she did the only thing she could think of. She lunged forward to grab the biggest knife in the block on the counter. The move forced her to come within inches of one of the reflections of the clown, and it snapped its teeth together with a resounding clash that made her skitter back across the kitchen.

The thing laughed again, so loud this time she could feel it in her bones. She wanted to resist, to fight, but the sound was so disturbing she thought her very bones might shatter like glass falling victim to a high-pitched scream.

Gripping the knife, she slid down the wall to the floor, squeezing her eyes shut and covering her ears with her forearms. It didn't help. The laughter continued to cut through her soul, even as the horrible stench of death and rot returned, pushing her mind to the brink.

A part of her recognized that her claws were out. Her fangs, too.

"This isn't real," she murmured, tears pouring down her face. She didn't care if the clown heard her. "You're having a breakdown. This is just a hallucination. You're going to open your eyes and this will all be gone."

The laughter suddenly ceased and was replaced with a slow, soft chuckle that was ten times worse.

"I already told you this is real," the voice whispered as

the demented chuckles continued. "As real as our first meeting in that graveyard. Only this time, things will end with you bleeding to death at my feet."

With a sob, Rachel scrambled to her feet and fled the kitchen at warp speed. She should have run for the door, but her inner werewolf took over and pointed her toward the bedroom—and the weapons in there. Though what the hell she was supposed to shoot was beyond her.

"Run, little wolf." The clown's leering grin mocked her as she sped past her dresser and the large mirror attached to the top of it.

Rachel ignored the taunting voice, slowing long enough to wrap her claw-tipped fingers around the mirror atop the dresser, ripping it off with a growl and slinging it out the bedroom door and into the living room, where it smashed into pieces.

Scrambling for the nightstand, she grabbed the .380 she'd left on the top, then yanked open the top draw and grabbed her Sig. Somehow, she ended up in bed, back against the headboard, handguns pointed in two different directions, steady despite the terror tearing through her like a storm.

"You can't run and you can't hide," the voice said, the deep sound seeming to fill the very air around her. "You'll never be free until I'm done with you, and by then, you'll be begging for me to end it all."

Rachel screamed so loud and so hard it felt like her vocal cords were being ripped out. The laughter continued no matter how much she begged the monster to leave her alone. A little voice inside told her to get the phone and call her pack for help. But the thought of getting off the bed and going into any part of her apartment that might have a reflective surface terrorized her so much her body refused to even consider it.

So instead, she sat there on her bed, hugging her knees, weapons in both hands, sobbing uncontrollably as endless waves of fear washed through her body.

Knox grinned as he guided his motorcycle across town. A little while ago, he'd driven Ben home in one of the DAPS vehicles. It had been interesting, to say the least. He'd expected to spend the time talking to Ben about how to excavate his butt out of Addy's friend zone, but instead, the kid had used the entire drive attempting to convince Knox that he had a legitimate shot at getting Officer Bennett to be his girlfriend. Knox would have laughed if it wouldn't have hurt the boy's feelings.

So, he'd bitten his tongue, nodded his head at the appropriate moments, and agreed he'd give it a shot. As soon as an opportunity presented itself, he'd let Rachel know he was interested in her.

"You shouldn't wait," Ben told him firmly, his face far more serious than a sixteen-year-old kid should ever be. "I waited around and look where it got me. Addy could have gotten hurt. Heck, she could have died. You should go see Officer Bennett tonight."

Knox pointed out it wasn't quite that dramatic for him and Rachel. She wasn't in danger. Besides, it would be well after midnight by the time he got to her place. She'd be asleep and wouldn't be thrilled to have him show up on her doorstep.

"You really sure about that?" Ben asked.

"What part?" Knox wanted to know.

"Any of it," Ben said, sounding wise beyond his years.

After dropping off the teenage Yoda, Knox had gone home, changed clothes, then jumped on his bike, headed for Rachel's place. He had no idea what the hell he was going to say when he got there. But something inside—maybe his inner werewolf—told him this was the right thing to do. Given his track record of decision-making as of late, he was slightly leery of this approach, but he hoped if he let his wolf make the call, the outcome would be better this time.

He thought the ride over in the cold night air would clear his head and help him come up with a clever reason why he was showing up at Rachel's place. Unfortunately, by the time he pulled to a stop in an empty space in front of her apartment complex, he was still at a loss.

Killing the engine, he climbed off the bike and took off his helmet, leaving it on the seat, then walked into the building. As he took the stairs up to her floor, he tried to come up with a plan.

The first thing to do was knock on her door, of course. But what would he say when she opened it? Especially if she was pissed about him waking her up. Did he charge in boldly and admit how much he'd enjoyed the kiss they'd shared? Or should he slip into the situation a little more smoothly, maybe say he wanted to make sure she was okay after tracking Addy and Aaron through the school? Because he was pretty sure that red glow in her eyes meant she'd lost time again.

He was still trying out different variants of *are you okay* when he heard what sounded like whimpering from somewhere on the second floor.

Rachel.

He didn't know how he knew it was her, but he did. She was in trouble.

Knox took the last five steps in a single leap, claws and fangs extending as he raced down the hall. He was grateful that it was so late and there was no one around to see him. Not that he cared if there was. Rachel needed him and he'd do anything—face anything—to get to her.

The whimper turned into screams before he was even halfway to her door. Didn't anyone else hear them? But then he remembered her saying she had nightmares a lot. Maybe her neighbors had gotten used to it.

Knox didn't slow as he approached her door, instead lowering his shoulder and slamming through it at full speed. He'd thought he'd take the whole thing down, but the door swung open, dumping him into the middle of a war zone.

Pieces of wood and shattered glass from a mirror covered the living room floor, as if something had exploded. But before he could even consider how all of that crap had gotten there, another scream from the bedroom ripped through the apartment. He kicked the door closed behind him without thinking, then pulled his Glock from his holster and headed for the bedroom, expecting the worst.

He looked left and right as he stepped into the bedroom, finger poised on the trigger of his weapon, preparing himself for absolute carnage. But as he swept the room, he found it was empty except for Rachel. She was sitting with her back against the headboard, looking terrified. Even though he was standing right in front of her, it was like she didn't see him.

Rachel was dressed in a long T-shirt, her knees pulled up

to her chest, her arms wrapped around her head like she was trying to shield her ears from a noise as tears ran down her face. Her claws and fangs were extended, and she was clutching two guns in her hands. He looked for signs of violence, but there wasn't a mark on her. He frantically looked around again, trying to find whatever the hell had attacked her.

Knox was peeking under the bed when another heart-rending scream tore through him. The sound was filled with so much pain and terror that he stopped worrying about whatever—or whoever—had done this to her and hurried over to her.

Even though he'd made no effort to move quietly up to this point, it wasn't until the mattress dipped under his weight that Rachel seemed to realize someone was in the apartment with her. Both arms snapped straight, two automatics pointed at his face, her fingers tense on the triggers.

"Rachel, it's me," he said as firmly but calmly as he possibly could considering the barrels of two weapons were aimed at him.

She must have recognized it was him because her arms slowly lowered until she dropped both weapons onto the bed. Before Knox could take a breath to ask if she was okay, Rachel threw herself into his arms, deep sobs shaking her whole body.

Knox wrapped his arms around her, pulling her in close even as Rachel crawled into his lap and buried her face against his chest. He desperately wanted to know what had happened, but he knew she wasn't ready for that. Not yet. So he holstered his Glock, carefully moved Rachel's weapons to the nightstand, then focused on calming her down. He sucked at stuff like this, but he did his best, rocking her gently, rubbing his hands softly up and down her back, and making quiet shushing sounds he hoped were soothing.

"It's okay," he murmured. "I've got you. You're safe. I won't let anything happen to you, I promise."

He knew the words were absolute babble, but he kept saying them over and over because he had to do something. Hearing her cry was more painful than almost anything he'd ever experienced in his life—like every tear that fell from her cheeks carried a piece of his soul with it.

He must have been better at this comforting thing than he realized because after a few minutes, Rachel's sobs began to fade to whimpers, then slow to exhausted sighs. Only after her heart rate returned to normal and her breathing became regular did he finally ask the question he needed her to answer.

"What happened, Rachel? Who did this to you?"

When she didn't answer right away, Knox thought she'd fallen asleep, but then he felt warm air brush against his neck and realized she was trying to speak. But her words were so thready and fragile, it was almost impossible to hear them, even for a werewolf.

"My nightmare came to life and tried to kill me," she whispered.

Knox pulled back a bit to see her face, waiting for her to say more—something that would help him understand what she'd meant. But when all she did was gaze up at him with broken, fear-filled eyes, he knew if he wanted to know more, he would have to ask.

"You mean you had another nightmare? Is that what happened?"

He said the words carefully, not wanting to make it seem

like he was making light of what she was going through. People threw the term *nightmare* around like it was something trivial, and he supposed that for some, their nightmares were little more than bad dreams. But he knew firsthand how powerfully incapacitating they could be. How it almost seemed like they could pull the life from a person.

Rachel hesitated. "I guess so, but it seemed so real. The clown was here." She stopped, looking confused, then shook her head. "Or I thought he was here. I could see his face in the mirror, and the glass of the microwave—everywhere. He told me that I'll never get away from him."

Tears spilled down her face again, and Knox pulled her in close. "Shh. It's okay."

"I'm scared, Knox," she sobbed against his chest. "It's like I'm going insane and it's getting worse every day. I can't handle this on my own anymore."

Knox recognized the symptoms of extreme PTSD. He'd seen it before—he'd felt it before. The nightmare of that damn clown's attack was tearing her apart from the inside out.

He wrapped his arms around her more tightly, wanting to somehow protect her from every horrible thing that had ever happened to her with nothing more than his physical presence. "You don't have to handle this on your own. I've got you and I won't let anything happen to you. We'll get you help and get through this together."

They sat like that for a long time, Knox holding her close while she cried. When it seemed as if she was too exhausted to cry anymore, he felt her body relax until he was sure she'd fallen asleep. He held her a few minutes longer, then started to reposition her on the bed, figuring she'd be able to sleep better if he covered her with the blankets.

But the moment his arms loosened, her eyes shot open, full of panic. "Don't let me go!" she practically shouted. "When you hold me, he feels far away and I feel safe."

Knox wanted to check the door to her apartment to make sure it was closed, but he knew he couldn't do that, at least not right now. So he lay back on the bed and pulled her onto his chest, wrapping her tightly in his arms again. Then he kissed her head and made the same soothing sounds as before.

"I'm not going anywhere," he promised. "I'm never going to let you go."

It seemed like only seconds before she was asleep again, and as Knox held her close and watched over her, he realized he'd never felt anything so perfect in his life.

CHAPTER 10

Rachel woke up wrapped in warmth and comfort so perfect all she wanted to do was lay there and revel in it. Following her instincts, she buried her face deeper into the pillow under her only to realize the pillow was harder than she was used to sleeping on...and had a heartbeat. Lifting her head, she opened her eyes to discover she'd been sleeping on a man's chest.

She glanced up to see Knox asleep on his back with one arm casually thrown over his head, the other wrapped around her. He looked so edible lying there with the first rays of the morning sun lighting his scruff-roughened jawline.

He'd gotten a blanket over her at some point during the night, but it was the bare, muscular arm tucked around her providing the real warmth...and comfort. A quick check under the aforementioned blanket confirmed she was wearing her favorite orange-and-white Tennessee sleep shirt while Knox had on a pair of tight boxer briefs that were the same deep blue as his T-shirt. She dropped the blanket, guessing that meant they'd actually slept together instead of had sex. Rachel wasn't sure if she was relieved or disappointed.

With a sigh, she rested her head on his chest again, replaying the events that had gotten her here.

She remembered the nightmare about the clown from last night, but here in Knox's arms, it felt distant, like she was seeing a movie of an event she'd been involved in a long time ago. The terror had been so overwhelming it had driven her to some dark place in her head she thought she'd never escape from. But then Knox had shown up and everything she'd been afraid of had somehow receded into the background.

That was when she'd given in to the exhaustion that had been building for so long and fallen into the deepest, most relaxing sleep she'd gotten since that frigging clown had tried to kill her back in Chattanooga.

Rachel pondered that as she listened to Knox's heart beating under her cheek, the scent of his body enveloping her like a second blanket. While she wasn't comfortable putting a name to it, she knew there was something special about him and the way he made her feel. For the first time in a while, she wasn't holding her breath waiting for the next panic attack to hit or the next shadow in the corner to scare her to death. With Knox there, she felt normal again.

She didn't know if it was all the moving around or the noise of her overactive mind that woke Knox up, but either way, his arm tightened around her momentarily before he placed a tender kiss on top of her head.

"I didn't wake you, did I?" he asked softly, tracing gentle circles on her back and shoulder with his fingers.

"No, it wasn't you," she murmured against his shirt, wondering how much nicer it would be if his chest were bare. "I always wake up the minute the sun shows its face. It's been that way since I was a kid. Used to drive my parents bonkers."

"I can see why," he said with a chuckle. "Did you sleep okay?"

The concern in his voice was unmistakable, and Rachel

smiled. “I slept great.” She tipped her head back to look up at him. “In fact, it was the best sleep I’ve had in a long time. Actually, it’s nearly the only sleep I’ve had in a long time. So, thank you.”

He looked confused for a moment, but before he could say anything, Rachel moved a little higher on his chest and kissed him. It was impulsive as heck, and if someone had asked why she’d done it, she wasn’t sure she’d be able to put it into words. But after everything that happened last night, it felt right.

She’d intended it to be a quick kiss, nothing more than a little added emphasis to her words. But the moment their lips touched and she felt the zip of electricity pass between them, she knew there was no way she could be satisfied with one little peck. When Knox pushed aside the blanket and urged her up higher, so she was lying fully atop his body, Rachel knew she wasn’t the only one feeling the tingle.

Knox slipped his tongue between her lips, deepening the kiss. She might have moaned a little at the taste of him, but if she did, she refused to be held accountable. It wasn’t her fault he was so damn delicious.

They made out for a long time, her hands resting on his chest, his tangled in her hair while their tongues slow danced. She couldn’t remember the last time she’d kissed a guy like this. Then it hit her. She couldn’t remember it because she’d never kissed a guy like this. Sure, she’d kissed guys before, but it had never felt like this. Her whole body was humming with a combination of excitement and arousal, just like it had on the dance floor last night. If the growing bulge under her thigh was any indication, Knox felt the same way.

She was disappointed when Knox broke the kiss and

gently pushed her away to study her. But the smoldering heat in his warm brown eyes told her the pause was temporary.

"Don't get me wrong," he said softly, twirling a lock of her hair around his finger. "You can kiss me like that anytime you want and twice on Sunday, but please don't feel like you have to pay me back for staying here with you last night. I did it because you needed me, not because I thought I'd get something out of it."

She smiled, shocked at how warm and gooey his words made her feel inside. "I know, but that doesn't mean I don't appreciate it. I'm not trying to exaggerate here, but I'm pretty sure you saved me from a complete mental breakdown."

It probably said a lot that Knox didn't argue with her.

"I was serious last night. About getting through this together." He pushed her hair back from her face. "I'll help you find someone to talk to and go with you to the sessions if you want."

She lay there on top of him, stunned at the offer. How the hell had this happened? One day he was a hunter who wanted to kill her kind, the next he was a werewolf who needed her help, last night he'd turned into the only person who could help her stay sane, and now he was in her bed making unbelievable promises. How was it possible for Knox to go from the worst possible human being to the man she couldn't seem to do without?

Rachel didn't bother pondering it too long because thinking at this point was wasting time they could use doing something better. So, instead, she clasped his shoulders and dragged herself up his body like it was a Slip 'N Slide. Then she covered his mouth with hers and kissed him hard.

Knox groaned, sliding his hands down her back until

they cupped her butt through the thin material of her T-shirt. Dang, she knew he had really big hands, but they felt even larger as they squeezed and massaged her ass. The sounds of appreciation she made were probably ridiculous, but she didn't care.

"I think I just found one of your happy places," he murmured against her lips as he slowly worked her T-shirt up to expose her butt.

She swore she heard sizzling when his warm hands came into contact with her bare skin. Okay, she really didn't. But man, did it feel good. The sensation had her writhing all over him, right up to the point that his underwear-covered hard-on became wedged in the cleft between her legs. Then she started doing some serious wiggling.

"Mmm, I think you've found another one," she breathed, forced to break their kiss so she could sit up a little and grind against him more firmly.

Rachel was so caught up in the moment she didn't realize Knox had gotten a grip on the hem of her T-shirt until he'd lifted the material up to take it off. She raised her arms, leaning forward a little to make it easier. And just that fast, she found herself completely naked while Knox was still half-clothed. But when he gazed up at her with an expression of utter adoration on his face, she decided she could get used to the disparity. It turned out she liked being regarded as if she were a goddess.

When Knox had gotten his fill from that vantage point, he rolled her over on the bed until she was on her back with his hands positioned possessively to either side of her shoulders, legs straddling her hips.

"Let's see if we can find a few more of your happy

places," he murmured as his mouth came down on her neck and he began to kiss, lick, and nibble his way along her jawline from earlobe to chin, then down to her collarbone, fire following his path.

She arched like a bow as his warm lips found their way down to her breasts, teasing and nipping at first one nipple, then the other. Rachel reached down to thread her fingers into his silky hair, scraping her nails along his scalp in encouragement as his tongue traced little circles around her nipples, then the curved undersides of her breasts, and finally, the valley between them. She about lost her mind as he took his time exploring every part, finding erogenous zones she'd never known existed.

But then she felt Knox tense, his mouth hovering above the upper slope of her left breast. She looked down and saw him gazing intently at the two-inch-long and quarter-inch-wide scar there. It was a shade lighter than the rest of the skin around it and barely discernible. There were several tiny lines branching away from the main scar where the doctors had to cut her open to deal with the internal injuries. The way Knox was studying them, it was almost like he was thinking about the pain she'd endured.

"Yes," she said without him asking. "That's where Horace Watkins stabbed me. The blade missed my heart but got the top of my lung and nicked a vein. I have another scar on my right shoulder in back."

Knox lifted his gaze to hers, and she was stunned to see that his normally brown eyes were swirling with gold. Why, she couldn't say. Without a word, he lowered his head again and ever so gently kissed the scar, murmuring something even her werewolf ears couldn't make out. A moment later, he continued his way down her body, nipping along her ribs and down her abs, spending a few extra seconds making love to her belly button.

"I think you've found a new happy place," she sighed, wanting to let him know she'd appreciate it if he hung around that area a while longer.

He didn't disappoint her.

Knox's amazingly careful inspection of her body led him to her right hip, where he slowed again with a soft chuckle. "A tattoo of a wolf's head with the word *SWAT* above it? Is that an inside joke or something?"

Rachel let out a throaty laugh as his lips and tongue traced the outline of the wolf's head. "It's a pack thing. Each member gets one as soon as they're accepted onto the team."

"So, you have to be part of the team then, huh?" He snorted. "I guess that means no wolf's head tat for me."

She opened her mouth to tell him it wasn't like that, but the words got lost as he continued his exploration, following the crease of her thigh as he slowly spread her legs. Then his lips found that sensitive place in between them, and any meaningful thoughts she'd been having completely evaporated.

Knox definitely knew what he was doing down there, sliding his tongue up and down the folds of her pussy, occasionally moving upward to trace slow, methodical circles around her clit. It felt absolutely incredible, and she was sure she'd orgasm if he kept doing what he was doing. But every time she got close, he'd pull away and lick her folds again. She grabbed his hair, trying to guide him to her clit, but he stubbornly refused to follow her helpful suggestions.

Just when Rachel thought she might actually have to

resort to force to get him to stop teasing her, Knox slid two fingers inside her wetness, finding that perfect spot like he had a GPS tracker telling him where to go. At the same time, his mouth came down over her clit and he began flicking his tongue in perfect rhythm.

It couldn't have been more than a few seconds before her entire body clenched up and she was hit with an orgasm that made her whole field of vision go bright white, like a sun had exploded into a supernova right above her. Knox rode with her through it, his fingers and tongue making waves of pleasure wash over her.

By the time she'd collapsed back onto the bed in a sweaty, loose-limbed pile of melted goo, she was sure Knox—or at least his tongue—had ruined her forever.

Rachel suddenly felt a tickling sensation along her body, and she looked down to see her hero-turned-lover kissing his way up her tummy until his face was directly above hers.

He grinned. "Sorry to bother you in your moment of orgasmic bliss, but do you happen to have a condom somewhere? If not, I guess I could do with some duct tape and a rubber band. Though I'm not too sure of the reliability of that particular method."

She couldn't help but laugh. "Top drawer of the nightstand. You might have to dig around a bit to find them. It's been a while."

He leaned across her body, opening the drawer and rummaging around, finally coming up with a foil-wrapped packet. The molten expression in his eyes as he stepped off the bed to get undressed was enough to make her tingle all over again. She hadn't really been thinking about round two, since round one had turned her head to mush, but now that it was about to happen, she had to admit she was excited at the prospect of having him inside her.

Knox reached over his shoulder to grab the back of his shirt, pulling it over his head. Rachel sighed contentedly. As fetishes went, this one was mild, but she'd always loved watching a guy get undressed, especially when they yanked their shirts off that way. Most women got undressed pretty much the same way they got dressed. It was all about smooth, careful moves so they never tore a stitch or stretched a seam out of line.

Guys, on the other hand, ripped off their clothes like they didn't care if the shirt survived the event. They were so rough about it…sexy. Maybe she spent too much time noticing things most people didn't, but in this case, she definitely appreciated what she noticed.

Long before Knox's clothes had started coming off, she'd figured out that he was built. But seeing his bare chest and broad shoulders and—*oh my goodness*—those rock-hard abs made her realize she'd been selling him short. The man wasn't simply amazing—he was sublime.

Rachel gawked without shame, taking in the thick muscles of his smooth chest, the sexy slope of his traps from neck to shoulders, the ripples of his stomach as he worked his underwear down and off. The happy trail of dark hair that led from his belly button to a shaft that was absolutely perfect in every way. He was the complete package and looked so yummy she felt her fangs aching to come out so she could take a bite.

Knox reached for the condom packet, but she grabbed it first, scooting her butt to the edge of the bed.

"Let me," she said softly.

Smiling as he moved to stand between her legs, Rachel reached out and wrapped her fingers around him, caressing up and down along the long length a few times. She told herself it was to make sure he was hard enough to put the condom on him. But she knew he was already hard enough to hammer nails. She simply wanted to get her hands on him before she put the big guy under wraps.

Knox groaned when she dipped her head forward and swiped her tongue across the head of his hard cock. She let out her own sound of appreciation. He tasted delicious, making her assume it must be another one of those werewolf things because he was more scrumptious than any man she'd ever been with.

Rachel was tempted to keep going—sure Knox wasn't going to complain—but she was hungry to see what came next, so she pulled back with a promise to herself to definitely do this again later, then got to work getting the condom on before she changed her mind.

She scooted back on the bed as Knox climbed on, spreading her legs and inviting him in. Giving her a smoldering look, he dipped down to take a nibble of her inner thigh as he moved up her body. She laughed at the electric sensation, stunned she was so comfortable with a man she barely knew, a man she'd been more than ready to hate only a short time ago.

No matter how ready for this they both might have been, neither of them seemed to want to rush. Instead, Knox took his time teasing her opening with his hardness before finally gently sliding in. Rachel gasped when he pushed in deep, reveling in the sensation of his thickness spreading her wide, filling her completely.

His forearms came down on either side of her body, his mouth finding hers as he slowly made love to her. He slid all the way out until only the tip was inside her, then plunged back in with a firm thrust, bottoming out hard enough to let her feel the impact of his hips against her inner thighs. She kissed him back, wrapping her arms and legs around him, holding him tightly and locking her ankles together behind his back, content to let him set the pace. While it wasn't fast, the force of his movements shook her body until she was trembling all over. Something told her this orgasm was going to be even better than the first one, but if he wasn't going to rush it, neither would she.

Knox nibbled on her lips, her earlobes, her neck, even her collarbones. And the whole time he teased her with his mouth, he never slowed his pace, making tingles start in her middle, then gradually spread outward until her whole body was vibrating. She gave herself over to the sensation, her perception of everything else around her blurring at the edges. She knew for sure she would have already orgasmed if Knox hadn't been holding back.

"Harder," she urged breathlessly in his ear. At the same time, she squeezed him tighter with her legs and scraped her nails down his back, making sure he understood how much she wanted this.

Knox pulled back a little to gaze down at her, his eyes an iridescent gold now. The way he looked at her was awe-inspiring, as if she was the most important thing in the world to him. She nodded, trying to convey without words that she felt the same. She hoped that would do because, right then, she'd have had a hard time expressing everything going on in her head.

His mouth closed on hers, and if the kiss hadn't taken her breath away, his sudden hard thrusts would have. He plunged into her over and over, touching her in places she hadn't known she had, his pelvic bone doing a delicious number on her clit every time he thrust.

The tingle deep in her tummy became a lightning bolt faster than she would have thought possible, and her teeth found their way to one of those perfect shoulder muscles of his as she bit down on him to hold back the torrent of screams that fought to burst out of her.

The rush of pleasure was almost too much as she tumbled off a cliff and kept right on falling. Then Knox followed her off the precipice, half groaning, half growling as he orgasmed.

Rachel wasn't sure what happened after that because the details were kind of fuzzy, but the next thing she knew, she was lying on top of Knox instead of under him. It was seriously comfortable and she didn't plan on going anywhere. So, she stayed glued to his awesome chest, listening to his heartbeat return to normal and enjoying the tremors of pleasure that continued to rock her body every few seconds.

It must have been a good fifteen minutes before she had enough energy to think, much less move. But when she finally did, she pushed herself up on Knox's chest to smile at him.

"On a scale of one to ten, that was probably a hundred," she told him.

He reached up to cup her face, his touch a caress, his dark eyes soulful. "Yeah, it was."

She bent to press a tender kiss to his lips, prepared to go

into detail about how much she loved what they'd just done when a thought occurred to her.

"Not to change the subject, but I'm almost certain I locked my door last night. How did you get in?"

He ran a finger up and down her arm, mouth edging up. He had a gorgeous smile. "It was locked, but when I heard you scream, I kicked it in. Don't worry, though. I slipped out of bed after you fell asleep and wedged a chair from the kitchen table under the door handle so no one could get in without some serious force."

That answer led to about a dozen others, such as why he'd shown up at her door in the first place and how he'd been able to get her to calm down when she couldn't figure out how to do it herself. But then a bigger question came to mind and everything else suddenly took a back seat.

"When you offered to help me find someone I could talk to about my nightmares, you said you'd be willing to come to the sessions with me." She hesitated, praying he really had said that and she hadn't dreamed it. "Did you truly mean that? You'd come see a shrink with me? Hold my hand and crap like that."

Knox nodded, his expression suddenly sincere. "Yeah, I was serious. I know how hard it can be to open up about stuff like this. If it will help, I'll be there for you."

Rachel once again wondered how the hell she'd stumbled across someone like him right when she needed him the most. But at the same time, she also realized Knox seemed to have some personal experience when it came to dealing with stuff like this. What else explained his ability to calm her down last night or his confession about knowing how hard it was to open up about things?

"I'm not trying to dig into your personal life or your past, but something tells me you've been through the same thing I'm going through now," she said. "Did you?"

"Wait, what just happened?" Knox sputtered, gazing at the beautiful, sexy woman lying on his chest, baffled by the sudden turn in the conversation. "One second we're talking about me going to therapy with you, and the next, we've somehow jumped to the topic of my traumatic experiences."

Rachel folded her hands on his chest, resting her chin on them and regarding him with a genuinely hurt expression. "Sorry. I was only asking. If you'd rather not talk about whatever happened that gave you so much experience with stuff like this, you don't have to. Really. I honestly wasn't trying to pry."

Ah, hell. Now, he felt like a jerk. Last night, Rachel had opened up her personal suitcase of issues and dumped them all out for him to see, yet here he was acting like his secrets were too special for her to know about.

"I know you weren't prying," he said, gently running a finger down her cheek. "You caught me a little off guard, that's all."

Rachel regarded him silently for a moment, then slipped off his chest to pull the blankets up over the both of them. When she had the covers the way she wanted them, she didn't climb on top of him again, but instead put her head on the pillow beside him. While they were technically still close enough to almost touch, it felt like a tremendous space had opened up between them.

That feeling bothered the crap out of him.

"I was with a four-man SEAL team in Nairobi," Knox said softly, turning to stare up at the ceiling. "It's not something that makes the evening news very often, but the extremist Islamic activity there can be as bad as anything you'd see in Iraq. We were there to do some low-level surveillance work and start a dialogue with members of the Kenyan Ministry of Defense and National Police about future joint operations. We didn't expect to directly engage with hostile forces, which was why I had two newbies fresh out of BUDs with me."

Knox didn't mean to stop there, but thinking about that day was enough to start the scenes replaying in his head—memories he'd tried like hell to forget.

"But?" she prompted.

Knox jumped a little at the softly spoken word. How long had he been lying there trapped in his head, alone with his dark thoughts?

"But there was a terrorist attack at an office complex near where we were meeting." He remembered every second of the fight like it was yesterday, instead of more than a year ago. "It had nothing to do with us, but we became involved anyway. The ministry officials we were with were high-level officers and were armed. Fortunately, the officers from the National Police were, too. Even with them, we were heavily outnumbered. One of the new guys on my team, Lawrence Vasquez, was hit in the chest and went down before he even had a chance to fire his weapon."

He swallowed hard. He'd never forget the expression on Lawrence's face as he stared at the blood pumping out of his own chest. Knox had slapped a self-sealing combat bandage over the wound, but it hadn't helped. Those bandages were amazing, but there wasn't much you could do on the battlefield with an injury that severe.

"I'd been in so many firefights that I'd stopped counting them," Knox continued. "I'd seen a lot of people die, including fellow SEALs, but nothing hit me the way Lawrence's death did. The damn guy had been through nearly a year of the most intense, grueling training that had ever been created just to prepare him for that moment, and he died from a random gunshot in less than a minute. I watched him die right there in front of me, and there wasn't a damn thing I could do about it."

Rachel rolled onto her side and rested her warm hand on his chest. It felt good. "Is what happened to Lawrence the reason you got out of the navy? When you talked about it before, you never really said."

Knox didn't turn his head to look at her. His commander, team members, friends, and family had all asked the same thing. "I lied to myself and said it had nothing to do with him. I reasoned that one death out of all the deaths I'd seen while I'd been a SEAL shouldn't have that kind of power over me. Hell, I'd barely had a chance to talk to Lawrence, much less get to know him. How could his death affect me so much?"

"But?" Rachel prompted again, making Knox think that she'd missed her calling. She should have been a shrink.

"I found out that lying to yourself doesn't help. I didn't have nightmares as bad as yours, but I found myself reliving the moment when Lawrence died," he said. "It frustrated me. I mean, I know that good people die all the time, but in the end, I couldn't shake the feeling that Lawrence's death was different. It wasn't until later, after I'd gotten out of the navy and was wandering around trying to figure out what came next, that I realized why his death had shaken me so much. It was because he'd died without having a chance to even live. His life had been wasted. All that skill, the training, the potential...it was all gone in the blink of an eye."

"What happened to Lawrence wasn't your fault," she said quietly.

"I know," Knox murmured. "Well, I do now anyway. It took me a while to get to this point. In the days and weeks after Lawrence died, I blamed myself. The way I saw it, he'd been fresh out of training, but I had eight damn years of combat experience. Why hadn't I been able to do something? The doubts tore me apart a little more each day. If I couldn't save someone like Lawrence, what good was any of it?" He sighed. "It wasn't long before I was questioning everything I believed in, everything I thought was important to me. That's why I ended up getting out of the SEALs. Not because of the nightmares and all that other crap, but because I stopped believing what I was doing mattered. It was like I lost my purpose in life."

Rachel moved closer, resting her head on his chest. He wrapped an arm around her shoulder, loving the feel of her smooth skin against his. "Did you talk to a therapist? Is that how you were able to stop blaming yourself?"

"I didn't exactly talk to one," he admitted. "A lot of the VA hospitals in the country offer walk-in counseling. Others have group sessions that are open to anyone who needs them. Sometimes, when I was out on the road trying to get my head back on straight, I'd stop in and sit in the back row and listen to what everyone else had to say. They got me to talk a few times, but I didn't say too much. Like I said, mostly I just listened. Knowing I wasn't the only person out there dealing with this stuff helped. I won't try to convince you that I did things the right way, especially since I rarely saw the same counselor more than once, but one thing I'm sure of: I don't believe a person gets better from something like this. The memories of your trauma will always be there. I think the goal is to find a way to come to peace with them without them being so devastating for you."

Rachel pushed up on her forearm to give him a dubious look. "I don't know about that."

He gave her a small smile. "It won't happen right away, but if you work at this, it will get better over time. I promise."

Her lips curved. "You know, for a former hunter, you're really good at this personal advice stuff."

Knox snorted. "How long are you going to hold that hunter stuff over my head? I made one lousy decision and ended up on the wrong side—temporarily, I might add. You'd think taking a bullet for you at the wedding reception would balance the scales."

She smacked his shoulder playfully. "Balance the scales? You wouldn't have needed to take that bullet if you weren't there to kill werewolves. If you're looking to apologize to me for being a hunter, you'll need to come up with something better than that."

Rachel climbed astride his body, silently helping him come up with a damn good way to start that apology, but as he put his hands on her naked hips, there was a horrendous crashing sound from the living room. Cursing, Knox set her aside and jumped out of bed, scrambling for the clothes he'd left on the floor and the Glock holstered there.

Footsteps approached the bedroom just as he came up with his gun. He pointed it toward the door, finger on the trigger. Out of the corner of his eye, he saw Rachel reaching for her weapons on the nightstand. But then she froze, diving back into bed and dragging the blanket up to cover her breasts.

Knox had a moment to notice his claws and fangs were halfway out before a man charged into the room. Knox came damn close to shooting the guy, every instinct he had urging him to protect Rachel, when he realized the intruder was her SWAT teammate Diego.

"What the hell, Diego?" Rachel shouted, clutching the blanket in her clawed hands, eyes glowing an angry green.

Diego halted in his tracks a few feet inside the room, an automatic in his hands pointed directly at Knox. And yeah, Diego's claws and fangs were out, too. His eyes were glowing so golden yellow they practically sparked with the promise of violence.

Knox kept his weapon aimed at Diego, wondering when the shooting was going to start. For the moment, at least, the other werewolf was too busy taking in the scene before him—a naked guy standing there holding a gun on him, an equally naked, furious woman in bed under the blankets, and clothes strewn all over the room.

"What the hell?" Diego repeated, confusion obvious on his face and in his tone as his gaze settled on Rachel. "That's what I'd like to know. The door to your apartment looks like it's been kicked in, then wedged shut, and while I'm trying to decide whether to kick it in myself, I overhear you saying Knox is a frigging hunter."

He stopped, like he expected Rachel to say something. When she didn't, he continued.

"Tell me I heard wrong. Tell me you aren't sleeping with a hunter who tried to kill you, me, and the rest of our pack mates."

Rachel glowered at him. "Put that damn gun away and turn around!"

She gave Diego less than a second to comply before she whipped back the blanket and climbed out of bed. She marched over to the dresser, moving with the grace and intensity of a pissed-off angel. Neither he nor Diego said a word as she pulled out underwear and a SWAT-issued T-shirt, then grabbed a pair of matching tactical uniform pants from the closet and got dressed. Knox took the opportunity to put his weapon away and get his own clothes back on.

Once Rachel was dressed, she walked over to stand in front of Diego.

"First off, if you broke my door, you're paying for it," she said, her eyes flashing green again, her voice a low growl.

Diego opened his mouth, probably to point out that the door was already broken when he got there, but Rachel cut him off with a glare that would scorch paint. Knox felt like he should provide backup or something, but he knew he'd only get in the way. Besides, he didn't want her looking at him like that.

"Secondly, yes, I am sleeping with a hunter." She took a step closer to her pack mate, glowering at him so hard he actually took a step back. Her claws might not have been out, but she still looked like she was half a second from ripping him a new one—literally. "And while he's actually a *former* hunter who never hurt a werewolf and instead took a bullet meant for me, the only thing you need to get through that thick skull of yours is that I decided to sleep with him.

That means I learned everything I needed to know about his past and his involvement with the hunters and came to the conclusion that he's a good person."

Diego opened his mouth to say something, but she cut him off again.

"Notice that at no point did I mention running over to one of my best friends in the Pack to get his okay on whether I should climb into bed with Knox. That's because I don't need your approval or anyone else's before I decide to sleep with someone. I'd expect my friends to trust me to make that decision for myself."

Knox felt almost bad for the other werewolf as Rachel blasted him. At least Diego had the intelligence to look chagrined. But before the guy could apologize, Rachel held up her hand, silencing him.

"And for what it's worth," she added. "Knox is here because I had a major meltdown last night, complete with delusions that someone was attacking me. It was so bad I ripped the mirror off the dresser and threw it into the living room, then grabbed my weapons. If it weren't for him, I'd probably be in a psych ward somewhere right now. He's even talked me into seeing a therapist and agreed to go with me when I do."

Diego gave Knox a look that seemed partly grudging appreciation and partly something else. Knox wasn't sure, but he thought it might be jealousy. Which didn't make a lot of sense, since Rachel said Diego was nothing more than a pack mate and friend.

"You're going to go see Dr. Delacroix?" Diego asked Rachel. "I wish it hadn't taken so long for you to do it, but I guess that as long as you do it, that's all that matters."

An uncomfortable silence filled the room until Diego finally cleared his throat. "So, I originally came over to pick you up for our shift. You still want a ride to the Lloyds' place?"

Rachel shook her head. "I'm at the courthouse today. Jennifer is having a meeting with the judge and defense lawyers, and I'm backing up Khaki there."

Diego looked back and forth between Knox and Rachel before nodding. "Okay, I'll see you later at the Lloyds'. Or the compound. Or wherever."

Rachel muttered a curse as he walked out of the bedroom. "Diego, hold on a second."

Knox hung back in the bedroom as Rachel hurried into the living room to catch up with her pack mate. He wasn't trying to eavesdrop, but with his werewolf hearing, it was kind of impossible not to. She was asking Diego not to say anything about her and Knox—or the meltdown—to the other members of the Pack. Diego agreed but pointed out she was going to need to tell their pack mates at some point.

"Preferably before this all blows up in your face," Diego added.

Knox thought the conversation was over, but then he heard Rachel ask if they were good. There was a moment of silence before Diego chuckled, saying they'd always be good. There was a rustling of fabric and Knox guessed they were hugging. It was a short hug, but Knox still didn't like it. Neither did his inner wolf.

Rachel thanked her pack mate for kicking in her door to come to her rescue, even if she didn't need it. "Maybe next time, though, knock first?"

A few moments later, she returned to the bedroom.

"Sorry about that. Diego crossed about a dozen lines with that crap."

Knox shook his head. "Don't worry about it. He's a friend and he was worried about you. It's cool you have people who care about you enough to do something like that."

Rachel didn't say anything but, instead, eyed him like she was worried he was going to bolt or something.

He ran his hand through his hair and let out a breath. "What time do you need to be at the courthouse?"

She walked over to him, her lips curving into a smile as she reached up to wrap her arms around his neck. "I could hang around for another fifteen or twenty minutes if I skip breakfast. What do you have in mind?"

He placed his hands on her hips. "I was thinking I could clean up that mess in the living room, then maybe try to fix your door while you pack a weekender."

Rachel eyed him with a baffled expression.

"My extended-stay hotel isn't much more than a small bedroom and a living room with a kitchenette, but I thought you might want to have a place to stay for a while that isn't inextricably linked to the nightmares you've been having." When she didn't say anything, he added, "It was just an offer. If you'd rather not, I understand."

She continued to regard him silently for a moment before going up on her toes and kissing him. Then she stepped back with a smile that made it feel like a weight had been taken off his chest.

"I'd like to stay at your place," she said softly. "I'd like it a lot."

CHAPTER 11

Rachel made her way up the stairs to the second floor of the Frank Crowley Courts Building, doing her best not to gawk at the arc of glass that made up the roof of the atrium. It reminded her a little of the underwater tunnel at the Chattanooga Aquarium. Without the fish and the water, of course. Regardless, it was dang pretty.

She followed her nose and found Khaki sitting on a wooden bench outside one of the courtrooms, reading something on her cell phone. There weren't many people around, so it wasn't like keeping an eye on the doors was too difficult.

"There you are." Her friend stuck her phone in the cargo pocket of her uniform pants and slid over to make room for her on the bench. "Marshall's lawyers have been in there arguing with Jennifer for almost an hour and it doesn't sound like they're going to finish up anytime soon. I get the feeling Marshall's side is getting desperate because they're throwing anything in front of the judge they can think of. Jennifer keeps trashing everything they bring up. I wouldn't be surprised if this trial wraps up in another few days. Regardless, I already called and told the DAPS guys out front to go get a coffee or something if they want."

Rachel nodded as she sat down beside Khaki. She'd been wondering why she hadn't seen any of Knox's coworkers guarding the front of the building when she'd come in.

Reaching into the brown bag she'd brought with her, she

took out a Boston cream donut before handing the bag to Khaki. Her friend's face lit up like a Christmas tree when she saw the monster-sized pastry left inside.

"What?" Rachel said, putting on a hurt expression. "Did you really think I'd stop for breakfast and forget about my best friend and how much she loves apple fritters?"

Khaki laughed and started to take a bite, but then stopped. Frowning, she took a deliberate sniff of the donut in her hand before leaning over to do the same to Rachel. Her friend's dark eyes widened.

"I can't believe you're sleeping with another werewolf and didn't tell me." Khaki looked half-shocked, half-overjoyed. "When did you meet him? Where did you meet him? I want details, so spill!"

Rachel stared at her pack mate, speechless. *Crap.* She should have known Khaki would pick up Knox's scent all over her. She was a werewolf, for Pete's sake. And her best friend. So why was she so uncomfortable with the idea of Khaki knowing about her and Knox? She certainly trusted her not to say anything to anyone.

Besides, Diego already knew.

The problem was that Khaki would want to know details Diego hadn't even considered. Diego had seen her in bed with Knox and immediately focused on the physical aspect of this relationship. Khaki would want to know about the emotional part. That's what women cared about.

Unfortunately, that was the part Rachel was least sure of. She knew she liked Knox. Okay, maybe she more than liked him. Being with him felt right in a way it hadn't with any other men she'd dated. But the PTSD she was dealing with—the nightmares, the feeling of constantly being on edge, and the hallucinations—made her doubt what she was feeling for him. How could she know if any of this was real?

"What's wrong?" Khaki asked. "I would have thought you'd be happier about something like this."

"I am," Rachel said quickly. "But…it's complicated."

Khaki lifted a brow. "My soul mate is also my squad leader, and we have to keep our relationship hidden from the rest of the Dallas PD so the HR department doesn't get wind of it and force one of us to drop out of SWAT. Trust me, I'm good with complicated."

Rachel couldn't argue with that.

"He's one of the guys from DAPS." She bit into her donut as the cream filling did its best to escape. "His name is Knox Lawson, and he got out of the Navy SEALs a little while ago. He's only been a werewolf for a couple months."

Khaki nodded, nibbling on her apple fritter. "I think I heard Diego mention him. He said you volunteered to help Knox learn what he needs to know about being one of us. I thought that was pretty cool considering you just met him."

Rachel took a deep breath, ready to throw herself into the deep end of the pool.

If Diego could handle the truth, Khaki should be able to as well, right?

"Technically, I ran into him before we met at the Lloyds' place," she admitted softly.

"You did?" Khaki asked. "Where?"

Rachel met her friend's gaze. "At Max and Lana's wedding reception. He was with the hunters."

She held her breath, waiting for Khaki to go ballistic, but her friend took another bite of apple fritter, chewing thoughtfully before slowly nodding.

"Crap," Khaki said. "That *is* complicated. How did he end up as a werewolf and, more importantly, in your bed? Assuming that's where you did the deed, I mean—your bed."

Rachel laughed, relaxing. This was Khaki she was talking to, the woman who'd been her bestie since she'd walked into the SWAT compound that first day. "Knox fell in with the hunters without realizing what they were really about. For reasons he has yet to clearly explain—if he even knows—he stepped in front of another hunter and took a bullet meant for me. That's what turned him. Since then, he's been hanging around Dallas to be close to me while he tried to figure out how to ask for my help."

"Seriously?" Khaki blinked. "That has got to be the most romantic thing I've ever heard—or the creepiest. Not sure which." Her brow furrowed for a moment as she tried to decide. "So how did things go from stalking to sex?"

Rachel studied the half-eaten donut in her hand. "Honestly, I'm not sure. When we talked in my apartment that first night, I wanted to hate him. But then he told me about saving my life and swore he'd never harmed a werewolf, and the next thing I know, I'm offering to teach him the ropes." She shrugged and nibbled on her Boston cream in between recounting the story. "The more time we spent together, the easier it was to forget he used to be a hunter. Then last night, I kind of had a meltdown at my apartment in the form of the worst waking nightmare ever, and when Knox showed up, the horrible images I kept seeing and terrifying things I kept hearing all went away."

"And then you slept with him?" Khaki prompted when she didn't continue.

Rachel frowned as she realized her donut was gone. She

should have bought two. "Yeah, though in the interest of full disclosure, I have to admit, after the meltdown last night, all we did was sleep. The other part came this morning. Right before Diego showed up at my apartment and found us naked in bed."

"No way!" Khaki's eyes went wide, then laughed. "I would have loved to see that. Does he know Knox used to be a hunter?"

Rachel nodded. "He overheard Knox and me talking about it. He thought I was in danger, so he kicked in the door of my apartment. But he promised not to say anything and to give me time to tell everyone myself."

"And how exactly do you plan on telling the Pack you're dating a former hunter?"

Rachel let out a sigh. "I have no idea. I'm not even sure if I need to tell them. I mean, I've known Knox for less than a week and we've slept together a grand total of once. It could fall apart by tomorrow for all I know, which would make telling the Pack a moot point."

Khaki arched a brow. "Please. The man took a bullet for you, stayed in Dallas to be close to you, then held you after one of your nightmares. And from the look in your eyes when you talk about him, it's obvious the bond isn't one-way. The same way it's clear you're already falling for him, even if you did just meet him. That isn't so surprising, though. That's the way it works when you meet *The One.*"

Rachel started to agree with her friend's assessment of the situation until she got to that last part. She did a double take.

"Wait. What?" she sputtered. "Knox can't be *The One* for me. I mean, he used to be a hunter. Besides, we only just met. There's no way he's *The One.* I'd know if he was, wouldn't I?"

Khaki reached into the brown paper bag and picked out a crumb she'd missed, popping it into her mouth. "You're aware whoever is in control of the whole soul-mate thing doesn't care about your excuses, right? Then again, maybe this is just a case of *the woman doth protest too much.*"

Rachel opened her mouth, then closed it again, not sure what to say to that. Before she could get her thoughts together, the courtroom doors opened with the babble of conversation and the clatter of footsteps.

Rachel was immediately on her feet, as was Khaki, who crumpled the brown paper bag and discreetly stuffed it into her cargo pocket.

"Gage wants me to stay with the judge," Khaki said. "There's been some concern he might be targeted along with Jennifer. He's headed somewhere right after this, so I'm taking him out the west exit like normal, while you take Jennifer through the back. DAPS has a security motorcade waiting for you there."

Rachel nodded. While the stuff about guarding the judge was new, the route she'd take Jennifer out of the building this morning wasn't. It had been planned out last night.

Rachel thumbed the radio on the shoulder of her vest. "We're on the way," she told the DAPS guys waiting outside.

Khaki slipped through the crowd of nearly a dozen men coming out of the courtroom with Jennifer. Rachel would have preferred to grab Jennifer and slip away quickly, but unfortunately, the ADA was still arguing with several men in expensive suits in the middle of the hallway. A few of them looked more like bodyguards than lawyers.

Rachel moved closer until she was standing at the prosecutor's side as she faced off against a tall man with aristocratic features and a slight bit of gray in his dark hair. Rachel recognized Alton Marshall from the photo the chief had shown her and her teammates the other day.

"By all means, feel free to exercise your legal rights and take the stand to testify on your own behalf, Mr. Marshall," Jennifer said. "I'm sure you think your charm will have some effect on the jury, while I look forward to cross-examining you on any statements you might make."

Jennifer's heart beat fast as she faced down the crime boss. They were staring at each other, waiting for the other to break. Knowing there was no way the prosecutor would be the first one to walk away from the confrontation, Rachel leaned in to interrupt the impasse.

"Ma'am, it's time to go," she murmured in the woman's ear. "Your car is waiting."

Jennifer threw Rachel a grateful look, but before the DA could say anything, Marshall spoke.

"Officer Bennett, what a pleasure," he said.

Rachel gazed at him coolly. She wished she could say the same. "Mr. Marshall."

He regarded her thoughtfully. "I understand ADA Lloyd owes her life and her daughter's to you. Surviving an ambush from three highly trained assassins, then almost chasing down their getaway vehicle on foot is quite impressive."

Rachel felt like reaching over and ripping the guy's throat out, but instead, she smiled. "I can't honestly say if those men were highly trained, since the two who got away ran for the hills pretty damn fast. I personally think whoever hired them got ripped off."

Marshall didn't even blink, but if the tension in his body was any indication, he was pissed off as hell, something that pleased Rachel to no end.

Taking Jennifer's arm, Rachel guided her to the stairwell at the end of the hall. Pushing open the door, she took a quick look before they headed down the steps. Rachel was watchful but not overly concerned anyone would try anything in the heavily guarded government building. That was good because Rachel's head was still spinning with the possibilities of what she and Khaki had talked about.

Could Knox really be *The One* for her? What kind of crazy, mystical force out there would put a werewolf together with a hunter? Even if there were extenuating circumstances. Was that why she'd let him get away all those months ago at the SWAT compound?

One of the DAPS security team members announced over the radio earpiece she wore that they had the prosecutor's vehicle ready and waiting and that the rear loading dock area was secure.

"My daughter can't seem to stop talking about you. I think Addy idolizes you," Jennifer said, jarring Rachel out of her thoughts as they continued down the steps.

It would have been simpler to walk out the front door, but they'd all decided that option was too dangerous. There were dozens of tall buildings nearby that could serve as the perfect location for a sniper. The back was more secluded.

"Addy is an amazing girl," Rachel murmured as they reached the basement level of the building, forcing herself to stop worrying about soul mates for a while. "And I'm sure she idolizes you just as much. She's probably talking about me more because I'm around her so much lately."

The basement level of the courthouse had a lot of offices but seemed to be used mostly for file storage, hence the nearly overwhelming smell of old paper. She heard a few people moving around, but other than that, it seemed relatively quiet.

"I think we both know my daughter doesn't think much of me right now." Jennifer's voice was soft and full of regret. "Her father and I haven't been getting along very well lately, and unfortunately, Addy's been caught in the middle of it."

Rachel remembered Addy saying as much the other day at the mall. She hadn't felt comfortable getting into it then, and she didn't want to talk about it now, either. She led the way along the long central corridor that led to the back loading dock. To their left and right they passed open doorways, endless rows of filing cabinets filling each room.

But she had to say something. "I'm sure everything will work out."

Jennifer sighed. "I hope you're right. As soon as the trial is over, I plan to do everything I can to make it up to her and my husband. They both deserve more from me."

Recognizing yet another minefield she wouldn't be stepping into, Rachel simply nodded and kept walking.

She was still waiting for the next awkward thing to come out of Jennifer's mouth when two men stepped from one of the rooms ahead of them. Both guys were wearing work coveralls and there was a trolley cart loaded with the kind of boxes copier paper came in.

One of the men—a middle-aged guy with a slight paunch straining to slip out the front of his partially unzipped coverall—smiled at them warmly. A split second later, he grabbed the handgun that had been hidden under one of the boxes and opened fire in their direction. The move was so smooth Rachel never saw it coming. There hadn't even been a single tingle of her normally hypersensitive werewolf senses. She hadn't even smelled any gun oil.

A bullet smacked into the wall beside Rachel and it was only then that she realized she could barely hear the sound of the gun going off. They were using silencers. *Crap*. That meant they were more professionals.

Cursing, Rachel wrapped her arm around Jennifer and spun around, not only to put her body between the woman and the incoming bullets, but because the only way out of there was the way they'd just come. She made it half a step before catching sight of two other men in coveralls tucked away in opposing doorways halfway down the corridor. They were far enough out of the line of fire so they wouldn't get hit by their buddies' bullets while still clearly making it impossible for Rachel and Jennifer to escape.

Rachel considered turning back and attacking. It would be unexpected and since the first two guys apparently only carried handguns, she might have a chance. But then the reality of leaving Jennifer unprotected in the hallway struck, and she knew fighting back wasn't an option.

Tucking the trembling woman close to her body, Rachel ran down the corridor toward the two men guarding their escape, then darted into the nearest filing room just as a round caught her in the calf. The wound didn't hurt much, but the impact of the high-speed bullet almost took her leg out from under her and she stumbled, clipping the doorframe with her shoulder. Unfortunately, Jennifer's head hit it, too.

Rachel flinched hard at the grunt of pain Jennifer let out

as they both tumbled to the floor of the filing room. But when she heard the sound of pounding footsteps outside, Rachel knew she didn't have time to check on the woman. Dragging a woozy Jennifer to her feet, she ran toward the back of the room, getting as many heavy steel filing cabinets between them and the approaching bad guys as possible.

A quick look around confirmed she was in a square-shaped windowless room with only one way in or out—the door they'd just stumbled through.

Two men charged through the door as Rachel ducked down behind the last row of cabinets and gently eased the prosecutor to the floor. There was a small gash along the left side of Jennifer's head and blood was already running down her cheek and neck. Head wounds always bled a lot, but this one didn't look too bad. Still, the impact with the doorframe had been bad enough to knock Jennifer senseless. She wasn't unconscious, but damn close to it.

Grabbing her weapon from its holster, Rachel popped up from her hiding place and fired off a half dozen rounds in rapid succession to get the bad guys to duck a little. Then she dropped back down and thumbed her radio, first sending a quick SOS to the DAPS people waiting outside the loading dock, then flipping the channel button and putting out an Officer Needs Assistance call on the DPD main channel.

Her nose and ears told her all four men were in the room now. Rachel didn't wait for a reply on the radio. She stood and shot off another few rounds in the men's direction. She didn't have much of a chance to aim because all four of their weapons were unloading on her at once, but she wasn't too worried about that. Her DAPS backup was seconds away.

All she had to do was hold on until they arrived. Then they'd have the four hired guns trapped.

But minutes later and already down to her last spare magazine of ammo, her backup still hadn't arrived. She tried to call them again but got nothing. It was like there was no one on the channel, even though it was the same one she'd used to talk to them before she and Jennifer had come down here. Maybe the signal was blocked because they were in the basement. But that shouldn't have mattered. The DAPS guys still should have heard the shooting. They were only a couple hundred feet away. Had more bad guys taken them out?

She had to stop worrying about that because the four men trying to kill her and Jennifer had split into two teams, each moving toward them from a different direction. Rachel was hesitant to leave the still nearly unconscious ADA alone, but if she stayed where she was, she'd draw the killers right to the woman.

Having no other choice, Rachel shoved Jennifer into a small space between two cabinets. Praying she'd be safe there, Rachel darted toward the nearest of the two approaching kill teams. She stayed low so they wouldn't see her head above the cabinets, letting her nose and ears guide her toward her targets. As she moved, Rachel let her body shift as far as it would go, claws fully extending, fangs hanging over her bottom lip. She wasn't too worried about the men seeing her like this because, in a minute or two, they'd be dead—or she would.

Rachel lifted her Sig as she reached the end of the row she was moving along, taking a breath and readying herself. These men were clearly experienced. They moved with a silent confidence that nearly matched her own and she had little doubt they'd go for a head shot if they had a chance. A bullet there would put even a werewolf down for good.

She only hoped seeing someone with claws, fangs, and glowing, green eyes popping out in front of them would stun them long enough to give her a chance to take the first shot.

When she stepped out from behind the cabinets, she got exactly what she wanted. Both men stood there stock-still, stunned to silence. But instead of pulling the trigger, Rachel was also frozen in place because the man closest to her suddenly had frizzy hair, a face covered in white greasepaint, a permanently demented smile, and red, glowing eyes.

"Hello, pumpkin," the clown whispered in a horribly familiar voice. "I've been waiting for you."

Rachel panicked, her heart beating so fast she thought it would explode. She'd be hyperventilating too, if she could breathe. Fear clawed its way up from her belly and into her throat. Any second now, she was going to scream. Something told her that this time, she wouldn't stop until she was dead.

Then the guy on the left—the one who didn't have a clown's face—lifted his weapon with shaking hands to shoot her in the head. She flinched just in time for the bullet to tear through her left shoulder. She was so numb with terror she barely felt the injury, but it was enough to jerk her inner wolf to growling, snarling life.

Rational thought disappeared as instinct took over and she simply reacted. It felt like someone else controlling the strings of her puppet body as she jerked her gun up and shot the clown in the face. Seeing him go down, her heart sang with perverse joy, knowing he'd never haunt her again.

The second man lifted his weapon to shoot her again, and her body reacted, her left arm sweeping out, her claws ripping through the man's throat.

Rachel had no time to think about how she was going to explain a gruesome injury like that to anyone, not when the other two men were already closing on her from the far side of the room.

She spun just as one of the silenced weapons went off. The bullet grazed her side where it wasn't covered by her bulletproof vest. The wound seemed to hurt more than the one to her leg or shoulder, and a part of her knew it was because she was too terrified from that damn clown to function at full strength.

She instinctively ducked behind a file cabinet as gunfire rained in her direction, then immediately popped back up to return fire. Until the upper receiver on her Sig locked back on an empty magazine. The men immediately charged, probably trying to reach her before she had a chance to reload. But they slowed as they realized she was already out of ammo, one pulling a knife as he crept closer. Rachel wasn't sure why he'd bother with a knife when he was already holding a gun.

She tensed to leap at them, something telling her it was better to get in close than to let them shoot holes in her from a distance.

But as she started to lunge, one of the men stopped where he was. His face suddenly changed right before her eyes and he became the clown of her nightmares. The thing grinned, then began to laugh, the sound echoing in the room all around her.

Rachel froze, the fear stronger than ever, and she

couldn't do anything but stand there and wait for the clown to do his worst.

Knox weaved his bike in and out of rush-hour traffic, knowing without looking at the speedometer that he was doing over 120 as he raced for the courthouse. At least he prayed that's where he was going. He still didn't know his way around Dallas very well. He knew it was a big building with lots of glass somewhere off Commerce Street. How hard could it be to find?

He slowed only long enough to turn onto West Commerce, then hauled ass again, maneuvering in between cars and trucks, running every light he came to. Drivers swerved to avoid him, honking their horns, but he didn't slow. More than a few people shouted obscenities out their windows, but he ignored them. Considering this was Texas, he was lucky no one had taken a shot at him—yet.

Even if someone had, he wouldn't have slowed down. Rachel was in trouble, and it was taking him effing forever to get to her.

After leaving her place, he'd stopped at Starbucks for coffee on his way into the DAPS office, needing caffeine before dealing with Theo. He'd just reached the counter when Rachel's voice came through his radio earpiece, shouting for backup. Even though he wasn't technically working the protective detail today, he'd slipped in the bud out of habit. Now, he was glad he had.

Knox didn't even remember leaving Starbucks. One moment he was there; the next he was on his motorcycle speeding off and hoping he wouldn't get killed before he got to the courthouse. Luckily, he'd been less than two miles from the Frank Crowley Courts Building when he'd heard the SOS.

As soon as he raced onto the bridge over the Trinity River, he spotted what had to be the courthouse. The building was made up of two squat high-rises separated by some kind of arty-looking glass center section. But it wasn't the size of the place or all the glass that told him he'd guessed right. It was the pure pandemonium of terrified people flooding out of every available doorway, running for their lives.

Knox didn't bother heading for the parking lot on the side of the courthouse complex. Nor did he stop on the sidewalk along the front of the building. Instead, he yanked on the handlebars of his bike and jumped the curb before heading straight up the concrete stairs leading to the main entrance. There were a lot of steps, and people running down them had to throw themselves aside to avoid getting run over, but he was too worried about Rachel to care. Even from here, he could hear the gunfire inside the courthouse.

He managed to get his bike stopped before crashing through the large glass doors, but only barely. He leaped off the bike, letting it fall to the pavement instead of wasting time getting the kickstand down. Then he was pushing, shoving, and fighting his way through the flood of humanity still trying to get out the main doors. He heard a growl from deep in his throat, and he prayed his fangs and claws stayed where they frigging belonged. That was all he needed, to incite even more panic by looking like a damn monster.

But he had to admit, it was nice being a werewolf when

it came to getting through the crowd. He never would have made it otherwise.

When he finally broke through the wall of bodies, a courthouse security guard—an older guy whose wide eyes and hammering heartbeat confirmed how freaked out he was—motioned him back toward the doors.

"We're evacuating the building," the man said, trying to sound authoritative. It didn't work. He sounded as scared as all the other people running through the arch covered atrium. Knox didn't blame him. "You need to leave."

Knowing that identifying himself as an employee of Direct Action Private Security wouldn't do shit in this situation, even if his company had been hired to protect one of the city's prosecutors, Knox instead yanked out the leather holder with the cheesy security guard badge Theo had given him when he hired him and flashed it quickly at the man.

"Dallas SWAT!" he shouted, not even slowing down as he headed for the stairs.

The guard looked confused, no doubt wondering why Knox wasn't decked out in all the requisite tactical gear. The man opened his mouth to say something, but an angry growl echoed up from somewhere downstairs. The poor old guy went pale and turned to join the rush of people trying to get out of the area.

The main stairs in the atrium didn't lead down to the basement, so Knox ran for the door at the far end of the hall. He hit the steps, letting his nose and ears guide him downward, praying his barely developed instincts didn't steer him wrong. He hadn't heard any more gunshots since coming inside, but he hoped that growl meant Rachel was still alive.

When he reached the basement level, he sprinted down

the corridor, wondering where the hell his DAPS teammates were. If Rachel was in trouble, those assholes should have been here already to help. Then a disturbing thought hit him. What if the other security team had shown up and were dead?

He pushed those thoughts aside, focusing all his efforts on finding Rachel. It wasn't difficult to know which way to go. Even his inexperienced nose could figure out which direction the scent of burnt gunpowder was coming from. There was another scent on the air with it, tangy and metallic. He made a conscious decision to ignore what that smell might mean.

Another growl came from a room just up ahead.

Rachel.

Knox ran faster.

He had his weapon out and finger on the trigger as he entered the room, ready to do anything he had to do to protect Rachel, but what he saw froze him solid.

Two men lay on the floor, their bodies twisted unnaturally. A third man was draped across the top of a row of filing cabinets. The dead bodies weren't what shocked Knox, though. No, what stunned him was the amount of blood spattered around the room.

Rachel stood in the middle of it all, her back to him as she struggled with a man he couldn't get a good look at even though the guy had to have a good half a foot on Rachel and at least a hundred pounds. Knox started forward to help her when she let out a loud snarl and ripped the man's throat out with her claws. Blood spray coated the nearest cabinets and wall in a fine mist of red, mixed with larger droplets that immediately began to run down every surface they landed on.

Realizing there weren't any more threats in the room, Knox holstered his gun. Figuring it'd be best not to startle Rachel, he opened his mouth to let her know he was here, but before he could say anything, she spun around, crouching low and growling at him, like she thought he was another enemy about to attack.

He knew what it was like in combat, when you fell into a zone where you stopped thinking and simply reacted to things around you, so her response wasn't surprising. Especially since her eyes were glowing red. But it was the knife sticking out of the front of her shoulder that had him more worried. The blade was sunk in at least two inches deep and had to hurt like hell.

Knox stepped toward her without thinking.

The claws coming his way were a blur, but he got a hand up and caught her wrist, stopped them inches from his throat. Rachel bared her teeth in a snarl.

Shit. She'd lost it again.

"It's okay, Rachel," he soothed. "It's me—Knox."

He thought for a moment she might take another swing at him with her other hand, but instead, she lifted her nose and took a good sniff of him. That seemed to calm her a little, but he continued to make comforting sounds until the red glow faded from her eyes. The moment it did, all tension left Rachel's body and she collapsed against him. Well, as much as she could with a knife sticking out of her shoulder.

Hating to do it but reminding himself she was a werewolf, Knox pulled the knife out as gently as he could and tossed it on the floor. Then he wrapped her in his arms and held her as tears ran down her face. While she wasn't nearly as hysterical as she'd been at her apartment last night, it tore his soul out to see her in pain all the same.

They were still standing there a few minutes later when Diego and a female cop moved cautiously into the room. The duo took one look around before putting away their weapons. Knox recognized the tall, dark-haired woman as another werewolf from the Dallas SWAT pack, and based on previous conversations with Rachel, he was fairly sure her name was Khaki.

Diego moved around Knox and Rachel toward the back of the room, talking softly on his radio, telling the other cops currently on their way there at high-speed to slow down, that the threat had been neutralized. When he was done, he ducked down behind a row of cabinets and came up with a semiconscious Jennifer Lloyd in his arms.

Shit. Knox had been so concerned about Rachel he hadn't given a single thought to the woman they were supposed to be guarding.

"I'll take her outside and get her checked by the paramedics. That should give you guys a few seconds to come up with something that's going to explain all this." Diego motioned with his chin at the bloody walls and mauled corpses lying around. "Good luck with that by the way."

As Diego walked out, Rachel pulled away to wipe the tears from her face. She still looked out of it, kind of like she had immediately following the incident at the mall and the one at the school dance. Except this time seemed worse.

Khaki walked over to stand beside them, looking at him and Rachel expectantly. "Well, any idea how we're going to spin this?"

"I told the chief and the crime techs your versions of events," Gage said, looking from Knox to Rachel, then to her teammates Diego and Khaki. It had been an hour since the fight in the courthouse and now they were all outside by the SWAT SUV. "Including the part about how the knife brought to the scene by one of the suspects is to blame for all the damage. I'm not sure anyone believed that, but at least they're not outright calling me a liar...yet. It helps that the DAPS security team is taking so much of the heat for supposedly not hearing your call for backup."

Yeah right. Knox ground his jaw. He'd talked to the guy who'd been the team leader of the DAPS security detail at the courthouse. One of Theo's buddies, the dickweed swore their radios had never picked up Rachel's call for help, claiming it must have been poor reception. Knox knew that was a load of crap. If he had to guess, he'd say the guys out on the loading dock had chickened out when they heard the shooting, then came up with the radio reception bullshit to cover their asses. He hadn't mentioned his suspicions to Rachel or any of her SWAT teammates, but he'd sure as hell sent a text to Theo, letting the man know he was currently employing a bunch of cowards.

Knox looked up when he realized Gage was still staring intently at Rachel, serious thoughts apparently rolling through his head.

Gage pinned Rachel with a look. "I hate to do this, but you'll be riding a desk until Internal Affairs finishes their investigation."

Standing beside Knox, Diego, and Khaki, Rachel groaned.

"Desk duty?" She pushed away from the SWAT SUV she'd been leaning against. "You're seriously taking me off the Lloyd detail after I saved Jennifer's life?"

Gage's eyes flared yellow gold for a moment and the expression that crossed his face right then had Knox—and everyone else—take a step back. The guy was an alpha just like the rest of them, but after being in his rather pissed-off presence for a while, Knox could understand why all the other alphas in the Pack accepted him as their leader. The man was a little intense to say the least.

But if the set of Rachel's jaw was any indication, she seemed to be in the mood to challenge her alpha. Right after the ambush, she wouldn't have been capable of it, but now, after an hour of answering questions and being interrogated over and over, she was almost back to her old self. Getting away from the bodies and all that blood had probably helped, too.

"Yes, you saved Jennifer's life, but can you look me in the eyes and tell me you honestly remember exactly what was going through your head as you ripped those men apart down there?" The SWAT team commander's voice was level, but there was still a hint of anger there. "Do you even remember any of it?"

"I got there at the end of the fight and can confirm Rachel had no choice but to kill the last one," Knox volunteered when Rachel remained silent. "She was out of ammo and the guy had already put a knife in her shoulder."

The team commander leveled Knox with an expression that made him feel like he was five years old again and his grandpa had just pointed out kids were better seen and not heard.

"I'm not questioning whether it was self-defense," Gage said calmly before turning back to Rachel, who was currently busy staring at the cracks in the parking lot asphalt. "And I'm not trying to embarrass you, Rachel. But I'm serious when I ask if you remember what happened in that room earlier. Because based on the lack of details in your statement, something tells me a lot of parts are missing."

Rachel lifted her head, meeting her alpha's eyes. "I remember going into the room and hiding Jennifer between two cabinets, then turning around to engage the four men. After that, it's kind of a blur."

Knox didn't miss the hitch in her voice. There was something she was leaving out, something she didn't want her boss to know. Knox didn't even want to think what it might be.

Gage frowned. "Is this the first time that's happened to you?"

Rachel shook her head. "Nothing like this, but enough times that I'm thinking I should see someone about it. Diego said he'd help set something up with Dr. Delacroix."

Gage pinned Diego with a hard look. "You knew Rachel was having problems and you didn't think to mention it to me?"

Diego shrugged. "I thought the most important thing was supporting my pack mate and making sure she got help. If I thought she was a danger to herself or the team, I would have told you."

Knox had a newfound appreciation for Diego's willingness to put himself between Rachel and their boss, especially since Gage's jaw was flexing so hard it looked like he was about to grind his teeth to dust.

"You're right." Gage nodded. "Getting Rachel the help

she needs is the most important part." He gave Rachel a stern look. "But that doesn't mean I can overlook the problem now that I know it exists. Go talk to Delacroix and take all the time you need to get your head straight because I can't put you back on duty until she gives me the all clear."

Rachel nodded, but Knox could see how much it bothered her to be taken off active duty. After seeing the tail end of what happened in the courthouse, he could understand Gage's stance. Rachel needed help before it was too late.

Gage left a little while later, taking Diego and Khaki with him and telling Rachel to take the rest of the day off.

Knox moved closer to her as her teammates walked away. "You ready to head over to my place?"

"Don't you need to go into work?"

"I'm sure Theo can live without me for a while." He gave her a small smile. "You're more important right now."

It wasn't even 1600—4:00 p.m.—by the time they got to his hotel, but Knox could tell Rachel was already wiped out. Between the shootout in the courthouse and the hours of questioning, followed by her boss putting her on indefinite desk duty, it had been a really long day for her. Thankfully, Diego had sent them a text as they'd been walking down the hall to the room, saying Rachel had an appointment with Delacroix tomorrow at nine in the morning.

"If you want to take a shower and get cleaned up, I can fix us something to eat and you can crash early." He dropped her weekender bag on the floor in the bedroom, then walked back into the living room. "You look exhausted. And before you ask, I have no problem sleeping out here on the couch. My offer didn't come with any strings."

Rachel wrapped her arms around him, resting her cheek against his chest and squeezing him tightly. "Well, when I accepted your offer, it sure as hell came with strings. So, don't think about skipping out of taking me to bed and holding me all night. It's probably stupid, but the truth is, I only feel safe when I'm in your arms."

Knox couldn't describe the sensation hearing those words created in him. It wasn't like anything he'd ever experienced before. Figuring he'd sound like an idiot if he mentioned it, he kept the thought to himself and settled for squeezing her tighter.

"I lied to Gage today," Rachel whispered against the material of his shirt. "When I said that what happened at the courthouse was a blur, I mean. I actually remember almost everything."

He didn't know if that was good or bad. "Is there something in particular you didn't want him to know?"

"I saw the clown again." She shuddered in his arms. "I know it sounds insane—that *I* sound insane—but when those four men attacked, one of them turned into the clown from my nightmares. He looked like him, sounded like him, even smelled like him—like something dead and rotting. He was the one I shot in the face. I had to do it to shut him up. But then one of the other men turned into the clown, laughing and taunting me. But when I killed that one, it was like the clown jumped out of that guy's body and into the last one. That's when things did get blurry. I don't remember how I ended up in your arms. I remember killing the last guy, then you were there."

Knox continued to hold her, rubbing soothing circles on her back, hoping it would make her feel better. At the same time, he wished he could make this all go away. But he didn't know how.

"I know you won't believe it—heck, I don't believe it myself—but I swear I could feel the evil in that room with me," she said. "It only left when you got there and put your arms around me."

Rachel didn't say any more and Knox didn't ask any more questions. Taking her hand, he led her into the bathroom and helped her get her clothes off, then joined her in the shower. He spent a long time washing her hair and massaging her shoulders, suds and warm water streaming down her beautiful body. Then, when he'd rinsed her off and dried her with a towel, he carried her to bed and made love to her until she was too exhausted to think about anything.

CHAPTER 12

"You don't have to lie on the couch unless you want to."

Rachel dragged her gaze away from the leather sofa against the far wall to see Dr. Hadley Delacroix smiling at her from across the big cherrywood desk that dominated the office. Rachel couldn't help but find her amusement disarming.

"Honestly, most people prefer to sit right where you are, and we talk like two good friends."

Rachel nodded and sat back a little more in the stuffed armchair in front of the desk, settling in for what she feared would be a long, painful experience. It would have also been nice if Knox could have come in with her, so he could have told the story from his perspective. But Hadley wanted to start the session with just the two of them. The one saving grace was that Hadley Delacroix didn't fit with Rachel's preconceived idea of what a shrink was supposed to look and act like. Instead of the dry, colorless person she'd built up in her mind, Hadley was friendly, had crazy-long fingernails painted bright fuchsia, and wore a colorful flower print dress with high heels. Even the reading glasses she wore were stylish.

As they sat there in silence, Rachel glanced around the room before turning back to Hadley, in part to take in the modern, slightly edgy decor, but also to give herself a chance to get a read on the woman behind the desk, a woman she'd only just met yet was somehow supposed to bare her soul to. It was a daunting proposition. It had taken all Rachel's courage to talk about her nightmares to her two pack mates—and to Knox. She couldn't imagine how she'd be able to do it with Hadley.

Even using the doctor's first name felt odd. They'd gotten that issue out of the way while the two of them had been standing in the reception area with Knox and Diego, shaking hands and exchanging names. Hadley seemed to think it would be easier to talk if they kept things informal. Rachel wasn't so sure of that. She could walk up to any random stranger in the street and call them by their given name. That didn't mean she wanted to confess to them that she was a complete mess.

"I can only guess what's going through your head right now, but trust me when I say you aren't the first person who's sat in that chair, feeling apprehensive about opening up and talking about the things that scare them," Hadley said. "Things they'd rather keep buried."

"But we can't keep scary things buried, can we?" Rachel murmured, not sure if she was talking to Hadley or to herself. "Or they'll come out on their own."

Hadley nodded, her dark eyes full of empathy. "Unfortunately. Our minds have a way of forcing us to confront our issues whether we want to or not. And it seems like the harder we fight the process, the more painful it becomes. But I suspect you already know a little something about that."

Rachel rested her elbows on the arms of the chair, clasping her hands on her lap. "How much did Sergeant Dixon tell you about what happened yesterday at the courthouse?"

While Diego had texted her yesterday to say Hadley would see her this morning, Gage had been the one who'd set up the appointment.

"Very little, actually. He mentioned there were issues you needed help with and asked if I could fit you in this morning, but he didn't give me any details."

Rachel sighed. She appreciated her alpha had gone out of his way to help her while still keeping her secrets, but in some ways, it would have been a lot easier if Hadley already knew everything. Then Rachel wouldn't have to be the one to tell her.

"Maybe it would be easier if we started out with you telling me why you're here," Hadley suggested when Rachel didn't say anything. "Don't worry about why Sergeant Dixon thought you might need my help. What do you want out of these sessions with me?"

Figuring she was going to have to start talking at some point, Rachel took a deep breath and threw herself in the deep end of the pool. "I'm here because I keep seeing and hearing things that aren't there. I think I'm losing my mind, and I need your help to get my head screwed back on straight before I end up killing someone I care about."

Hadley placed her reading glasses on the desk, then sat back in her leather chair, a surprised look on her face. "Having someone be so honest this early in the conversation is refreshing to say the least. Knowing I don't need to worry about you grasping the importance of these sessions makes my job much easier, that's for sure."

Even though there was nothing remotely funny about the situation, Rachel gave her a small smile. "I thought you'd appreciate my desire to get everything out in the open. I wouldn't have agreed to come if I didn't think this was serious."

"Out in the open is good," Hadley replied with a smile. "So, let's start with why you think you're losing your mind, which is a completely unacceptable phrase, by the way. I've been doing this for a long time and I've never found anyone's missing mind hidden in the couch cushions or under a coffee table."

Rachel couldn't help but laugh. Thank goodness she'd found a therapist who could make her do that.

So she told Hadley about the clown attacking her in Chattanooga, leaving out the whole werewolf thing, but being honest about the endless nightmares, visions, phantom smells, and her sudden aversion to mirrors.

"I've known for a while I was experiencing symptoms that are probably associated with PTSD, but yesterday at the courthouse, it all came to a head," she added. "Right in the middle of an assassination attempt on an ADA by four highly trained killers, I saw the scary-ass clown from my nightmares. I froze. Actually, I pretty much lost it. That's why I'm here."

Rachel thought she'd done a good job of summarizing the situation, but Hadley asked a lot of questions about things she hadn't included, like what the clown looked like, how bad her injuries had been after the attack in the graveyard, and whether she'd talked to a psychologist when she'd still been at the Chattanooga police department. Although she didn't like thinking about the clown, they were all easy enough to answer. But then Hadley wanted to know how she usually dealt with the stress of her job, what her sex life was like, and about her relationship with her family. Rachel didn't think of herself as shy, but Hadley seemed to have no problem digging into parts of Rachel's life that were usually off-limits.

"You said before you're worried you'll kill someone you care about," Hadley said, changing the subject so quickly Rachel almost got whiplash. "Is there anyone in particular you think is in danger?"

Rachel considered that. "My teammates on SWAT. The civilians who trust me to do my job. And Knox, of course."

Hadley sat forward, resting her forearms on the desk. "Is there some reason why you think Knox is in more danger than the other people you mentioned?"

She shrugged. "I suppose because Knox always seems to be the one around when I have an episode. On the bright side, he's also the only one who seems to be able to put me back together when I lose it, so maybe I shouldn't complain."

Hadley regarded her thoughtfully for a long time, and Rachel could practically see the wheels spinning in her head. What the hell had she said that was so interesting? She was about to ask when Hadley tossed her another question out of left field.

"You used the term *episode*," the therapist finally said. "Could you describe what one of these episodes is like and exactly what you're doing right before it occurs?"

Deciding she didn't even want to try and explain the impossibilities of her and Knox chasing down a speeding SUV in a mall parking garage or how she'd ripped out a few throats in the basement of the Dallas County Criminal Courthouse, Rachel instead decided to go with a trimmed-down version of what happened in her apartment the other night. But that wasn't what Hadley was looking for.

"Now, tell me the story again, this time in detail."

"What kind of detail?" she asked, afraid she already knew.

"I want you to close your eyes and walk me through the episode from the moment you walked into your apartment until it ended. Do you think you can do that?"

Rachel groaned silently. She wasn't thrilled about the idea, but she supposed she could handle it, especially if Hadley thought it might help. So she took a deep breath and closed her eyes, then plunged right in. It wasn't long before she realized why Hadley wanted her to close her eyes. It definitely forced her to go deeper into the memories than she would have done.

She described the smell that had hit her in the shower and how much it rattled her, the way she'd rushed out of the bathroom expecting to find something dead right there in her living room. Of course, the worst part of rehashing the event in that level of detail was the way it brought the events rushing back with a clarity that was almost eerie. For a moment, she imagined she could actually pick up the rancid odor right there in Hadley's office. She shook it off, knowing that wasn't possible.

As she was relating what had happened in the kitchen, Rachel felt goose bumps along her arms, then down her back, like cold air had brushed across her body. Distracted, she stumbled to a halt with the story, but when Hadley didn't say anything, Rachel got it back together and kept going.

She'd reached the part where she saw the clown's face in the glass door of the microwave when a sudden, familiar chuckle made her jump out of her skin.

She opened her eyes and just about died. Hadley was gone and in her place was the clown she knew all too well sitting behind the desk. A split second later, the clown was out of the chair, launching himself across the desk, his hands going for her throat.

Rachel screamed.

"I think the receptionist is interested in you," Knox said softly as he and Diego sat in the waiting room of Dr. Delacroix's office. The room was surprisingly large, with potted plants everywhere and a water feature against one wall that gave the room a tranquil feel. "She's been eyeing you since we sat down."

The dark-haired Diego casually glanced at the pretty, blond receptionist at the desk near the entrance. The woman must have noticed the surveillance because a smile immediately curved her lips even though she was going out of her way to keep her eyes focused on her computer.

Diego wordlessly turned his attention back to the wall in front of them, but Knox didn't miss the slight grin tugging at the man's lips or the way he kept looking at the receptionist out of the corner of his eye. Knox opened his mouth to inquire whether Diego was going to ask her out, but the other werewolf spoke before he could.

"So, you're a hunter who became a werewolf," Diego said in a low voice, not looking at him. "You realize how incredibly ironic that is, right?"

Knox had been wondering when the guy would bring up the hunter thing. "Yeah, Rachel made the same observation.

She also grilled the hell out of me concerning every stupid decision I've ever made, of which there were many. But in the end, she must have decided there was something redeemable about me, since she agreed to help."

Diego seemed to consider that answer for a moment before nodding, his mouth twitching again. "Rachel's pretty sharp when it comes to judging people. Which is why I was shocked when I found out she'd gotten close with you. I'd assumed that, given your background, she would have reacted differently."

Part of Knox wondered if Diego was pissed Rachel hadn't slapped cuffs on him and dragged him off to jail, while another part of him wondered if the other werewolf was jealous. Rachel might have said she and Diego were just friends, but it seemed like there was more to it than that.

Since he sure as hell wasn't going to ask, Knox decided to go with the truth—for his part at least. "To be honest, I was a little surprised when she said she'd help me. Considering I assumed the best I could hope for was a little advice on how to keep this werewolf thing under control, I definitely never expected all this."

"All what?" Diego asked, still not looking at him.

Knox opened his mouth to explain but closed it when he realized he had no idea what the hell to even say.

"It isn't that difficult a question," Diego said. "What didn't you expect?"

Knox leaned forward to rest his forearms on his thighs. "It's complicated."

"There's a woman involved. Of course it's complicated." Diego chuckled. "And since that woman is Rachel and a werewolf, it's also confusing."

Knox snorted. "I'm not exactly sure what this thing between me and Rachel is or where it's going," he admitted. "All I know is that, when I'm with her, I'm happier than I've ever been in my life. I know it sounds cliché, but being with her simply feels right."

Diego finally turned and regarded him thoughtfully, though in some ways he also seemed almost deflated. "It's not so crazy really."

"No?"

"I'm going to ask you a simple question and I want you to answer it without thinking. Just go with your instincts."

Where the hell was Diego headed with this? "Go ahead."

"If Rachel comes out of her session with Dr. Delacroix and says she needs to move to the Amazon rainforest and live in a grass hut to keep her sanity, what would you say?"

"I'd go with her," Knox said without hesitation, his dislike of rainforests be damned. The thought of Rachel going somewhere without him made his stomach twist itself into knots.

Diego looked both disappointed and resigned at the same time. "Yeah, I thought you might say that. Has Rachel ever mentioned *The One* to you?"

Knox frowned. "The one what?"

Diego let out a sigh. "It's complicated, but basically, it's a theory about werewolves and soul mates and how you know when you find that person."

"Soul mates?" Knox made a face. "Isn't that...I don't know...make-believe?"

The receptionist glanced their way, and Diego flashed her another smile before turning back to him with a scowl. "Make-believe? You mean like werewolves and vampires?"

"Okay, I guess I see your point. So you think Rachel and

I are soul mates? How is that even possible? I mean I was a frigging hunter for Pete's sake."

Diego's mouth edged up. "That's the magic of it all—it pulls two people together against all odds. You're *The One* for her and she's *The One* for you. Where you both started doesn't matter. It's where you end up."

Knox thought about everything he'd gone through the past year—seeing Lawrence bleed out, leaving the SEALs, falling in with the hunters, locking eyes with Rachel at that wedding reception, getting shot and becoming a werewolf, chasing Rachel all over the place. Now that he thought about it, maybe everything in his life had happened exactly like it was supposed to so he could end up here with Rachel, a woman absolutely perfect for him—a woman who gave him the one thing he'd always seemed to be searching for.

Two chairs over, Diego let out a short laugh and shook his head. "You know, when Rachel showed up and joined the team, I was kind of hoping she'd be *The One* for me."

So Knox was right about the jealousy thing Diego had going on. He should have felt the green-eyed monster breathing down his neck, too, but he didn't. Did being *The One* mean you never got jealous because you knew no one could ever come between you and your mate?

He sat back in his chair. "Does she know you feel that way about her?"

Diego's smile was rueful as he shook his head. "No. She's always thought of me as a friend and I never said anything. The moment I saw you two together yesterday, I knew she and I are meant to be just that—friends. I'm okay with that."

Knox wasn't sure if it was that easy, but before he could say anything more, a nasty smell hit his nose, almost making him gag. He thought for a moment it was his imagination, but then Diego sat up straight, his eyes locking on the door to Delacroix's office.

"What the hell?"

He and Diego were already on their feet when a blood-curdling scream from the doctor's office tore through the air and right through Knox's soul. He charged for the door, his fangs and claws extending whether it was a good idea or not. Diego was on his heels, a growl rumbling through the man's chest.

Knox shoved his shoulder against the door, telling himself to be ready for anything, but what he saw on the far side of the office froze him solid because it didn't seem real.

Or possible.

Hadley Delacroix was gone—though heaven knew where she went, since the door he'd busted in was the only way in or out—and now a clown wearing white face paint, a garish, red smile, and frizzed-out, fiery-orange hair was in the room with Rachel. The thing had one hand wrapped around her neck and was choking the life out of her as she dangled a foot above the floor. Rachel struggled to free herself, but the clown was too strong.

Knox cursed, forcing his body to move. He was halfway across the room when the reality of what he was seeing finally hit him. It was the clown from Rachel's nightmares and it was trying to kill her.

It was *real*.

The clown must have noticed Knox coming at them because the thing turned its head and gave him a creepy smile. With an evil chuckle, it tossed Rachel bodily across the room toward Knox like she was a toy.

Knox barely had time to catch Rachel before she crashed to the floor. Even then, they both took a tumble. Tightening his arms around her, he twisted his body in midair, so his shoulder and back took the brunt of the impact.

Out of the corner of his eye, Knox saw Diego heading for the clown, clearly intent on taking the monster down. But instead of shying away from the heavily muscled werewolf, the clown stepped forward and backhanded Diego across the room. Diego slammed into the wall beside the door, knocking off the landscape painting hanging there.

Knox jumped to his feet and strode toward the clown with a snarl, his claws extended further than he'd ever seen them. The clown squared off against him, that same demented smile on his ugly face.

"Don't hurt it!" Rachel shouted from behind him. "Hadley is in there!"

Knox slowed, not sure what the hell Rachel was talking about at first, but then he realized the clown wore the same colorful dress Hadley had been wearing when he'd met her in the waiting room earlier. It made no sense, but somehow, the clown was *inside* Delacroix's body.

Shit.

Knox retracted his claws. Rachel was right. He couldn't hurt the woman. The clown. Whatever the hell this thing was. Unfortunately, the clown didn't have the same issues with causing damage. Taking advantage of Knox's hesitation, the thing surged forward and punched him in the center of the chest.

It was like being hit by a truck, and Knox swore he heard a crack as something near his sternum broke. He didn't even realize he was flying through the air until he slammed into the big wood desk. It collapsed under him, wood fragments going everywhere—including into his back.

He would have preferred to lay there and groan for a while, but the clown was already heading for Rachel again. She stood there immobilized, terror in her eyes.

Scrambling to his feet, Knox sprinted across the room and tackled the clown from behind. The thing quickly squirmed free, backhanding him across the face hard enough to crack his jaw. How the hell could anything Delacroix's size be so frigging strong?

Knox grabbed the clown around the waist as the thing tried to get away. Luckily, Diego showed back up, throwing himself on the clown's legs to help hold it down.

Trying to restrain someone as strong as the clown without hurting the body the thing was using as a host was like fighting with one arm tied behind his back. Every time he and Diego got it pinned down, a fist came flying out and another bone in his body or Diego's would crack. It didn't help that the damn clown laughed like crazy the entire frigging time they fought. The sound was so disturbing it made goose bumps run up and down Knox's spine.

Then Rachel leaped into the fray and got her hands on the clown's face. Greasepaint smeared everywhere as Rachel shouted at the clown to leave Hadley alone. It seemed like a ludicrous demand, but suddenly, it was like a switch had been flipped and all the fight went out of the clown.

Knox was lying across the clown's body, pinning one of its hands to the floor, so he couldn't see its face very clearly, especially with Rachel now entirely blocking his view, but a moment later, he heard Hadley ask what was happening in a soft, confused voice.

Figuring it was safe to release her, Knox sat back on his heels as Diego did the same down by Hadley's legs. To his relief, the clown was gone and the therapist was back. Eyes glazed and a dazed expression on her face, some of her dark hair that had been up in a neat twist was hanging down around her shoulders in complete disarray.

"What happened?" Hadley asked again, scanning the room, a frown furrowing her brow as she focused on the three of them again. "How did I end up on the floor? And why are you all looking at me like that?"

Rachel glanced at Knox and Diego but didn't answer. Knox couldn't blame her. How could anyone explain anything that had just happened?

CHAPTER 13

Rachel buried her face in Knox's pillow, breathing in his scent and letting it lull her back into that fuzzy place where things weren't nearly so complicated as her real life seemed to be right now. Of course, no matter how much she'd rather lay there in his comfortable bed and continue to forget her problems for a few more hours, there was a part of her that knew it wasn't the mature, adult thing to do.

Sometimes, being an adult sucked.

Sighing, she shoved the blanket down a bit and rolled onto her back, gazing up at the ceiling for a while before glancing at the clock on the nightstand. She blinked when she saw that it was a little after 9:00 p.m. Crap, she'd slept for more than eight hours. She thought for sure it hadn't been more than an hour or two. Then again, watching your therapist turn into the clown from your nightmares and kick the crap out of you and your friends was somewhat exhausting.

Rachel considered reaching over to turn on the lamp beside the bed but then decided against it. She might be awake, but that didn't mean she was ready to get out of bed yet. She still needed time to think about and process everything that had happened.

She could hear soft murmurs from outside the bedroom as Knox and Diego talked. While she was grateful for their support, she wasn't eager to face them yet. So instead, she lay there reliving the morning's events and letting herself believe the warmth provided by the blankets was actually Knox's arms around her.

If she weren't a cop, she would have been shocked at how fast law enforcement and paramedics had shown up at Hadley's office after the clown disappeared. Then again, the psychologist provided trauma counseling for quite a few cops and paramedics over the years. They'd recognized her address and gotten there quickly.

She and Diego had immediately identified themselves as fellow DPD officers, saying Knox was private security currently working for the DA's office. But when the responding officers had seen the freaked-out receptionist, not to mention the big dent in the wall, the questioning had become intense.

Hadley had been so dazed she was barely able to say anything, which was probably good. As far as the doctor could remember, one moment she'd been talking to Rachel, the next she was on the floor with Rachel, Diego, and Knox holding her down. Diego—a master of creativity—suggested Hadley had suffered from a violent seizure, and it had taken the three of them to restrain the woman. Rachel hated implying Hadley was somehow responsible for everything that had happened, but the cops and paramedics seemed to buy it, so that's the story they stuck with. The officers who'd responded to the call spent a little more time taking down everyone's statements and contact information but left soon after paramedics had taken Hadley to the hospital.

That had left Rachel with Knox and Diego. The three of them had stared at each other, none of them eager to be the first to talk about what had really taken place in Hadley's office. Finally, they'd all decided to take the conversation to Knox's hotel room, figuring it wasn't something to talk about over lunch at a restaurant.

But other than confirming they'd all indeed seen the clown taking over Hadley's body—and kick their asses without breaking a sweat—their conversation hadn't yielded any solid conclusions. In some ways it was nice for Rachel to discover she wasn't alone in her insanity, but the thought that perhaps she'd somehow infected Knox and Diego with her condition didn't make her feel very good.

Rachel sat up in bed and ran her fingers through her hair. Lying there reveling in Knox's scent was a guilty pleasure she didn't have time for. She needed to figure out what the hell was going on with her. Getting up, she pulled on jeans and a T-shirt over the bra and panties she wore, then shoved her phone in a pocket and stuck her feet in a pair of mule sneakers before heading into the living room.

Knox and Diego were sitting on the couch, staring intently at a laptop. They glanced up as she entered the room. Soda cans, junk food wrappers, and pieces of notebook paper covered in writing littered the coffee table. As she got nearer, she looked at the papers curiously but realized she couldn't read the scribble no matter what. Both of them had atrocious handwriting.

"How are you feeling?" Knox asked, concern evident on his handsome face. "You slept for a long time."

Rachel didn't say anything as she opened the fridge to take out a Diet Coke, thankful Knox had bought her some so she wouldn't have to overdose on sugar by drinking the Mountain Dew he preferred. Back in the living room, she stopped by the open bag of Hostess powdered mini-donuts and grabbed a handful. She could eat donuts for breakfast, lunch, and dinner, then mix in a few for snacks in between.

She flopped on the couch beside Knox, wolfing down one of the powdered donuts before answering. "I feel good. That fight this morning in Hadley's office must have worn me out. Or maybe I finally had a chance to catch up on all the sleep I've been missing out on over the past few weeks. Either way, I feel as good as new."

Knox and Diego exchanged looks but didn't comment, so Rachel wasn't so sure they believed her. She wasn't sure she believed it herself.

"What have you two been up to while I was napping?" she asked, biting into another donut.

"Research," Diego said. "We've been trying to find anything that might help us understand what the hell happened this morning."

Rachel raised a brow at that, not sure how a person would go about researching a complete mental breakdown involving four different people. Were there chat groups for something like that?

"Have you learned anything?"

"Well, to start with, Horace Watkins is dead," Knox said.

Rachel stopped chewing, the previously delicious donut suddenly dry and tasteless in her mouth. "Why would you even check on something like that? It's not like Horace Watkins slipped into Hadley Delacroix's office and changed into her clothes when I wasn't looking. Or into my apartment. Or the basement of the courthouse."

Knox exchanged another quick glance with Diego before turning his attention back to her. "We know that, but what happened this morning wasn't some kind of mental breakdown. That thing was real. It attacked all of us and damn near killed us. The fact that Horace was made up as a clown when he attacked you, and now you're being terrorized by a clown that looks exactly like him isn't something we could ignore. Unfortunately, it was a dead end. The prison said he hung himself while in solitary confinement ten weeks ago."

The idea of Horace Watkins somehow being personally involved in these episodes seemed insane. But then again, seeing her nightmare come to life and throw one of her pack mates through a wall was also more than a little insane. So, maybe it was time to suspend her disbelief for a while and try to accept the craziness of this situation.

"Are they sure it was ten weeks ago?" she murmured, trying to understand why that time frame seemed so important. "Why was he in solitary anyway?"

"They couldn't give us a specific time of death," Diego answered. "I got the feeling the guards hadn't been checking on him as often as they were supposed to. Apparently, Horace had gone completely ranting, raving, foaming-at-the-mouth crazy and attacked the guards dozens of times."

"Why are you so interested that it was ten weeks ago?" Knox asked. "Is that significant?"

She thought about it, then shrugged. "Maybe it's a coincidence, but ten weeks ago is about when my nightmares started up again really bad. Before that, they'd almost disappeared."

Knox frowned and grabbed a piece of notebook paper already covered with scribbles and wrote down something that looked like the words *ten weeks* and *nightmares*.

"What else have you two been doing?" she asked. "There are a lot of notes here."

Knox picked up a stack of papers and handed them to her. "We surfed the web, looking for other accounts that sounded anything like what happened this morning. Some of them are probably bullshit, but a few seem legit. It's kind of scary, but there's a lot of weird crap going on out there in the world—even weirder than vampires."

Diego continued, "We dug some more, and when we realized there might be a legitimate explanation, we got in contact with Davina DeMirci to see if she might know something. She said she'd do some digging and get back to us. We figured we'd keep looking while we waited."

Rachel nodded, not bothering to do more than glance at the pieces of paper, since she couldn't read them anyway. Davina was a rather odd woman they'd met out in LA. She owned a nightclub that served an extremely unusual clientele of the supernatural variety. The woman definitely knew a lot about things that go bump in the night. It probably wasn't a bad idea to talk to her.

She opened her mouth to ask how they'd described the clown attack to Davina but was interrupted by a buzzing coming from her butt. Reaching back, she pulled out her phone and found a text waiting for her.

"What's up?" Knox asked, looking up from his laptop and a chat loop dedicated to the creatures frequently appearing on the TV show *Supernatural*. She had no idea why he'd be looking there.

"It's Addy. Her parents got in a huge fight earlier, and now there are a bunch of lawyer types at the house. She thinks they're talking about getting divorced and wants to know if I can come over and hang out with her."

"I don't think that's a good idea," Diego said quickly

even as Knox nodded in agreement. "After this morning, I think you should stay here, where we can keep an eye on you. Besides, doesn't she know you've been taken off her security detail?"

Rachel felt her gums and fingertips tingle at the idea of Knox and Diego thinking they were going to keep her there for her own protection. She appreciated their concern, but she was a big girl who could take care of herself. Okay, maybe she couldn't exactly take care of herself—at least not when the clown showed up—but she'd made Addy a promise that she'd be there whenever the girl needed her. Rachel wasn't going to go back on that promise now. She just needed to stay away from any dangerous, adrenaline-filled situations—or ones that involved her thinking about the clown. Neither of those scenarios should come up during a girl-to-girl chat in the safety of the Lloyd mansion.

"Addy doesn't need a security guard. She's scared her parents are getting divorced and she needs a friend." Rachel stood and shoved the phone back in her pocket. "I'll be fine going over there."

Knox immediately got to his feet. "I'm with Diego on this. What if that...thing...comes back? Why can't Zane or Trey sit and talk with her?"

She lifted a brow and put her hands on her hips. "For one thing, Addy can't talk to Zane or Trey because DAPS is guarding the house tonight and they aren't there. For another, no teenage girl on the planet is going to talk to a bunch of guys about her parents' impending divorce. And lastly, the clown isn't going to make an appearance as long as I don't think about him and stay calm. That seems to be the only time he shows up."

That whole speech might have constituted the equivalent of whistling past the graveyard, but it was either believe she had at least some control over her life, or check herself into a mental facility.

Going into the bedroom, she picked up her small backup weapon and strapped the holster around her ankle underneath her jeans, then grabbed her jacket, slipping it on as she walked into the living room.

Knox looked dubious, trading yet another glance with Diego. "Are you really willing to take a chance on that with Addy in the room?"

Rachel sighed, knowing Knox meant well. Reaching out, she caressed his stubble-covered jaw. "I agree that I'm better when I'm around you, but I refuse to let this thing—this fear—control my life. Addy needs me, so I'm going to go to her. And before you ask, no, you don't need to come with me. I'll run over there and talk to her for a while, get her calmed down, then come right back. I'll only be gone a couple of hours."

When Knox looked like he still wanted to argue, she stepped closer. "Knox, I need you to trust me on this because I need to be able to trust myself. Okay?"

Knox finally nodded. "Okay. But if you start feeling weird, call me. And please, text me when you get there so I know you arrived safely, okay? And let me know when you're on your way back here, too."

"I will." Rachel leaned over to kiss him, stunned at how touched she was at his concern. "Don't worry. I'll be fine."

Rachel's phone chirped again as she pulled out of the parking lot of Knox's hotel, so she checked it at the next stoplight. As she suspected, it was Addy.

> *Are you almost here? A bunch of men from that security company my dad hired are walking all over the house, including the jerk who owns it. He keeps staring at my butt and totally perving me out. Why couldn't that cute one, Ethan, be here tonight?*

Rachel snorted at the comment about Ethan. She hadn't really noticed, but she supposed she could see why Addy would think he was cute.

> I'm on my way, but it will be at least 20–25 minutes. If any of those DAPS guys bother you or you don't feel safe, find a place to hide, okay?

Addy sent back a thumbs-up emoji.

Rachel put her phone away, then waited for the light to turn green, hoping she hadn't made a mistake in leaving the hotel room. Maybe Knox was right and she was putting Addy at risk by meeting with her. Rachel knew she was prone to episodes where she lost time and became violent. Now, here she was going to help a teenager whose parents were having a nasty marital spat. This was probably a really dumb idea. But the moment the thought popped into her head, she dismissed it. *Screw that noise.* She was stronger than this and refused to let fear keep her from helping a friend.

The drive over to the Lloyd mansion didn't take quite as long as expected, and she got there in little more than fifteen minutes. But as she approached the front of the property, her inner wolf stirred, telling her not to pull into the driveway, so she drove past it. As she did, she couldn't help but notice the large number of guards at the wrought-iron gates, ones she didn't recognize from DAPS at all. She couldn't put it into words, but something told her asking them to open the gates wouldn't go well, even if she flashed her badge.

She drove several blocks down the street until she found a place to pull off. Killing the engine, she hopped out of her Fiat 500X SUV and moved quickly toward the house, wondering if she was being silly. But the closer she got to the Lloyd property, the more unsettled her nerves became. Her gums and fingertips tingled like they were on fire, and she couldn't help thinking something was wrong. Even so, she didn't mention her suspicions when she texted Knox to let him know she'd made it to the Lloyds' safely. There was no reason to alarm him.

Rachel stopped in the shadows of the high stone wall along the south side of the residence to text Addy and let her know she was almost there.

Hurry up. The fighting is getting worse.

Rachel cursed. This was obviously what had her inner wolf so restless. It sounded like this potential divorce thing was turning nasty.

Where are you now?

Under the bed in the last guest room at the end of the hallway upstairs.

Stay put. I'm coming to get you.

Switching her phone to vibrate, Rachel slipped it into her pocket, then moved along the wall to a place where she knew the security cameras couldn't see and hopped over. Dropping into the shadows on the other side, she knelt there for a moment, waiting to see if there were any guards on this side of the house. She wasn't sure if she was happy or concerned there was no one out here at all.

Where the hell were the DAPS guards that should have been roaming the property?

She moved across the side yard, keeping to the dark shadows until she reached the house. She dipped down and headed to the back of the mansion, using the hedges for cover. She slowed when she heard voices, poking her head up carefully to look in a window.

The first person she saw was Conrad Lloyd. Jennifer's husband looked tense as he stood talking to a group of half a dozen men dressed in suits. Rachel glanced around the room—as much of it as she could see—but she couldn't see Jennifer. She swung her gaze back to Conrad when it occurred to her that several of the men were pretty big guys. She did a double take. *Crap.* Those were the men who'd been at the courthouse yesterday—with Alton Marshall.

She dropped to the ground under the window, her head spinning. *WTF?* Why would men involved with a dirtbag like Marshall be *at* the Lloyds' place? If they were talking to Jennifer, it might be one thing, but these men were obviously acquaintances of her husband.

Rachel was still trying to work it all out when she heard the sound of leather shoes on stone floors. Peeking over the windowsill again, she saw Theo walk into the room.

"My guys have your wife secured in a room near the garage," Theo told Conrad. "Your call on what we do with her, but if you need help getting rid of the body, let me know and we'll take care of it."

Rachel's eyes went wide. She'd heard that wrong...right?

"I appreciate the offer, but Marshall's associates are going to take care of it for me," Conrad said.

Theo looked a little disappointed. "Well, if you change your mind, let me know."

Conrad assured Theo he would, then waited for the man to leave before turning back to Marshall's goons. "Before you take care of my wife, I want you to find my daughter. I don't want her to have any idea what happened to her mother. And I don't want any of this to get traced back to me, either. It has to look like an accident. Understood?"

The men grumbled something in answer, but Rachel was too busy scrambling through the hedges as she headed for the other side of the house. She only prayed she could find an easy way inside and up to the second-floor guest rooms.

Pulling out her phone as she went, she sent a quick text to Knox, telling him Conrad and DAPS were working with Marshall and they were going to kill Jennifer. Calling probably would have been better, but she didn't have time for a long conversation. She had to get to Addy and her mother fast.

Bring help ASAP, she added.

It wasn't until Rachel reached the back of the house and the unlocked French doors there that she wondered why she'd texted Knox instead of Diego or her other pack mates. But as she silently slipped inside, she decided it didn't matter.

CHAPTER 14

"Do you really think it was a good idea letting Rachel go out on her own like that?" Diego asked without looking up from the website he'd been skimming through.

Knox finished the last few powdered donuts he'd been working on polishing off. "What was I supposed to do, lock her in the bedroom and slide donuts under the door for her to live on? I haven't known Rachel as long as you have, but I have no doubt she'd never let anyone force her to do something she didn't want to, even if it's for her own good. I have to trust that if she senses trouble coming, she'll tell me."

Diego regarded him thoughtfully. "I think Rachel may have gotten far luckier than she knows when you took that bullet for her. There aren't many men strong enough to handle a woman as wild and free as she is. Most would try to hold on too tightly and end up losing her. You two really are meant to be together."

Knox was about to deny it, not wanting to rub the relationship he had with Rachel in the other man's face. Then he realized that was stupid. Diego was putting into words what they both knew to be true. Of course, that didn't keep Knox from feeling a little bad for Diego. He was quickly coming to consider the other man a friend, and regardless of what Diego might say, the guy was still dealing with the pain of knowing Rachel wasn't meant to be with him.

"You're going to find *The One* for you, Diego," Knox

said. "It'll happen, and when it does, I'll be right there to tell you I told you so."

Diego snorted and went back to perusing the Internet. "Yeah, sure it will happen. But knowing my luck, I'll meet my soul mate only to find out she's serving a ten-year prison sentence or married already, or has a kid who will hate my guts."

"Damn," Knox muttered. "Aren't you just a ray of sunshine?"

Diego opened his mouth to reply when the laptop dinged and a Skype notice popped up. Diego immediately clicked on it and the video image of an attractive middle-aged woman with the bluest hair Knox had ever seen filled the screen. Hell, it practically frigging glowed. She was seated at a desk and there was an old-looking tapestry on the wall behind her.

"Davina, this is Knox Lawson," Diego said, gesturing to him. "He's Rachel's mate and is helping her deal with this thing. Please tell us you found out something about this frigging clown."

The woman glanced at Knox before focusing on Diego again. "Is there something in the water out there in Texas that attracts werewolves, or is it simply the barbecue?"

"How did you...?" Knox started, but Davina cut him off.

"I can tell what most people are by looking at them. It's my thing. But we aren't here to talk about me. We're here to talk about what's attached itself to your pack mate."

Knox was about to point out he wasn't technically in Rachel's pack, but before he could, Davina stood up from her desk and moved out of view of the camera. A moment later, she was back with what looked like an enormous encyclopedia. Opening it, she turned the book to face them, holding it up to the camera. Knox leaned forward, straining to make out the details of a very dark Gothic-looking painting. There was a creepy-looking creature perched on the stomach and chest of a half-dressed woman draped across a bed. In the background was what Knox assumed was a horse. He had no clue what the hell a horse was doing in a woman's bedroom.

"This is a painting titled *The Nightmare*. It was done in 1781 by an Anglo-Swiss artist known as Henry Fuseli," Davina explained. "The popular theory is that the creature on her chest is an incubus, while the horse is supposed to be a mare, representing nightmares. Turns out that's only half-right. The thing on the woman's chest represents a creature called a *nachtmahr*, also referred to as a mare, *mara*, *maron*, or half a dozen other names, depending on the culture you're dealing with."

"Sorry, but that thing doesn't look anything like the clown that attacked us," Knox said, hating to interrupt but not interested in an art history lesson.

Davina dropped the book on the desk with a thud, making the camera shake. "Really? If you want clowns, go find a circus. The *nachtmahr* is a malicious entity—a spirit that feeds on its victim's fear. It creates that fear by scaring the crap out of them, appearing to each victim as whatever terrifies them the most. In Rachel's case, it's a clown."

"But *we* saw the clown too," Diego pointed out. "I couldn't give a rat's ass about clowns, so if this thing changes its appearance for each victim, why appear to Knox and me as a clown?"

Before Davina could answer Diego's question—which

seemed very logical—Knox's phone dinged. He glanced at it long enough to see that it was a text from Rachel saying she'd arrived at the Lloyd mansion. He breathed out the tension he hadn't realized he'd been holding.

When he looked up, Davina was frowning, like she was disappointed in their lack of intelligence. "Because you weren't its victim—Rachel is. You were collateral damage. You mentioned this guy Horace attacked her as a clown over a year ago, then Horace died in prison. That's how the *nachtmahr* works. It finds a victim it likes the taste of, then rides that victim until they're dead, usually by their own hand. Then it jumps to a new victim and starts the process all over again. It must have gotten a tiny nibble of her fear when Horace tried to kill her and decided she'd be fun to go after next. I'm not sure how much Rachel has told you, but I'm willing to bet this all started with little stuff—strange smells, cold chills, shadows out of the corner of her eye."

At Knox's nod, Davina continued. "The horrifying nightmares come next, wearing down a person's defenses, physically exhausting them. It's downhill from there—hallucinations, sounds—until finally the creature creates a crack in its victim's mind. That's when the physical manifestation comes. Like the incident that happened today. The shocking thing is that it's taken so long. From everything I've read in my books, most victims don't manage to make it more than two weeks before they completely lose it."

"Then what?" Diego asked.

Davina sat back in her chair. "My understanding is when the *nachtmahr* has taken complete control, it will force Rachel to do things she'd never consider doing, so it can feed off her fear and her horror. She'll kill innocents, like

Horace tried to do with that girl in Chattanooga. Then at some point, she'll come after those closest to her, like the two of you."

"Rachel would never do anything like that," Knox growled.

"She will," Davina insisted. "She won't have a choice."

Diego cursed. "How do we find this fucking thing and kill it?"

"The first part is easy," Davina said. "It's obsessed with Rachel, so while it might jump out for short rides in other people, like those killers in the basement of the courthouse or that therapist, it's tied itself to Rachel for the long term. Killing it, on the other hand, is both easy...and hard."

"What the hell does that mean?" Knox snarled, his fangs and claws coming out. He had no interest in playing riddle games with Rachel's life.

"Like I said before, a *nachtmahr* is a malicious spirit, and spirits are damn hard to kill," Davina said sadly. "There are only two ways to do it. You must either drown them in salt water, or incinerate them in fire. Obviously, they have to be in a host at the time and you have to do it when there aren't any other people around, or the thing will jump to another host. That's how the thing got from Horace to Rachel. Once it finds someone it wants, it creates a link, so it jumped from person to person like a damn parasite until it got to Rachel."

"You have to be shitting me," Knox whispered. "There isn't some way to draw it out? Someone must have destroyed one of these things before."

Davina shook her head. "I don't know of any way to draw it out of a host—it simply jumps from one to another. And as far as someone trying to destroy it, there are two reported instances of it. One in the mid-1800s, when a sailor possessed by one took his ship alone into the middle of the Atlantic by himself and jumped overboard, and another in Hawaii in 1910, when a possessed woman ran to the top of a volcano by herself and jumped in." She sighed. "I'm sorry, but that's all I've got. You can't get this thing out unless it wants out, and if there's anyone else within twenty or thirty feet when you try to kill it, the thing will simply jump to their body. At least that's what the documents I found lead me to believe."

Davina shut down the connection shortly after that, telling them she'd keep looking, but she wasn't holding out much hope.

Knox couldn't do anything but sit there, staring at the blank laptop screen. "What the hell are we going to do? We damn sure can't tell Rachel any of this. She'll sacrifice herself without a second thought to save everyone around her."

Before Diego could answer, Knox's phone dinged again. He picked it up from the coffee table, expecting to see a text from Rachel saying she was heading back. He was right about who it was from but wrong about the rest.

"Shit," he muttered, shooting to his feet.

"What is it?" Diego asked, now standing.

"Rachel just sent me a text saying Conrad and DAPS are working with Marshall, and they're about to kill Jennifer," he told Diego as he headed into the bedroom to grab his Glock and extra ammo clips. "She needs backup. Now!"

CHAPTER 15

RACHEL SLIPPED INTO THE KITCHEN, PAUSING TO LET her senses take in everything around her in the huge home. She'd been at the Lloyds' place a lot, so she instinctively knew what scents and noises were the everyday kind, but there were a lot of people she didn't know moving around, which made things difficult.

Reaching down, she pulled out her .380 automatic from her ankle holster, wishing like hell she'd brought her Sig. Being without it felt like she was missing a part of herself—an important part with lots of large caliber ammo. The little double action she carried was okay in a pinch, but if things degraded to a shooting match with these a-holes, it would almost be laughable.

Rachel pushed thoughts of shooting matches aside as she carefully made her way through the house, silently slipping past some of the men without them seeing her. She recognized several as the DAPS guys she'd worked with over the past several days, but now it was clear their allegiance was to whomever was paying them—and right now, that seemed to be Alton Marshall.

She wished she could move faster, especially since she had no idea how much longer Jennifer had before Marshall's men either took her away or killed her right where she was. But with so many people in the house, she was forced to duck and hide several times. The delay was frustrating as hell, but if there was a silver lining, it was that her snail's pace would give Knox and her other backup time to get there.

Rachel heard a few of the men talking about not being able to find Addy. One even suggested she'd slipped out of the house earlier to go see her boyfriend. That wasn't true, of course, and thankfully Rachel had no problem following Addy's scent straight to the last guest bedroom at the end of the hallway on the second floor.

Stepping inside, Rachel silently closed the door behind her, then stood there in the darkness. A moment later, she picked up Addy's heartbeat. The poor girl was so scared it sounded more like a hummingbird than a sixteen-year-old kid.

"Addy?" she called softly. "It's me—Rachel."

There was a gasp, then a rustle as the girl scrambled out from under the bed like there was someone chasing her. Rachel almost fell over backward when Addy threw herself in her arms and buried her face in her shirt, soft sobs of relief shaking her.

Rachel shushed her as quietly as she could, patting Addy's back and hugging her. She understood the girl was terrified, but if one of those goons she'd seen below heard them, *bad* wouldn't even begin to describe it.

Gently pulling away, she took Addy's hand and led her over to the window, where a patch of moonlight filtered in.

"Honey, this is going to be hard for you to hear, but it's important you understand the situation we're in, okay?" Rachel whispered.

Addy's eyes widened and for a moment, Rachel felt horrible for putting her in this position. But in the end, there wasn't a choice. Rachel had to get Addy—and her mom—out of there within the next few minutes, before it was too late.

"What's wrong?" Addy asked in a broken whisper. "Is it my mom and dad? Are they…?"

Rachel shook her head quickly. "No, your parents are both still alive. I promise."

She immediately cursed herself for making such a vow. The truth was, she really had no way of knowing if Jennifer was still alive. Rachel prayed she was right about that. But standing here talking wasn't helping the situation. They needed to move.

"Addy, your mom is being held at gunpoint by some really bad guys in a room somewhere close to the garage." Rachel hesitated, wishing like hell she didn't have to put it all out there like this. "I don't know all the details, but your father is somehow involved with Alton Marshall, the man your mom is trying to send to prison. I think your father and Marshall may be working together."

Addy's eyes went wide. "Working together? Are you sure?"

Rachel nodded. "I'm sure. I wish I weren't, but I am."

Addy swallowed hard. "There's a workshop behind the garage. Dad used to work on old cars when I was little as a hobby. He hasn't done it in a long time, though."

"Do you think you can help me find a way to get there without anyone seeing us?" Rachel asked.

Nodding, Addy reached up to wipe the tears off her cheeks. "There's a back staircase at the far end of this floor that leads to that end of the house. If we're careful, we should be able to get to the workshop without anyone seeing us."

Addy reminded Rachel so much of Hannah in that moment she wanted to hug her. But they had no time for hugs.

Taking Addy's hand, Rachel headed for the bedroom door, pausing only long enough to confirm there was no one in the main hallway. Then they both hurried as fast as they could along the hardwood floor.

Rachel was glad she had Addy with her or she would never have found the back staircase or followed the myriad twists and turns that led to the area behind the garage so quickly. She got the feeling this part of the house had been added on after the original construction and the passageways had been necessary to connect the various rooms.

"There's a long hallway around the next corner," Addy whispered, pointing ahead of them. "If you go left at the end, you get to the garage. If you go right, it's the workshop."

Rachel nodded.

If they were going to stumble across any of Marshall's men, this would be the place, Rachel thought as they moved. But they made it down the dimly lit corridor and all the way to the workshop before Rachel smelled anyone. Unfortunately, there were two men with Jennifer, on the other side of the closed door to the workshop. That sucked. But on the bright side, she could make out three heartbeats in there, which meant the prosecutor was alive.

Rachel could have kicked in the door easily, ripped it off the hinges, and gone in shooting. But that would have alerted everyone else in the house, and that wasn't something Rachel wanted to deal with, not when she had to worry about Addy and her mom.

Turning to the girl, she motioned her back down the hallway, then followed.

"Your mom is in there, but there are two men with her," Rachel said. "I need you to stay here while I deal with them. Then we'll get out of here."

It was obvious from the look on Addy's face that she had

a hundred questions, but Rachel didn't give her a chance. Motioning for her to stay, she slipped her small pistol into the back pocket of her jeans, then headed for the workshop.

Rachel pushed the door open quietly, not wanting to alert either the men or Jennifer that something unusual was coming their way until the last possible second. The two dirtbags were leaning back against a workbench, eyes focused on Jennifer. The ADA was sitting on the floor with her back to a built-in cabinet, dirt on her clothes and a bruise forming on her cheek.

The men were so focused on Jennifer they didn't realize Rachel was there until it was too late.

As they reached under their jackets for their weapons, the urge to extend her claws and tear out their throats was difficult to ignore, but she did—not only because she couldn't let Jennifer see something like that, but because she had no desire to give the clown an opportunity to make an appearance. She wasn't completely sure there was a direct connection between her inner wolf and the clown, but every time she'd been in high-stress situations—chasing the killers at the mall, trying to find Addy when Aaron had slipped away with her, the shootout at the courthouse, the therapy session with Hadley—the clown had come out. She hoped that staying completely calm would keep it from happening now.

That was hard to do as the men aimed their guns at her, but she forced herself to stay calm as she closed the distance between them, intent on ending this as quickly—and as quietly—as possible.

Before the man closest to her could pull the trigger of the large-caliber automatic in his hand, Rachel grabbed his wrist and slammed a palm into the underside of his elbow. It snapped easily, but before the man could scream in pain, she punched him in the throat as hard as she could.

Rachel was in the second guy's personal space before he could even understand what was going on. She batted his gun hand aside, then drove a knee into his crotch. While he was busy trying to recover from that, she got one hand on his chin and the other in the hair at the back of his head and twisted. The crack his neck made echoed in the room like a gunshot.

She glanced at Jennifer to make sure she was okay, ignoring the stunned expression on the ADA's face as she collected up the dead men's weapons. They were large-frame Glocks loaded with 10 mm ammo. They were too big and unwieldy for her hands, but they were better than the little .380 she'd brought. She was rummaging through the men's jackets for spare magazines when Addy peeked her head around the corner of the doorway.

Addy slowed when she saw the two bodies on the floor, but then ran over to her mom, hugging Jennifer even as she tearfully helped her mother to her feet. Rachel hated to break up the moment between mother and daughter, but she had to.

"Jennifer. Addy. We need to go."

They both looked at her as they wiped away tears.

"Does that door lead to the garage?" she asked, pointing at the far side of the workshop.

Jennifer nodded. "Yes. My car is in there, but the keys are in my purse in the living room."

Crap. She'd been hoping Jennifer might have the keys on her.

"That's okay," Rachel said. "We're going to open the

garage door and the moment we can run under it, we're heading around the side of the house and the perimeter wall, then we'll hightail it to my SUV parked down the street. Sound good?"

Mother and daughter nodded, but when Rachel turned to lead the way, Jennifer put a hand on her arm. "You need to know that you can't trust the DAPS people. They're not being paid to protect Addy and me. They work for my husband and, by extension, Alton Marshall. If they see us, they'll kill us."

Addy looked devastated all over again—maybe because she'd been holding out hope that Rachel had been wrong and that her father wasn't wrapped up in this mess. Hearing her mother confirm it seemed to be the last straw and fresh tears filled her eyes.

"I know," Rachel said. "We won't let them catch us."

The moment they were in the garage, Jennifer hit the button to raise the door. Rachel said a silent prayer of thanks when she realized it was the quietest garage door she'd ever heard—or didn't hear. Rich people had all the nice toys.

The door was at knee level and the three of them were just about to duck under it when the scent of several men hit Rachel from outside.

Crap. They were screwed.

She was already dragging Addy and her mom back to the workshop as the door lifted high enough to reveal Theo and a bunch of his DAPS buddies. Jennifer was smart enough to grab Addy and run before the shooting started. Rachel only wished she'd put a bullet in Theo before turning and running after Addy and Jennifer.

As she followed them through the workshop and into

the maze of hallways beyond, Rachel tried to keep Theo and the other men from getting too close, but within moments, she realized the a-holes were herding them away from the exits and any possible escape. Instead, Theo and the other armed goons pushed them toward the depths of the house until they were trapped in a cul-de-sac created by the intersection of three different hallways. Rachel shoved Addy and Jennifer behind her as rounds started coming at her from every direction. She dropped to a knee and returned fire, forcing herself to time her shots. Even if it seemed impossible right then, she had to hold out until Knox and the rest of her backup arrived.

CHAPTER 16

Diego pulled his Mazda RX5 to the side of the road a few hundred yards short of the Lloyd residence, out of sight of the gatehouse. Moments later, a big SWAT SUV pulled up behind them. Knox opened his door and was heading toward the front gate without slowing down to think about what he was doing.

"Wait a second, dude." Diego ran around the car to catch up with him. "I know you're freaked out, but we can't go in there without a plan or we're not going to be any help to Rachel at all. If anything, we'll make things worse."

Knox growled, grinding his fangs together hard enough to almost break them off. His fangs and claws had made an appearance on the drive over, and it had taken all his energy to not jump out and run all the way to the Lloyds' every time they encountered the least little bit of traffic.

Before he could say anything, Zane and Trey jumped out of the SUV, concern on both men's faces.

"What did you mean when you called and said Rachel's in trouble?" Zane demanded. "She's not even supposed to be working."

"She went to see Addy," Knox said. "Apparently her parents got into a huge fight and Addy needed someone to talk to, so of course, Rachel ran right over. She didn't care about being off the detail. But it wasn't until we got her text saying Conrad Lloyd and DAPS are working with Alton Marshall and they're planning to kill Jennifer that we realized something was wrong. I'm just hoping she waited until we got here before doing something crazy."

"Bloody hell," Zane muttered.

Trey shook his head. "Yeah, well if Rachel thought for a second Addy was in danger, there's nothing in the world that'd keep her from going in there."

No frigging kidding. "Tell me something I don't know. If DAPS is working for Marshall, she's going to be heavily outnumbered."

Diego and Trey nodded in agreement, but Zane was frowning.

"First off, we have no idea if Rachel is still in there. She might have already gotten in and out with Addy and her mom," the British werewolf said. "Second, even if we go in, you aren't. You're not a cop, and we can't have civilians going in there, especially if you're with DAPS."

Knox didn't realize he'd lost control of his inner wolf and was moving forward to attack Zane until Diego intercepted him with a hand on his chest.

"Dude, relax. Zane won't try and keep you out. He knows better than anyone how impossible that would be for you."

"I won't?" Zane asked, confused.

Diego glanced at his pack mate. "He's *The One* for Rachel. And before you ask, I only found out about it myself yesterday. So don't bother trying to stop him, because it won't work."

The muscle in Zane's jaw flexed, and for a second, Knox thought he was going to have to fight the guy, but then Zane turned and walked to the rear of the SUV. He came back a few moments later carrying two SWAT tactical vests to match the ones he and Trey were wearing, a radio headset, and an M4 carbine. He handed a vest, the radio, and the carbine to Diego and the other vest to Knox.

"I don't have a radio for you, but the vest will at least make it look like you're one of us in case any DPD officers arrive on scene," Zane said. "The rest of the Pack is in Irving, raiding a drug dealer's place, so we're on our own for now."

Knox tossed his jacket, shrugged into the vest, and cinched down the Velcro straps. His urge to take over and establish the plan for moving on the mansion was hard to ignore after so many years in the SEALs, but he knew it wouldn't fly here, not with these guys having so much more experience at being werewolves than he did. "What's the plan?"

"We take it slow until we have a better idea what's going on in there," Zane said. "We'll jump the wall on the north side of the property, since there are fewer cameras there. Once we look around a bit, we'll go from there."

Okay, he could work with that, Knox thought.

As plans went, it was nice and simple. Too bad it barely lasted the two minutes it took them to move into position at the north wall and jump over. That's when they heard the chatter of gunfire coming from the far side of the mansion. A few moments later, half a dozen armed men ran out of the front door.

A stab of fear shot through Knox's chest.

Rachel is in trouble.

"Diego, you and Knox get into the house and find Rachel," Zane said. "Trey and I will work along the perimeter and attempt to draw as many of the bad guys out of there as possible to make it easier for the two of you."

Knox didn't wait for more instructions but immediately turned and ran for the house. Diego followed close enough to cover him but far enough away to avoid a single burst of gunfire getting both of them. There weren't any doors on this side of the mansion, but Knox didn't slow. He simply ran as hard as he could, the muscles of his legs and back flexing and twisting until he swore he heard bones crack.

He didn't slow as he reached the house but, instead, launched himself off the ground and right through a window. Glass shards sliced into the skin of his arms, but he ignored it. He hit the floor inside at a roll, then was on his feet and running again as Diego joined him.

More gunfire echoed from somewhere inside the house, but he couldn't trust the sound to lead him and Diego because it was bouncing off walls and floors, going in every direction at once. Instead, he allowed his inner wolf to pick up Rachel's scent and let that guide him. His nose led him down a series of corridors until they came up behind three men blocking the way and shooting toward the far end. One of the men must have somehow realized Knox and Diego were there because he turned to engage them.

Knox didn't hesitate and was glad to see Diego didn't, either. They simply kept running, putting all three men down before continuing along the hallway. At the end of it, he found Rachel, Jennifer, and Addy crouched down, doing their best to avoid being hit by all the bullets coming their way. The sight of blood running down one of Rachel's arms and staining the material of her jeans along both thighs had Knox close to losing it, but he had no time for that. Biting back a growl, he forced himself to run past her, emptying an entire magazine of ammo down one of the two hallways ahead of them, where Theo and a handful of other men hid. At the same time, Diego turned and fired down the other.

As Knox reloaded his weapon, he wished Zane had been able to provide him an M4 like Diego carried, but unfortunately, he'd have to make do with his Glock. It was enough though, and within seconds, Theo and the other guys from DAPS fell back and disappeared down the hallway. The same thing happened down the corridor Diego was firing, and for a few blessed moments at least, they weren't under threat of being overrun.

When Knox turned back to Rachel, it was impossible to describe the relief he felt at the sight of her beautiful face—even if she was bleeding. He would have pulled her into his arms and kissed her right then, but she was already dragging Addy and her mom up off the floor and down the hallway he and Diego had arrived from. They barely made it a few feet before they heard the stomping of feet coming toward them. Theo was coming back and he had help.

Shit.

"Diego, get Jennifer and Addy out of here," Rachel shouted. "Knox and I will slow Theo and his buddies down and give you time to get out."

Knox was prepared to argue his ass off, ready to tell Rachel to get Jennifer and Addy to safety herself while he and Diego stayed behind, but Diego was already hustling mother and daughter down the hallway.

With a growl, Knox turned to cover the hallway Theo's group had reappeared in, while Rachel handled the other corridor. Their position wasn't very defensible, but they held out as long as they could, knowing every second they delayed their attackers was another second Diego had to get Addy and her mother out of the house.

He and Rachel lasted another forty-five seconds before

they had to fall back. But even then, they made Theo and his band of gun-toting dickweeds earn every inch of floor space they gained. As he passed the three dead men on the floor, Knox leaned down and scooped up one of their weapons and a magazine full of bullets. The gun was a Glock—that was good. The 10 mm rounds, on the other hand, weren't his preferred caliber. But when his own weapon locked back on an empty magazine, he was damn glad to have it.

A few moments later, after both he and Rachel had been clipped by one of the dozens of bullets ricocheting off the floor, it seemed like their careful retreat was about to dissolve into an all-out withdrawal. That's when Knox looked over his shoulder and recognized the library was behind them. The first floor didn't have any windows, and he was hesitant to trap the two of them in there, but it wasn't like they had a shitload of options. He'd discovered that getting shot hurt, and he'd prefer not to have it happen again.

Grabbing Rachel's shoulder, he guided her backward, letting her cover them as they slipped through the doorway. He didn't stop moving until he reached the conference table near the glass-enclosed fireplace with its roaring flames. Momentarily taking his hand off her shoulder, he flipped the table on its side, then dragged her down behind it.

He heard Theo order some of the men to keep going after Jennifer and Addy, but he wasn't too worried about that. They'd easily given Diego enough time to get Jennifer and her daughter out of the house, if not over the wall and completely off the property. Now, he and Rachel had to keep Theo and the other men occupied until the cavalry arrived.

"I can't fucking believe you turned your back on your

teammates!" Theo called through the open door. "All for a piece of ass. Then again, that's your MO isn't it, running out on your team?"

Coming from someone he respected more, those words might have stung. "I only bail on people when they give me a reason to," Knox shouted back. "Like when I found out you're an asshole willing to kill women and children for profit. I have a strict policy against working for douche canoes, so I guess that means I'm going to have to quit your crap-hole organization."

That must have pissed Theo off because he leaned in the door and began peppering rounds into the thick oak of the table they were hiding behind. Thank God the Lloyds had a thing for quality antique furniture. The bullets weren't making it through that wood no matter what. Unfortunately, the moment he and Rachel ducked down, Theo and several other men took the opportunity to slip into the room, spreading out to get around the table. It was a foolhardy tack to take, but Knox had no doubt Theo was aware their time was running out. They had to kill everyone who knew what had happened here before the place was crawling with cops.

Beside him, Rachel nodded. A moment later, they both popped up and started shooting as fast as they could, no longer able to think about waiting for backup. For a few seconds, it looked like they had a chance. Until he and Rachel ran out of ammo.

Silence filled the room as their attackers realized he and Rachel were essentially defenseless. Then Theo stepped around the table with a superior smile. Lifting his gun, he pointed it at Rachel.

"Her first," he said to Knox. "Then you."

Knox didn't even think—he just reacted. His fangs and claws extended so hard and fast it actually hurt, but he ignored the pain as he went for Theo. He had no idea how to fight with these new weapons he possessed, but that didn't seem to be a problem, as his wolf instincts took over.

He didn't count on one of Theo's employees getting in the way. Knox slashed the guy's face with his claws, then picked him up and tossed him at Theo, messing up his aim and sending the bullet into the floor instead of Rachel's chest.

Something smacked Knox in the stomach, but he ignored the flare of pain as he reached out and tossed yet another man across the room. He hadn't been aiming, but from the corner of his eye, he saw the guy smash through the glass enclosure of the fireplace. He couldn't help cringing as the man's fire-engulfed body tumbled and rolled across the floor until it slammed into one of the bookcases, sending flames everywhere. The man tried to get up and run, but that only spread the fire more, and Knox was stunned at how fast flames roared up the wall of books the dying man finally stumbled into.

Knox was a little worried by how fast the fire spread across the room, but a scream from behind him made him forget all about it. He spun around to see Rachel with claws and fangs extended, staring straight ahead in total panic at one of the DAPS guys, who had turned into the clown.

Shit!

Everything went to hell then, as the rest of Theo's other guys all moved at once, either trying to escape the rapidly spreading fire or fleeing the *nachtmahr* as it savagely ripped into anyone it could reach.

Knox quickly hurried to help Rachel, who was standing in the middle of the room like a statue, but he didn't take three strides before Theo stepped in front of him, eyes filled with rage.

"I don't know what the fuck you and your girlfriend are, but you definitely deserve each other," he sneered, pointing his weapon at Knox's chest.

Knox was moving even as Theo pulled the trigger. The bullet clipped him somewhere along the left side of his chest, but he shrugged off the impact that threatened to spin him around in a circle and closed the distance between him and his former boss. Theo tried to adjust his aim, twisting to get the barrel up and pointing it at Knox's face, but Knox caught his wrist and squeezed hard, breaking bone as he pushed the weapon up toward the ceiling. Before Theo could react, Knox brought the claws of his right hand up and raked them across the asshole's face, then slung him across the room. Theo cried out in panic as he plunged into the flames and disappeared from view. There was so much fire and smoke it was impossible to see through to the other side of the room.

Knox would have followed anyway—just to make sure he was dead—but then Rachel screamed again and all he could think about was getting to her.

Turning, he found her on the far side of the library, backpedaling as she slashed and snarled at the clown relentlessly bearing down on her. Around them, bodies were scattered everywhere, but Knox didn't know if the clown or Rachel had put them down.

Blood ran down her arms and the front of her T-shirt, and it took Knox a moment to realize the clown was swiping at her with claws nearly as long and sharp as her own. Knox wondered for a moment how a clown could have claws like a werewolf, but then cursed his stupidity. The *nachtmahr* could be anything it wanted.

Knox ran toward Rachel, dodging flaming pieces of the collapsing ceiling as he crossed the floor. Knox wasn't sure what his claws would do to the damn thing and wished he'd gotten Theo's weapon away from him before tossing him across the room. But he hadn't, so he made do with what he had at hand—the heavy antique chair that matched the table he and Rachel had been hiding behind earlier. He scooped it up on the run and brought it down as hard as he could over the clown's head.

The chair broke, but so did the clown. Just to be sure, Knox hefted what was left of the piece of furniture—the back and one leg—and kept smashing. That was when he realized his inner werewolf had completely taken over, growling and snarling at the thing that had hurt his mate. It wasn't long before there wasn't much of anything left of the chair or the clown-faced *nachtmahr*.

Knox bent over, resting his hands on his knees, fighting to regain control. Letting the wolf have free rein for a few moments had been exhilarating, but the danger had passed and the creature was dead. He needed to pull back from the edge and fight the instinct to drop down on all fours for reasons he couldn't come close to understanding.

He took in a long, deep breath, almost scalding his lungs from the heat and smoke in the air. All of which reminded him that he and Rachel needed to get the hell out of this room before it all came down on their heads.

Knox straightened and held out his hand for Rachel, only to

see her standing several steps away, her red, glowing eyes regarding him with something close to curiosity—or amusement.

Even as he watched, her face changed, slowly shifting into a different shape. Then she grew taller, wider in the shoulders, and longer in the legs, until there was a man in front of him that he recognized. One that ripped his soul out.

"Why'd you let me die, Knox?" Lawrence asked. "You let me die before I even had a chance to live."

The man Knox knew to be long dead wrapped one hand around his throat and jerked him off his feet like he was a little stuffed toy.

"It's your fault I'm dead," Lawrence added, blood soaking through the chest of the camo uniform he wore, his hand tightening around Knox's throat so firmly he could barely breathe.

Knox's claws hadn't retracted from his earlier fight with the clown, and now they lengthened another inch or so as fear and panic fought to take over. He almost gave in to it, the instinct to lash out and tear the thing in front of him apart, fighting with what he knew to be true.

But this thing wasn't merely the *nachtmahr*. It was Rachel—his soul mate. To hurt it was to hurt her.

He couldn't do that—even to save his own life.

"Rachel," he gasped, gently covering the hand crushing his throat with both of his. He didn't fight, didn't claw to try and rip them away. Instead, he simply touched them, hoping she could feel him. "I know you're in there, Rachel, and I know you don't want to do this. But you have to fight this thing. The monster is trying to take over and make you hurt those you care about because it feeds on your fear. You have to fight for us. Please."

Saying any more was impossible after that. A moment later, his vision began to dim and he started to lose focus on the red, glowing eyes in front of him. The wolf inside him was torn, the need to fight for survival warring with the instinct to protect Rachel.

Knox was sure he was going to die when the thing suddenly let him go. He fell to the floor on his hands and knees, coughing and gulping for air. He was just starting to breathe normally again when he heard a growl followed by the most gut-wrenching sound he'd ever heard.

He jerked his head up to see Rachel on the floor on all fours, spasms and convulsions overtaking her body. Not sure what was happening, Knox leaned forward to help her, but he jerked back as one of her claw-tipped hands came up to shred the clothes off her back. Her jeans tore open next, then her spine, shoulders, and hips cracked and popped as light gray fur erupted from her skin.

The transformation from beautiful woman to beautiful wolf happened so fast it was unbelievable. When the change was complete, there was no red glow to her eyes now or anything to suggest there was anyone in that perfect form other than Rachel. She stood there gazing at him with the most intense, knowing expression he could ever imagine on an animal's face.

He started forward to wrap his arms around her—more than ready to hug a wolf for the first time in his life—but his body wouldn't move.

Knox felt the pressure in his head long before he began to comprehend what it was. The *nachtmahr* creeping into him to take over just as it had Rachel. He fought, mentally trying to shove the presence out of his head, but it kept coming until he swore he could feel the other creature in there with him, feel it taking control of his body. Fear like a cold freeze crept over him, slowly numbing his whole body, making him disappear. He knew when it was complete and he was shoved into a little, dark corner in the back of his mind, the thing would make him attack Rachel. He only prayed she would defend herself.

He didn't realize he'd clenched his eyes shut until Rachel made a chuffing sound in front of his face. When he opened them, it was to find the light gray wolf so close he could feel her breath on his skin, smell the scent of cinnamon and licorice in the air. Then she crouched down and crawled forward to rest her forehead against his.

He felt the fur.

Felt the heat.

Felt *her*.

Knox stopped fighting the creature and instead reached for the wolf, trying like crazy to reach out and touch its mate.

Bones snapped and muscles tore, but strangely, it didn't hurt nearly as much as he thought it would considering what he'd seen Rachel go through when she'd shifted. When Rachel had said it was possible to turn into a wolf, he hadn't been able to wrap his head around it. He was shocked to discover it was as simple as allowing it to happen.

The *nachtmahr* in his head fought like hell to stay there, ripping and tearing with mental claws that made him think of rusty fishhooks. But in the span of one bone breaking and the next, the presence—and the fear—disappeared from his mind like the popping of a soap bubble on a warm sidewalk.

He took a deep breath and immediately knew he was no

longer in his human form. The movement of his ribs against the hard floor only accentuated the fur covering his body. He inhaled again, relishing how everything smelled so much crisper and more alive—even the smoke and fumes that threatened to choke him.

Knox opened his eyes to gaze at Rachel. Seeing her through the eyes of a wolf, she was even more beautiful than in her human form, as unbelievable as that seemed.

He was also pretty sure she was smiling at him.

He was still sitting there gazing into the most perfect eyes ever when he heard a grunt and scrambling sound coming from the flames on the far side of the library. In a single synchronized heartbeat, both he and Rachel were on their feet. Turning around was complicated on four paws, but within a step or two, he got the hang of it.

The figure who leaped out of the fire already consuming most of the room was charred and bloody, smoke pouring off what was left of its clothing. The cracked and broken lips pulled back in a sneer, and even with the red, glowing eyes, Knox recognized Theo.

Understanding shook his core as he remembered something Davina had said. The *nachtmahr* was nearly impossible to kill because it would keep jumping into any available host. Any *human* host. The thing couldn't stay inside him or Rachel in their wolf forms, so it had sought out the only other living thing in range—Theo. Even though he was burned and damaged, the *nachtmahr* had still possessed him.

Rachel snarled at the creature charging toward them, its face going back and forth between the clown and Lawrence as it laughed. It was a horrible, guttural sound coming from a throat too scarred and damaged from the fire to do anything else.

Salt water or fire.

Either would kill the *nachtmahr*.

Knox didn't pause to think. He simply charged forward and slammed his fur-covered shoulder into the thing's chest, driving it back. Wicked, bloody claws swiped out at Knox, slashing deep into his flesh. He reared back and slammed into the creature again, knocking the monster into the flames.

The creature fell, raw flames racing to cover its arms, legs, and torso. The few remaining patches of hair singed away, yet the thing somehow crawled back onto its feet and stumbled forward again.

Rachel sprinted past Knox in a blur, ramming her shoulder into the *nachtmahr* and knocking it back into flames that leaped up as if hungry to devour it. This time, the thing didn't even try to regain its feet, instead crawling toward them on hands and knees as its face and body twisted from shape to shape. Knox recognized the clown and Lawrence, but there were many others. Interspersed among the misshapen monsters were figures that jarred his senses—a child with huge, innocent eyes, a woman in a wedding dress, a man in a fedora—and Knox instinctively knew he was seeing the forms the *nachtmahr* had used over the years to terrify its victims. And based on how many different shapes there were, he could only guess how many hundreds of years this thing had been alive.

Soon enough, the slide show of horrors stopped and a shapeless thing collapsed to the floor, flames continuing to lick across it. Knox held his breath, sure that at any moment, the creature would jump up and charge at them yet again. It didn't. Instead of going out with some dramatic whoosh of flames and sparks, the *nachtmahr* simply crumpled to glowing coals like a burned-out log.

Knox allowed himself maybe three seconds to rejoice in the victory before it became impossible to ignore the roaring flames all around them. He lifted his head to see that the fire hadn't merely engulfed the library but seemed to be consuming the entire mansion. The spiral staircase and the catwalk it led to were also gone. Large sections of the roof had disappeared, revealing the burning rooms above. The heat was beyond intense, and his fur began to curl up as it singed, the overheated air scalding his lungs with every breath. A quick glance toward the door—or at least where the door had been—confirmed they wouldn't be getting out that way. It was an inferno over there.

He looked at Rachel to see her gazing at him. She knew they weren't getting out of there, too. He could see it in her eyes.

Fear washed through him much like it had when the *nachtmahr* tried to take over. Knox realized the fear wasn't for his own death—it was for Rachel and what they could have had together if they'd been given the chance. Diego had been sure Knox and Rachel were soul mates, that she was *The One* for him. He liked to believe that was true, but now he'd never get a chance to know for sure.

Knox felt more than heard Rachel move closer to him. She looked deeply into his eyes for a moment, then rested her forehead against his. He ignored the heat and smoke then, letting himself absorb every sensation that was the woman he loved. He wished like hell he was in human form right then, so he could tell her how he felt about her before the end.

He was so lost in her scent and the softness of her fur against his that when the ceiling let loose and crashed down behind him, he barely flinched. Until Rachel moved back and let out a loud yelp. Thinking she'd been hit with a piece of flaming debris, he pulled back to look her over only to see her staring up at the roof.

A huge part of it had collapsed, crushing the ceiling. Even through the smoke and flames, he could make out a smattering of stars. But the night sky wasn't what held Rachel's attention—or his. Instead, it was the long section of slate-covered wood running in an incline from the floor of the library up to the roof. Fire was already licking at the bottom of it, but the top at least remained free of flames.

He threw a quick glance at Rachel, then they were both moving, scrambling, and slipping on the smooth tile, but making it up to the roof nonetheless.

The feeling of fresh air as they cleared the fire burning on the second floor and reached the roofline was exhilarating. Knox would have laughed if he could. Then he realized he actually was laughing, except it was coming out like a chuffing sound. He glanced at Rachel to see her standing there with her pink tongue hanging out, laughing, too.

Knox would have given anything to stay there with Rachel in that moment, but when the part of the roof they were on started to shake, he knew the rest of this mansion would be coming down soon—bringing them with it.

They ran then, slipping across sections of the roof where flames were already coming through, easily finding a way down to a first-floor landing, then onto the grassy lawn behind the mansion. They continued past the pond, heading for the woods beyond, and Knox prayed no one saw two huge wolves escaping from the burning building.

CHAPTER 17

Rachel was lying comfortably in the pine-straw-covered ground about twenty feet into the woods behind the house, enjoying the sensation of Knox's strong, furry body resting against hers and taking in the complete craziness going on half a football field away. The property was crawling with cops and firefighters, not to mention reporters, but luckily, everyone was too focused on the crime scene to notice two extremely large wolves hiding out in the forest.

Admittedly, she was a little concerned about how she was going to get back into her human form, since she had no idea how she'd ended up with four feet and a fur coat in the first place. She hadn't even consciously called on her inner wolf. All she knew was that she would have done anything to protect Knox from the clown. Clearly, the wolf inside her had felt the same, and she was immensely grateful for that. Even now, the memory of what the clown had almost forced her to do to Knox made her dizzy. As for the wolf thing, she was sure she and Knox would figure out how to change back at some point. Although, she had to admit, he made an extremely handsome wolf.

Shoving thoughts of how they were going to live as wolves for an extended period, Rachel focused on the good stuff that had happened tonight. They'd rescued Addy and her mom, killed the frigging clown, and managed to escape a burning building without being roasted alive. Overall, she had to admit it had been a pretty good evening.

Unfortunately, she doubted Addy and her mom thought the same, especially since it seemed like a foregone conclusion their house and everything in it was gone. But they were alive, and Rachel hoped they realized that was the most important thing. Something told Rachel it was going to take a while for Jennifer and her daughter to get over the reality of Conrad hiring someone to murder them.

Rachel wondered if Conrad had died in the fire and, if that was the case, whether he'd gotten off easy.

She and Knox were still lying there when Rachel saw Diego and Zane heading across the lawn in their direction, each carrying a navy blue duffel bag. Knox must have noticed them, too, because he lifted his head, his ears perking up.

Her pack mates walked into the trees, stopping in front of her and Knox. Zane looked a little awestruck at the sight of them, while Diego appeared smug.

"You owe me fifty bucks," Diego said.

Zane only scowled in answer.

Rachel exchanged a look with Knox, then gave her pack mates a confused tilt of the head.

"When Zane and I picked up your scents, I said you were both in your wolf forms, but Zane didn't think that was possible," Diego explained. "He insisted Knox is too new to be able to handle a full shift, and you're too...well...broken."

Rachel chuffed, the only response she could make in this form. But even if she'd been able to speak, she wouldn't have argued.

"But apparently I was wrong." Zane set down the duffel bag he was carrying and dropped to one knee in front of them, scanning their fur-covered bodies in the darkness. "You two okay? Any injuries or burns?"

Rachel let out another chuff, hoping they understood. Her first time turning into a wolf had been awesome—except for the whole demented clown trying to take over her mind—but now she was starting to discover what a huge pain in the butt it was not being able to speak.

"Needing new clothes is sort of an occupational hazard for us," Zane said, glancing at Knox. "We brought you some spare uniforms from the operations truck. The size probably won't be perfect, but it's better than walking around naked."

Rachel eyed the duffel bags. Crap, she hadn't thought about the fact that she was going to be naked under all this fur when she changed back. Shifting in front of Knox would be okay, but she wasn't thrilled at the idea of doing it in front of Diego and Zane. She felt her face heat—even under the fur.

"Not to rush you or anything, but could you guys go ahead and shift back now?" Diego glanced over his shoulder at all the people moving around outside what was left of the house. "I have no doubt a few people saw Zane and me walk into these woods. If we don't come out soon, they're going to start getting curious."

Rachel made another series of chuffing sounds at that, then shook her head back and forth as best she could, hoping her pack mates understood what she was trying to say. For a moment, they both stared at her in confusion, but then comprehension dawned on Zane's face.

"You don't how to change back, do you?" he asked, looking back and forth between her and Knox. "Either of you."

Rachel would have shrugged, if she could have figured out how to make her wolf shoulders perform a movement like that. So, she had to be satisfied with shaking her head again, even if the movement felt strange. She had a ginormous head.

"Don't worry," Zane said. "I can talk you through it."

Rachel hoped so. But before they tried it, she needed Diego and Zane to turn their backs. She motioned with her head, moving it in a circle the best she could.

Zane frowned. "I don't know what that means."

She repeated the gesture, but when her pack mates only continued to stare at her in confusion, she turned around, then back again, giving them a pointed look.

"Dude, I think she wants us to turn around," Diego said.

"Oh." Zane gave her an apologetic look. "Sorry."

Both her pack mates turned their backs to them, then Zane began to talk them through the shift from wolf to human.

"It's actually easier to go from wolf to human than the other direction," he murmured, his voice taking on that same calm tone she'd used with Knox the other night. "It's your natural form, so you won't have to work very hard to convince your body to go with it. Normally, I'd talk each of you through it individually, but since you're mated, I think I can have you shift back together."

She frowned, absently wondering what that expression looked like on a wolf as she tried to figure out what Zane meant. But then her pack mate spoke again, asking her and Knox to imagine they were touching each other, running hands and lips over bare skin.

Picturing doing something so sensual with Knox was a little difficult with Diego and Zane standing there, but as her pack mate continued to talk them through it, her imagination took over, and before she knew it, she was replaying the morning she and Knox had made love. And, oh man, did she focus on the details!

Rachel was so into it she swore she could feel Knox's warm skin under her fingers as she breathed in that perfect combination of leather and gun oil. She moaned a little, giving into the sensation as arousal throbbed through her core.

"I'd tell you to get a room, but first you'd need to get dressed," Diego said dryly, interrupting her extremely pleasant sensory immersion session. "Unless you want us to leave you alone here for a bit?"

Rachel opened her eyes to discover she and Knox were back in their human forms. She was lying in his arms, one hand on his chest, a leg draped possessively over him. Saying he was as turned on as she was at the moment was an understatement. Getting a pair of pants on was definitely going to be a struggle with that bad boy. Maybe hanging around in the woods for a while might be a good idea.

"Gage is going to want a full report of what the hell happened in the house, so you should probably hurry up," Zane said as he and Diego walked away, leaving her and Knox alone with their naked, warm bodies touching each other.

Knox lifted her chin with a finger and pressed a kiss to her lips. "You know, nothing says we can't spend an extra minute—or ten—getting dressed."

Rachel groaned. As much as she'd love that, they didn't have time. Giving him another kiss, she pushed herself upright, then reached over and grabbed one of the duffel bags, shoving it into Knox's hands.

"Get dressed, lover boy," she said. "I'm going to need

your help explaining what the hell happened tonight since I missed some of it."

Gage and a good portion of her other pack mates were standing in a group about a hundred feet from the front porch of the house—or at least where the front porch of the house would have been if it hadn't burned to a pile of cinders. Rachel and Knox had to pause as they made their way over there to let the people from the medical examiner's office pass with no less than eight gurneys. Some of the bad guys must have made it outside and fought with Zane and Diego. Hopefully, none of those bodies had been clawed up like the ones inside. That would be difficult to explain.

Rachel was still thinking about the bodies that would likely never be recovered from the mansion when she and Knox finally joined her pack mates. She was so wrapped up in her thoughts she didn't notice Brooks had drawn his weapon and was pointing it at Knox.

Crap.

Rachel immediately stepped forward to put herself between Knox and her big African American pack mate even as Knox tried to pull her back to safety.

"What the hell are you doing, Brooks?" Gage growled, moving closer and pulling the big man's arm down as he turned to look around them. "Put your frigging weapon away before the rest of the cops see."

That was all they needed. Half the DPD bearing down on them with guns drawn.

Brooks didn't put his department-issued Sig away,

regardless of what their alpha wanted. Instead, he held it down at his side, finger away from the trigger. His gaze locked on Knox as he ignored everything else around him, including Gage.

"He's a hunter," Brooks said softly, his eyes glowing gold.

The silence that followed his announcement was deafening as every single one of her pack mates regarded Knox with expressions ranging from dubious to curious to menacing. Out of the corner of her eye, Rachel saw Diego move to stand beside Knox. Zane took up a position behind them to cover their backs.

"Are you sure about this, Brooks?" Gage asked, his face unreadable. "Because from where I'm standing, Jennifer and her daughter wouldn't be alive if it wasn't for his help."

Brooks didn't blink or look away from Knox for even a second. "I'm sure. He was at Max and Lana's wedding reception. I remember him because he was limping from a gunshot wound to the leg. He only got away because Rachel didn't put a bullet in him when she had the chance."

Every eye turned to her. These were her pack mates, her friends, her family. The hurt and condemnation on their faces was almost enough to crush her soul.

"Is this true, Rachel?" Gage demanded. "Is Knox a hunter, and did you let him get away that night?"

While her alpha was clearly pissed, there was also disappointment in his voice. If she was being honest, that cut deeper than his anger.

"Yes, it's true," she said softly. "Knox was at the reception that night, and yes, I could have shot him, but I didn't. I didn't know why at the time and it wasn't until recently that I figured it out. Knox is *The One* for me. I couldn't have shot him that night no matter what. Fate wouldn't let something like that happen."

Gage stared at her, shock in his dark eyes. "He can't be *The One* for you. He's a hunter."

If any of this mess was funny, Rachel might have laughed at the sight of her big bad boss so baffled. He wasn't the only one who looked stunned. Her pack mates looked like they'd been hit in the face with a baseball bat.

"*Used to be* a hunter," Rachel corrected. "He had no idea what he was getting into. He never harmed a werewolf and the first time he had a chance to do the right thing, he did, by taking a bullet meant for me at the SWAT compound." She looked at Brooks. "Knox stepped into the line of fire of one of the other hunters who was about to shoot me. That's what turned him into one of us."

Before anyone could interrupt, she hurried on, telling them how Knox had shown up at her apartment looking for help and how she'd agreed. One thing had led to another, and before she knew it, she'd fallen for him. She thought she'd done a good job of explaining everything, but unfortunately, Gage didn't care about any of that.

"I've heard enough," he growled. "Dallas is still home for a lot of werewolves who lost people they cared about to the hunters. There's no way I'm letting a member of the Pack that's supposed to be protecting them associate with a hunter, even if you claim he's reformed—or whatever the hell you think he is. I can't put him in jail because I don't have any evidence, but he's not staying in this town. Not while I'm alpha of this pack."

Rachel swallowed hard. Talking wasn't going to fix this. She could tell Gage what Knox had done to save her life—and her sanity—but he and probably the rest of her pack mates were never going to see past the hunter label Knox carried, no matter what good he'd done.

"Fine," she said, reaching out blindly to take Knox's hand and hold on tight as she fought tears. "You don't want Knox to stay in Dallas, that's okay. We'll leave."

Gage looked at her like she'd slapped him. Clearly, he hadn't expected that. But before she could say anything else, Knox tugged her hand, pulling her around to face him.

"I appreciate what you're doing, but I can't ask you to leave your pack for me," he said gently. "You told me what they mean to you, what it felt like for you to find them after being on your own for so long. I'd never ask you to give that up."

She gazed up at him, realizing now that they probably should have had this conversation that morning they'd made love. But better now than never. Because she sure as hell wasn't letting him get away. The thought of leaving the Pack—her family—might hurt, but not nearly as much as leaving Knox. The idea was enough to make her feel like she couldn't breathe.

"I'm not doing it because you're asking." She reached up to caress his hair-roughened jaw, not caring that they had an audience. "I'm doing it because you're *The One* for me and I'm *The One* for you. That means we're supposed to be together regardless of who or what gets in our way. I love you, so stop talking. We're leaving. Just the two of us."

Knox looked stunned as hell but finally bent his head and kissed her. "As decisions go, this one might be certifiably insane, and while I'll be the first to admit to having a history of making hair-trigger decisions, I can definitely say that loving you isn't one of them. In fact, it's probably the smartest thing I've ever done."

Tears filling her eyes, she squeezed his hand with a laugh and, without looking at Gage, turned to lead the way past her pack and out of their lives forever when someone stepped in front of them.

"It won't be just the two of you," Diego said. "I mean, what kind of friend would I be if I let you guys walk away because you were dumb enough to fall in love? If you're moving out of Dallas to start a new pack, I'm going with you. Knox promised to help me find my soul mate, even if it does turn out she's serving a ten-year prison sentence and is married with a kid who hates my guts."

Rachel had absolutely no idea what that last part meant, but right then, she didn't care. Still holding on to Knox's hand, she wrapped her free arm around Diego and hugged him, amazed she was so lucky to have him as a friend.

She headed for the front gate again, this time with Diego in tow, only to pull up when Trey and Zane hurried around to step in front of them. She opened her mouth to tell them to get out of the way when they both announced they were going with them, too.

"Alyssa won't care where we live as long as we're together," Zane said of his mate as they walked.

They made it halfway down the driveway when someone else stopped them. This time it was Gage. Something told her he wasn't going to announce he was joining them, and she braced herself for another argument.

"If I told you that was all a test to see if you were really serious about Knox, would you believe me?" he asked.

She didn't buy that for a second but nodded anyway.

His mouth edged up. "Good. Then you passed the test. Now, what do you say we go back to the SWAT compound and figure out how we're going to make this all work?"

Rachel knew that was as close as she'd ever get to an apology from her alpha, but after giving Knox a questioning look and getting a nod in return, she decided to take what she could get.

She gave her alpha a smile. "That sounds good."

CHAPTER 18

"Man, I haven't played volleyball since high school. I forgot how much fun it is." Knox flashed her a grin. "I'm guessing this is a regular thing at these cookouts?"

Rachel nodded with a laugh as she and Knox left the sandy volleyball pit hand in hand to grab something to eat. It had taken a little over a month, but her entire pack had finally come to accept Knox—even Brooks. Acceptance had come a lot faster after Diego had explained about the *nachtmahr* and she'd told everyone how Knox had figured out how to kill it in the fire. Gage casually asking her to bring him to the monthly cookout was a formal acknowledgment of that fact.

Their six-person volleyball team, which included Zane, Trey, Khaki, and Xander, had won three straight matches and would have still been playing if it wasn't for the mouth-watering aroma of food coming from the line of grills near the main building. Diego was in charge of food today and whatever he was cooking smelled heavenly. From all the spices she was picking up, it was probably Mexican, which Rachel loved.

As they approached the grills, Rachel couldn't contain the laughter when she realized they were going to have to wait a little bit. Diego was busy serving Tuffie the pit-bull mix and Kat the cat, as well as Leo and Biscuit, two dogs who belonged to other members of the Pack. From the smell, it seemed Diego had given them all unseasoned meat he'd grilled for them. Like always, Kat refused to eat anything off the ground and would only eat her morsels of food off a plate. Rachel had never met a cat so finicky.

Rachel grabbed two oversized, disposable, plastic plates from the stack on the table beside the grill, handing one to Knox as she looked around for Addy, hoping the girl was eating something. She found Addy sitting with Ben at one of the picnic tables at the very end of the line, the two of them eating burgers by themselves. Rachel didn't like the way the girl was still isolating herself from everyone else, but at least she had Ben—and she was eating. It wasn't surprising that Addy was still having problems. She and her mom had almost died that night, but that was only the beginning. A few hours after the fire had finally been put out, her father had been captured at the Laredo border crossing, trying to slip into Mexico. He'd been sitting in jail ever since, awaiting trial for attempted murder, collusion, and money laundering. The endless stories in the local papers had reported that Conrad Lloyd had been in bed with the Marshall crime organization for years…literally. Apparently, his payment for helping to launder Marshall's money was a steady supply of prostitutes. The headlines had been lurid and impossible to miss. There was no doubt Addy had seen them.

If there was any bright spot in this mess, it was that Addy and her mom were closer than ever. With the Marshall trial wrapping up and the man heading to a lifelong stay in prison where he belonged, Jennifer had dropped most of her cases. She and Addy were even taking a two-week vacation to Italy in the summer.

Diego gave her and Knox a grin when they got to the front of the line and finally reached the grills.

"What'll it be?" he asked. "We have carne asada, Mexican barbecue chicken, and pork-and-chorizo burgers. Oh, and shrimp tacos that I made for our resident pescatarian werewolf."

If Rachel's mouth had been watering before, that was nothing compared to now. "Everything sounds so good and smells and looks even better. I'll take two of everything."

"Sounds good to me," Knox said.

Plates piled high, she and Knox grabbed a couple bottles of water and joined Trey, Connor, and Ethan. While most of the admin and logistics personnel from DAPS had been cleared of any involvement with Theo and his deal with Conrad, Ethan was the only field operative to make the cut. He and Knox had become good friends over the past month as Knox worked through the process of taking over the nearly bankrupt and heavily discredited company. Rachel wasn't so sure it was a good idea, but Knox and Ethan seemed to think they could make it work. Knox was currently working through résumés, knowing he needed people with sterling reputations if he was going to rebuild the company. The most interesting part of his proposed hiring strategy was the recruitment of some werewolves to round out the organization. Rachel thought that was a great idea.

"So, what do you guys make of Mike and Chief Leclair?" Trey asked.

"I am not even going there," Connor said firmly as he fed a few pieces of meat to Kat, who'd recently joined them at the table. She seemed to hang around him nearly 24/7. It was like the dang animal was in love with him. "That's just too weird to think about."

Rachel laughed, glancing over at the picnic table where Mike sat with Leclair, Gage, and his wife, but Mike seemed to only have eyes for their new boss. "As my grandmother used to say, it looks like he's sweet on her."

Everyone at their table glanced that way, but it was Trey who seemed to be the thoughtful one. "I never imagined I'd see Mike looking at another woman like that. Not after everything he went through."

Rachel was about to ask what that meant but was distracted by Knox taking a big bite of burger. Damn, he made enjoying his food look sexy. When she kept gazing at him, he motioned at her to eat, too. She studied her plate, trying to decide what to taste first. Did she go for the chicken marinated in cilantro, jalapeños, and a combo of lime and orange juice; the steak marinated in beer, lime, and garlic; or the burger of pork and chorizo with its generous helping of guacamole? Even the shrimp tacos were in the running, and she wasn't a big seafood girl.

Decisions. Decisions.

She finally went with the burger and almost moaned at how perfect the combination of spicy meat tasted.

"Hadley still hasn't asked you about what happened that day at her office, has she?" Trey asked, apparently moving on from the topic of Mike and the chief. "During any of the sessions you've had with her, I mean."

Even though she was no longer terrorized by the *nachtmahr,* Rachel had accepted she still needed help. The monster had found a comfortable home in her head because of the trauma she was still dealing with from the night Horace Watkins had tried to kill her. She'd been worried Hadley wouldn't want to see her anymore, especially after her office had been destroyed, but the doctor had been fine with it. And the sessions really were helping.

"No, thank goodness." Rachel took another bite of burger. "The doctors gave her a clean bill of health, so I think she chalked it up to stress."

A strange part of her therapy sessions—and the death of the *nachtmahr*—were her feelings toward poor Horace Watkins. After experiencing the terror of the creature firsthand, Rachel's heart went out to the man, despite what he'd done to her and Hannah. In reality, Horace had been a victim of the creature as much as she had. There was nothing the man could have done to resist the urges that had driven him to go after Hannah. It made her glad the *nachtmahr* was finally gone so no one else would end up like that.

She and Knox hung around for another few games of volleyball but then had to bail. They'd moved into a new condo a few weeks ago, and it was still a mess for the most part. This evening they planned on finally getting everything unpacked. Even with the *nachtmahr*—and the clown—gone, Rachel hadn't been able to face the thought of living in her old place anymore. It had cost a buttload to break the lease early, but it had been worth it to not spend another night in that place.

Rachel was pulling out pictures of her family and Hannah when she sensed Knox behind her. She turned to find him leaning against the wall in the hallway that led to their bedroom, watching her with an expression on his face that seemed almost like wonder.

She set down the framed photo she'd been holding and walked over to him. "What?"

He pulled her into his arms, wrapping her in his warmth, a smile tugging at his lips. "Nothing."

"Don't even try it," she said, poking him in the chest. "I can tell when you're keeping something from me. What is it? Are you regretting giving up your room at the extended stay hotel already?"

She tried to keep her tone light, because truthfully, she thought that might actually be it. Knox had no problem making knee-jerk decisions—following through seemed to be the problem for him.

"It's nothing like that," he insisted, the smile replaced by a serious expression. "It's just..."

"Just what?"

"It's just that I never expected you to pick me over your pack that night. Then, when I gave you a chance to backtrack and you didn't, I was stunned. Then you told me you loved me. I never expected that."

The words were beautiful, but she had to admit she was a little confused. "But Diego told me you two had talked about the soul mate thing. He said you knew I was *The One* for you. I thought you knew that meant I loved you?"

Knox nodded. "I guess I did. But knowing something in theory is completely different than hearing the words. When you told me that, it meant everything to me. I sort of realized that just now, as I watched you unpack your stuff here in the home we're going to share."

She smiled, wondering if she should rag on him for being a total romantic. "What brought on this sudden introspection?"

The grin was back, broader this time. "When I was running from one situation to the next over the past several months, I knew I was looking for something, but I never knew what it was until now. I finally figured out that it's you and this thing we have now. That's what I was searching for. You're my reason—my purpose. The woman I love more than anything."

There wasn't a whole hell of a lot she could say after something like that. Going up on her toes to kiss him, she took his hand and led him into their bedroom. So they could talk more about the reason they were together—without saying a single word.

ACKNOWLEDGMENTS

I hope you had as much fun reading Rachel and Knox's story as I had writing it! We knew Rachel would fall for the former Navy SEAL/hunter when we first added her to the SWAT team. What we didn't know was that the clown was going to be so evil. He definitely took charge of his character! And a special shout-out to our real-life friend and police officer, Rachel, for inspiring the heroine!

This whole series wouldn't be possible without some very incredible people. In addition to another big thank-you to my hubby for all his help with the action scenes and military and tactical jargon, thanks to my fantastic agent, Courtney Miller-Callihan; thanks to my editor and go-to-person at Sourcebooks, Cat Clyne (who loves this series as much as I do and is always a phone call, text, or email away whenever I need something); and all the other amazing people at Sourcebooks, including my fantastic publicist and the crazy-talented art department. The covers they make for me are seriously droolworthy!

Because I could never leave out my readers, a huge thank-you to everyone who reads my books and Snoopy Danced right along with me with every new release. That includes the fantastic people on my amazing Review Team, as well my assistant, Janet. You rock!

I also want to give a big thank-you to the men, women, and working dogs who protect and serve in police departments everywhere, as well as their families.

And a very special shout-out to our favorite restaurant,

P.F. Chang's, where hubby and I bat story lines back and forth and come up with all of our best ideas, as well as a thank-you to our fantastic waiter-turned-manager, Andrew, who makes sure our order is ready the moment we walk in the door!

Hope you enjoy the next book in the SWAT: Special Wolf Alpha Team series coming soon from Sourcebooks, and look forward to reading the rest of the series as much as I look forward to sharing it with you. Also, don't forget to look for my new series from Sourcebooks, STAT: Special Threat Assessment Team, a spin-off from SWAT!

If you love a man in uniform as much as I do, make sure you check out X-OPS, my other action-packed paranormal/romantic-suspense series from Sourcebooks.

Happy Reading!

ABOUT THE AUTHOR

Paige Tyler is a *New York Times* and *USA Today* bestselling author of sexy, romantic suspense and paranormal romance. She and her very own military hero (also known as her husband) live on the beautiful Florida coast with their adorable fur baby (also known as their dog). Paige graduated with a degree in education but decided to pursue her passion and write books about hunky alpha males and the kick-butt heroines who fall in love with them.

Visit Paige at her website at paigetylertheauthor.com.

She's also on Facebook, Twitter, Tumblr, Instagram, tsu, Wattpad, Google+, and Pinterest.

STAT: SPECIAL THREAT ASSESSMENT TEAM

Paige Tyler's all-new, pulse-pounding
SWAT spin-off series

COMING SPRING 2020

STAT—Special Threat Assessment Team—agent Jestina Ridley is in London with her teammates investigating a kidnapping when they cross paths with a creature that savagely kills everyone but her.

When Jes calls HQ for backup, they send her former Navy SEAL and alpha werewolf Jake Huang and his new pack. Convinced that the creature who butchered her teammates was a werewolf, Jes isn't too happy about it. But she'll need Jake's help if they're going to discover the truth and make it back home alive. And with everything on the line, Jes will have to accept Jake for who he is, or lose the partner she never expected to find…

"Paige Tyler has a fan in me!"

—LARISSA IONE, *New York Times* Bestseller

Also by Paige Tyler

SWAT: Special Wolf Alpha Team

Hungry Like the Wolf
Wolf Trouble
In the Company of Wolves
To Love a Wolf
Wolf Unleashed
Wolf Hunt
Wolf Hunger
Wolf Rising
Wolf Instinct
Wolf Rebel

X-Ops

Her Perfect Mate
Her Lone Wolf
Her Secret Agent (novella)
Her Wild Hero
Her Fierce Warrior
Her Rogue Alpha
Her True Match
Her Dark Half
X-Ops Exposed